Last First Kiss

Also by Lia Riley

Coming Soon
Right Wrong Guy
Best Worst Mistake

Last First Kiss

A BRIGHTWATER NOVEL

LIA RILEY

AVONIMPULSE
An Imprint of HarperCollinsPublishers

This is a work of fiction. Names, characters, places, and incidents
are products of the author's imagination or are used fictitiously
and are not to be construed as real. Any resemblance to actual
events, locales, organizations, or persons, living or dead, is en-
tirely coincidental.

Excerpt from *Right Wrong Guy* copyright © 2015 by Lia Riley.
Excerpt from *Heart's Desire* copyright © 2015 by Tina Klinesmith.
Excerpt from *Desire Me Now* copyright © 2015 by Tiffany Clare.
Excerpt from *The Wedding Gift* copyright © 2015 by Lisa Con-
nelly.
Excerpt from *When Love Happens* copyright © 2015 by Darcy
Burke.

EPub Edition JUNE 2015 ISBN: 9780062403773
Print Edition ISBN: 9780062403766

10 9 8 7 6 5 4 3 2 1

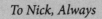

To Nick, Always

Acknowledgments

FIRST, TO MY agent, Emily Sylvan Kim, for unfailing optimism and helping the Brightwater series find its home at Avon Impulse. To my editor, Amanda Bergeron, who performs editorial magic and is encouraging and insightful. To Gabrielle Keck, for being so helpful and responsive.

A huge thanks to my critique partners on this book: Jennifer Ryan (hugs for the lovely blurb too), Jennifer Blackwood, Jules Barnard, and Natalie Blitt, for your kicks in the pants and much needed love notes.

Special love to Megan Erickson and AJ Pine. On good days and bad, you two are always there. It means the world.

A huge thank you to my family who put up with so much while I disappear to work or zone out in space. To J & B, I love you beyond words, and don't read Mama's books until you are much, much older. To Nick, this year has been nuts and I couldn't write half the words if it wasn't for your support. I love you.

The Legend of Five Diamonds Farm

(excerpt from
Brightwater: Small Town, Big Dreams)

ROWDY CATTLEMAN JERICHO KANE and quiet sodbuster Boone Carson were among the Brightwater Valley's first settlers. The story goes that in the late-nineteenth century, Carson sauntered into *The Dirty Shame Saloon* after a good harvest and bought into a poker game. Lady Luck must have perched on his shoulder because he quickly made three hundred dollars. His neighbor, Wild-J Kane, was also there, having lost everything but the shirt off his back.

"Carson," Kane allegedly said, "I'll stake half my ranch for your winnings on the next hand."

"Deal," came the reply. Carson's five-diamond flush

beat out the cattleman's three of a kind. He doubled his landholding and established Five Diamonds Farm.

And so began the famed Kane and Carson feud. The lingering grudge has withstood the test of time, driving the two families asunder, and rumors suggest the Eastern Sierras can now even boast of its own version of Romeo and Juliet. No dying, not unless you count the innocence of first love.

Chapter One

[draft]

Musings of a Mighty Mama

older posts>>

Dear Readers,
There were so many sweet but worried comments following my divorce announcement. Everything is ~~Screwed City, Population: Me~~ *okay. Gregor* ~~actually asked, "Annabelle, why limit myself to a single book in the whole library?"~~ *and I grew apart. No one's to blame.* ~~Only my high-waist underwear and lack of a sex drive.~~ *Yes, I went missing in action* ~~leading the charge on Operation Eat Your Feelings—good time to buy stock in Ben & Jerry's~~*, but for a fantastic reason. Ready for a little front-page news? (Insert the* ~~Imperial Death March~~ *anticipatory drum roll here.)*

Atticus and I are in Brightwater! ~~FML~~

We left Portland yesterday morning, drove to Reno, and then dipped back into California to arrive in the ~~fifth circle of Dante's Inferno~~ *Eastern Sierras. My* ~~don't-know-what-the-h-e-double hockey sticks I'm doing~~ *evil genius plan is to spend the summer at my family's farm, which includes a small orchard filled with* ~~ghosts and lost dreams~~ *heirloom apple varieties. My hometown is famous for* ~~two things: a hundred-year-old family feud and~~ *being the set location of* Tumbleweeds, *last year's* ~~overrated~~ *Academy Award winner for best picture.*

We'll be celebrating the start of our new adventure with a bang—at this week's Fourth of July fireworks celebration at the rodeo grounds. I'm contributing my specialty to the community potluck—cinnamon swirl coffee cake ~~infused with bitter tears~~.

Can't wait to share the natural beauty of this place, the snow-capped peaks, panoramic vistas, wild forests, and meandering rivers. It's high time to dust off my red cowgirl boots and wrangle you guys some shiny new blog posts. Brace yourself for a whole lot of goodness. ~~Kill me now. Use a hammer and make it quick~~.

Love, Annie

PS: Leave a comment telling me your favorite summertime potluck dish for a chance to win a set of organic silk play scarves for your little one from our lovely sponsor, Waldorf Whimsy

Draft Saved by Mighty Mama 12:45am in family life, baking adventures, summer fun | Permalink | comments (0)

THE KNOCK CAME as the last ice cube melted into her scotch.

What the . . . ? Annie Carson slammed against the chair, adrenal system upgrading from zoned out to Defcon 1. The vintage pig cookie jar stared back from the Formica counter with a vaguely panicked expression. Nothing arrived after midnight except lovers and trouble.

Annie didn't have a lover. And the biggest trouble she had tonight was trying to finish this blog post while forgetting all the reasons she fled from here in the first place. On the surface, Brightwater boasted a quaint Ye Olde West appeal. Nestled under the shadow of Mount Oh-Be-Joyful's fourteen-thousand-foot peak, the historic main street boasted a working saddlery instead of Starbucks, the barbershop offered complimentary sideburn trims, and tractors caused the only traffic jams.

Then there were the cowboys. Some women—fine, *most* women—would consider the local ranchers to be six kinds of swoon-worthy, but she'd learned her lesson ten years ago.

If you meet a cute guy wearing a Stetson, run in the opposite direction.

The next knock rattled the front door's hinges; whoever was out there meant business. Annie sneezed before drawing a shaky breath. Drinking wasn't a personal forte, but chamomile tea didn't do much to blunt the first-night-back-in-my-one-cow-hometown blues, even with extra honey.

Maybe if she took her time, whoever was out there would go away.

She closed her laptop's lid, stood, and walked to the sink, setting the tumbler under the leaky tap. Water drip, drip, dripped into the brown dregs. Dad's radio above the fridge, tuned to a Fresno classical station, piped in Mozart's requiem on the scratchy speakers, hopefully due to coincidence rather than cosmic foreshadowing.

More knocking.

This could very well be an innocent mistake. Someone had confused directions, taken a wrong turn, driven up a quarter-mile driveway to an out-of-the-way farmhouse ... to where she sat wearing a *Kiss Me, I'm Scottish* apron with a sleeping five-year-old upstairs.

She hadn't missed Gregor in months. Her ex-husband might be a metrosexual philosophy professor, but at least he stood higher than five feet in socks. Why, oh, why had she enrolled in yoga instead of kickboxing last summer in Portland? No way would a sun salutation cut the mustard against a crazy-eyed bunny boiler. An alarmed buzz replaced the hollow feeling in her chest. Brightwater was a sleepy, safe backwater. Had it grown more dangerous since she tore out of here on her eighteenth birthday? Meth labs? Cattle thieves? Area 51 wasn't too far away, so throw in possible alien abduction?

Well, she was alone now and would have to deal with whatever came.

As a rule, killers and extraterrestrials didn't announce themselves at the front door. Still, this was no time to start taking chances. She grabbed her father's single-malt by the neck and padded into the living room. The change from bright kitchen to gloom skewed her vision as blood shunted to her legs. Shadows clung to the beamed ceiling and brick fireplace. If the rocking chair in the corner moved, she'd pee her pants. That old gooseneck rocker starred in more than a few of her childhood nightmares— ever since her sister had mentioned that Great-Grandma Carson had died in it.

"Hello?" she called, her voice calm—but, darn, an octave too high. "Who's there?"

Silence.

The door didn't have a peephole. This was the Eastern Sierras, a place where shopkeepers left signs taped to their unlocked front doors saying "Went to the bank, back in five minutes."

Think! Think! What's the game plan?

Retreat—not a choice. But more whisky was definitely a viable option. She opened the bottle, and the gulp seared her throat. At least the burn helped dissipate the cold fear knotting her stomach. She pressed her lips together while screwing the cap back on. *Here goes nothing.* Brandishing the bottle like a club, she flung open the door.

A light breeze blew across her face, cool despite the fact it was early July. Five Diamonds Farm sat at four thousand feet in elevation. She glanced around the porch. Empty. Unable to stand the suspense, she stepped forward, her bare toes grazing warm ceramic. A baking dish sat on the mat. Annie knit her brow and crouched—a neighborly casserole delivery? At this hour? Fat chance, but one could hope. She removed the lid, and an invisible fist squeezed her sternum.

If hope was a thing with feathers, all she had was chicken potpie.

Literally.

A toothpick anchored a Post-it note to the crust.

Caught your hen in my tomatoes.
Chicken #2 will be nuggets.
Welcome home.

She tightened her shoulders. No name, but none was needed. This had Grandma Kane's fingerprints all over it. The crotchety old woman ruled the spread next door, Hidden Rock Ranch, like it was her own personal empire, and she regarded the Carsons as unwelcome squatters.

Annie smashed the note in her fist and hurled it as far as possible. Crud, such a crappy toss—the wadded paper barely cleared the bottom step. She couldn't even throw right. Three seconds later litterbug guilt struck, and she scrambled to retrieve it.

An engine roared to life near the barn, brake lights illuminating the ponderosa pine grove. Tires kicked up gravel and the horn tooted twice before turning onto the main road.

Enough was enough. The Kanes had once made her life a living hell, and that old woman's capacity to nurse a grudge went beyond anything remotely sane or rea-

sonable. The one-hundred-and-fifty-year-old feud had
to end. This was the twenty-first century, time to leave
behind the kerosene-lit dark ages once and for all. After
the last terrible year, she was due a little peace.

She tucked her chin to her chest and strode around
the house to assess the poultry situation. Five Diamonds
might have become a farm in name only, but at least the
chicken coop remained operational. As a girl, she loved
collecting the eggs, selling them for a few bucks a dozen.
The money went to her college fund, but that wasn't the
reason she took over the chore. She loved how when she
appeared with cracked corn, the flock approached at
warp speed, offering nothing but cheerful clucks. The
comical sight never failed to induce a giggle.

Tonight, the hens were quiet in the brooder box and
nothing appeared amiss. Relief drizzled through her
veins. Grandma Kane must be playing a joke. She probably shopped the poultry specials at the local Save-U-More
and—

"Oh, no." A corner of rusty wire bent at an awkward
angle. Annie yanked it as her groan rose to the moon-
less sky. Nearby, a coyote joined in, harmonizing with a
single, mournful note.

There was more than enough wiggle room, even for
the fattest hen, to escape. The back fields were overgrown,
the orchard was a gnarled jungle, and the house was more
weatherboard than paint. Backbreaking chores stretched
in every direction. Couldn't Dad at least have kept the
coop in one piece? She fought back a sniffle, dropped the
whisky bottle, and wiped her nose before twining the

wire around a nail, shaking it a few times to ensure the quick fix held. A better shoring of defenses would have to wait until morning.

In the distance, atop the low rise, a light flicked on. Grandma Kane must have been arriving home. She probably sat on a throne of chicken bones and gnawed drumsticks like a wrinkled Genghis Khan.

Annie clenched her jaw, eyes narrowing. As much as she wanted peace, all necessary recourses were on the table if that woman so much as inched a toe on her property again. There were laws, and they existed for a reason, such as protecting respectable people from bloodthirsty octogenarians. Five Diamonds and its inhabitants were now her responsibility.

Dad packed up his painstakingly restored '68 VW van and left for his artist residency in Mexico yesterday. He was ready to sell the farm and move on. Before leaving, he mentioned that offers had started to come in for neighboring properties last year—unsolicited and mindbogglingly high. Brightwater was on the map after *Tumbleweeds* filmed in the valley, won an Academy Award, and captured the public's imagination. *Sunset Magazine* followed up with a feature, "Last Best Secret in the West," and local property values skyrocketed, LA types snapping up second, third, even fourth homes.

Chest caving, she trudged to the front porch to gather what remained of the wanderlusting hen. A committed vegetarian for years, choking down even a single bite was out of the question. It was hard enough to swallow the fact that with Dad off to Puerto Peñasco and her sister, Claire, running a food truck in San Francisco, Annie was the only person left with the time to deal with Five Diamonds.

Her summer could be distilled to one simple goal—get the old farm ready for sale. With her share of the profit, she would be able to afford the astronomical housing in the Bay Area and move Atticus closer to his beloved aunt. Her mother died not long after Annie's birth, and Dad wanted to retire south of the border. This was a way for her and her son to have a taste of family life.

The city also had a vibrant tech scene, perfect for an ambitious blogger ready to re-enter the workforce. Atticus would start kindergarten in the fall, and at last she could blow the dust bunnies off her journalism degree. Perfect timing, as *Musings of a Mighty Mama* exploded this year, going from a hobby mommy blog to pulling in five figures in advertising revenue—low five figures, but a more than promising start. Gregor was legally committed to providing child support, but she needed to figure out a way to stand on her own two feet. A robust blog presence could open the door to a syndicated column on a national website, or a book deal, or—

Something.

But right now what she needed was more coffee cake. After scraping the potpie into the garbage, she snagged the last slice from the Bundt pan. Cinnamon sugar dusted her front as she trekked upstairs to bed. The bathroom's toilet ran while she brushed her teeth. Wonderful. Add another bullet point to the near-biblical-length "to do" list. Everything in Five Diamonds was leaky—including her.

No! No tears. She practiced water conservation as a rule.

"Nature doesn't deal in straight lines," Dad said once, while taking her on one of his "scouts" as he called it, hunting for inspiration. He'd spend weeks trolling river bottoms for just the right stones to place in just the exact swirl, or days creating an elaborate nest from twigs. People called him a genius, and perhaps they were right. He certainly didn't inhabit the same world as others, floating past broken chicken coops, leaking toilets, and dripping faucets as if they were background static. Reality didn't interest him, only the beauty and possibility hidden in flotsam and jetsam.

"Look at that tree branch, see the jags and bends?" he had muttered. "Or how about the groovy arc to that pebble? The world isn't a perfect Point A to Point B, Annie. Life's infinitely more complex."

It sounded nice the morning he said it beside the river bend, under cottonwoods starting to change color. But alone, in the dark, when you're almost thirty, divorced, without a clue where you're going—perfect lines, simple and clear-cut, were infinitely more appealing.

Growing up wasn't magical; it sucked.

Annie tiptoed into her childhood bedroom and quietly slipped into her pajamas so as not to wake her son. She could always crash in the master, but this room felt right. The matching brass beds, hers and Claire's, were still covered by the same nine-patch quilts they'd sewed during one long winter in their teens. Atticus slept in one, curled on himself, butt in the air, the awkward pose no adult would find comfortable but kids returned to time and again. She glanced at the empty bed and back to her little one. Not even a question, really. Crawling in beside him, the big spoon to his little, Annie inhaled his scent, a comforting blend of hot chocolate, fabric softener, and boy. The perfect antidote to the farmhouse's forlorn mustiness.

But the night was an honest time.

She was lost.

The pressure to keep a brave face and feign optimism since the divorce threatened to buckle her knees. But who wanted to hear that story? No one. She needed to be Mighty Mama, the superwoman who taught Atticus a hundred infant signs, ensured there was always a seasonal décor project on the go, and cheerfully concocted homemade laundry powder.

The suitcase against the far wall didn't hold thongs or sexy lace. It was time to hike up her practical cotton briefs, grab a glue gun, and get back on track. Her career, and more importantly, her son, counted on it.

"I'm going to take care of you, little man." Atticus stirred at her whisper, murmuring a few jumbled syllables. Outside, the coyote yipped again and the air seemed to vibrate from the melancholy pang. "I'll take care of everything."

Tomorrow she'd figure out how.

Chapter Two

GRANDMA'S CACKLE DRIFTED from the open barn door, never a good sign, especially in the middle of the night.

"All right, time to come clean." Sawyer Kane walked inside, telescope case tucked under his arm. "Where have you been?"

"Never you mind." Grandma slammed her truck door, dressed in red flannel pajamas, hair rolled tight in curlers.

"You can't drive around at this hour, remember what the doctor said? Your night vision isn't what it used to be."

"Pshaw. That quack couldn't find his way out of a wet paper bag."

Debatable. At her last physical, Doc suggested that with her gumption, Grandma could see well past one hundred. Sawyer didn't doubt it.

"You're up to no good." He followed her down the dirt path toward her house.

"Children should be seen and not heard."

Never mind Sawyer was a grown man, not to mention the sheriff of Brightwater. Here on Hidden Rock Ranch, Grandma's rule was law, and she never treated him any different than the lost five-year-old kid who came to live there with his two brothers after their parents died in a freak house fire.

His first memory was from the funeral, and the steady way Grandma gripped his hand as the minister intoned, "Ashes to ashes and dust to dust." He wished he could remember more than two holes in the ground. If he tried hard, sometimes there came the faint tinkle of his mother's laughter, or the sensation of his dad tossing him in the air. But they were only ever suggestions, a flash, nothing concrete.

At first glance, Grandma didn't appear formidable, rather skinny as a rail with her pointed nose and bifocals. But those bones were forged of titanium. She'd been widowed far longer than she'd ever been married, and she managed Hidden Rock Ranch through sheer force of will. She repositioned the once bankrupt six-thousand-acre property to ride the grass-fed, anti-antibiotic trends commanding high price points in the Bay Area and throughout wine country, branding the beef as "farm to table," and using the predominate peak in the valley, Mount Oh-Be-Joyful, as the logo.

She also showed no signs of handing over the reins.

Who'd take over after her eventual retirement was anyone's guess. Wilder, his older brother, high-tailed out of here years ago, becoming a smoke jumper in Montana. His younger brother, Archer, was more interested in wrangling and women than responsibility. Maybe the sprawling property would pass to one of their dozens of second or third cousins.

For now, though, Hidden Rock was Grandma's domain. Sawyer bought a few acres from her when it looked like he'd be settling down, before life kicked him in the teeth with the heel of a stiletto. Still, he held no regrets, at least not for the cabin, built with his two hands, the old-fashioned way. His log house wasn't a prefab made-to-order, shipped in and snapped together like Lincoln Logs. Instead, he spoke with neighbors, visited land, and selected trees he felled with his own axe, avoiding chainsaws wherever possible. He still had finishing work left, but for the most part the place was stout and snug, good enough, especially for a bachelor who lived alone with his dog.

Plus—blessing and a curse—he stayed close enough to ensure Grandma didn't get into too much trouble.

Apparently he needed to keep a closer watch.

Her pink-handled axe leaned against the log pile. "Were you chopping firewood?"

She waved her hand in dismissal. "Just a damn chicken."

"But you don't have a coop." An uneasy feeling washed over him. The Carsons' hens had been escaping for weeks. He'd returned the ones he'd found wandering before the coyotes had gotten hold of them, but Roger Carson only nodded an absentminded thanks, muttering Five Diamonds was "too much work."

Sawyer considered offering to do the repair job, but a man must respect another's right to run his land as he saw fit, even if Sawyer didn't admire it much.

"Where'd you find the chicken, Grandma?" he pressed.

She clomped up the backdoor steps and wiped her boots on the Go Away mat. "My conscience is clear."

"That's because you don't have one."

"I didn't find the chicken, it found me. The bird brain got in my garden, and you know how I feel about those tomatoes."

He knew Grandma loved him, in an abstract way, like the fact the sun rises, a law of nature, understood but little discussed. Grandma's veggie garden was a different story. Half her will to live seemed derived from growing things for the Brightwater County Fair, and her blue ribbons were proudly displayed above the living room fireplace.

If a Carson chicken had been so foolhardy as to wander into Grandma's tomatoes, no doubt it met a fast and furious end.

"I've had it to here with Kooky Carson." She raised her hand over her head. "That man couldn't pour piss from a boot if the instructions were printed on the heel. The girl needs to learn straight off—some things won't stand."

Something quickened deep inside him, the same way the west wind shook the aspen groves before a thunderstorm. "Girl?"

"Because the father is good as useless. You tell me, what grown man of sound mind spends his days gathering sticks and taking pretty pictures?"

Roger Carson's coffee table books sold in the high-end shops that started sprouting downtown, boutiques that filled long-empty store fronts. Word around The Baker's Dozen was that his photography sold for big bucks in places like Los Angeles and New York City.

"I think ol' Roger does fine for himself." Privately, he agreed with Grandma, but at least one of them had to observe her other oft-repeated and ignored rule, "If you can't say anything nice . . ."

"Well, he's gone." She sniffed as if to indicate *and good riddance*. She coveted Five Diamonds, had for years, clucking with disapproval after Roger ceased farming operations, focused on his art, and let the property go wild.

The Eastern Sierras were notoriously dry, most of the rain falling in the mountains. Brightwater River was the lifeblood to this harsh environment. After the Kanes lost the majority of their access in that unlucky hand of poker, the Carsons of old had been tight-fisted, allowing water access but forcing the Kanes to pay, nearly crippling the ranch. Grandma expanded their landholdings in other directions, and built back what they lost, but she carried the old grudge with dogged determination.

"Where'd Roger go?"

"That old hippie flitted off to Mexico. Imagine leaving with your roof in that condition, but what can you expect different from Kooky Carson? Remember the time he staged that whatchamacallit in the town square last year?"

"The hug-in?" Sawyer held back a cringe, remembering Roger, barefoot in a pair of overalls, strumming a ukulele between handmade signs that read, "Love is the Answer," "World Peace Starts At Home," and "Free Hugs."

A curious crowd sprouted on the sidewalk, but no one took Roger, or Kooky Carson, as he was known, up on his hug offer.

"I don't understand some people, I really don't. They wouldn't know how to find their backside if it was painted like a baboon."

She hadn't brought up "the girl," again, so he needed to proceed with caution. Grandma's senses were bloodhound good. She'd sniff him out unless he was mighty careful.

"Maybe I should pop around Five Diamonds in the morning and fix the coop."

"Nah, keep 'em coming. I've got a taste for fried drumsticks."

"Strange though, isn't it?" Sawyer hooked a hand behind his neck. "Not even Carson would leave the country and abandon animals."

Grandma gripped the handrail and turned, staring like he was a prize idiot. "Sawyer John. Do you have bricks for brains? Yes or no."

"Grandma—"

"Yes or no?"

"No." He smothered a grin. Grandma's annoyance overrode her suspicious nature.

"Five Diamonds isn't empty. That girl's back, like I told you, the little wild one who always looked like a half-starved chickadee. She never did grow right, probably didn't get enough protein."

So Annie Carson had come home at last. How long had it been? Ten years. She'd kept true to her promise, left Brightwater and never spoken to him after that disastrous graduation party. His last glimpse had been of her beautiful blue eyes, not gentle and warm, but sealed off like a frozen lake. She believed he'd betrayed her, set her up for the whole school to mock.

"You think my family is a joke, Sawyer Kane? That I'm a joke?" she'd choked out. "Guess what? The joke's on you because I'm going places, getting out of this nowhere town." She'd run in the opposite direction, surprisingly fast given her Birkenstocks.

Grandma wagged a finger. "Watch it, boy, you just tripped standing still. Why are you still here, anyway?"

Sawyer snapped to the present. "Wanted to see you home safe." Safe as she could be while plotting world domination and mass poultry murder.

Her face softened. Well, not exactly, but it turned a hair less severe. "You always were a good boy, Sawyer."

The unexpected compliment warmed his heart.

"But shave more. Because what we need to do is find you a nice girl."

"Grandma." The warmth faded fast.

"It's not right, you living alone in the cabin. This valley is our home and we need to keep it stocked."

"Stocked?" He shook his head, hoping he didn't hear her right.

"Breed the herd. Outsiders are coming in, more every day, thanks to that no-account nightmare." Grandma didn't think a great deal of the popular film *Tumbleweeds*, shot in the valley, and neither had much love lost for Buck Williams, the actor who played the blind cowboy. "It's time to get back in the saddle after Ruby."

"We're not talking about Ruby." His ex-fiancée, or Mrs. Buck Williams as she was now known.

When the film crew first rolled into town, Ruby's face and charm landed her a coveted role as an extra, and soon a new role all together, as a Hollywood up-and-comer's arm candy. It took a while before he realized what hurt wasn't her absence, but his ego. Her parting words ran on a loop in his head. "Moose, you're a Chevy and I have Rolls-Royce dreams."

"Remember your duty to Brightwater," Grandma snapped.

"I do." He shook his head to clear it. "Every day. I'm the sheriff, my whole life is duty."

She snorted. "You pull people over for traffic violations and bust bored kids spray painting the water tower."

"There's more to it than that." Hell, he'd been awarded a medal of honor from the governor for his role in dismantling a regional meth lab last fall. Domestic assault could go bad. Bar brawls weren't uncommon. His office was small, him and his two deputies, but they were capable and frequently called in to assist over in Sierra County. He and Maverick volunteered with the search and rescue in Yosemite's high country and the adjacent wilderness when hikers went missing.

Speak of the devil, his dog appeared from the shadows.

"Hey there, Mav." He crouched to scratch his black pointed ear. Some people thought German Shepherds were aggressive, but Maverick had nothing but heart. He failed out of K-9 school for licking the mock intruders.

"Roo roo roo," Maverick responded, in a tone that meant anything from "My day's been satisfactorily engaged in genital licking" to "Chewed a bone. Barked at a cat." Some days Sawyer wished for a dog's life. They didn't stress about bank account balances or gold-digging exes. They simply were. If in Sawyer's lifetime he got half as wise as Maverick, he'd consider himself one lucky son of a bitch.

"I'm tuckered out," Grandma snapped. "Time you get on home."

"Night, Grandma."

"Night, boy."

Maybe it should bug him more, how she refused to acknowledge he'd grown up and become a man with his own home and hearth, but instead it mostly amused him. He walked by the axe glinting in the moonlight and the smile slid from his face.

"Sawyer?"

He glanced over his shoulder.

Grandma poked her head back outside. "Something smells fishy."

Things always smelled fishy to Grandma. She started half the conspiracy theories in town. "How so?"

"Got one of those feelings."

Grandma and her feelings. He wanted to tell her it was gout, but even though he outweighed her by a good hundred pounds, she fought dirty. Probably hid brass knuckles in her pajamas.

"That girl is up to something, mark my words. She's Kooky Carson's next-of-kin, there's bound to be trouble. Big trouble."

"Night, Grandma."

The slamming door didn't do much to mask her dismayed grunt.

He strode up the hill with visions of a young, pixie blonde filling his mind. While he'd known who Annie was for years, they'd never directly spoken until the afternoon he discovered her poised on a cliff over the Brightwater River. He'd gone for a ramble down through the gulch behind Hidden Rock and froze beneath the cottonwoods. Her lean, naked body glinted in the dappled light, and as she jumped without a trace of hesitation, raw need took root in his stomach, blooming into an unfamiliar ache.

Wonder if she's changed at all.

At the cabin, he hoisted the telescope bag on his shoulder and kicked the dirt off his boots before walking up the wide front steps. He never wanted to study astronomy. Law enforcement had always been his path, a way to serve and protect, make a difference to the community. But he loved the stars. And when he set his mind on buying a telescope, he waited, saved, and the one he eventually bought was damn near professional grade.

Maverick kept to his heels, and before he turned on the bedroom light, another appeared, in the dark, down the hill at Five Diamonds Farm. A breeze ruffled the plain white curtains and he released a breath. Once upon a time, the split-rail fence separating his life from Annie's had been breached. The two of them spent time together at the swimming hole. Cliff jumped. Talked. Ignored the old grudge and the roles they were supposed to play, that of "Brightwater High's popular star pitcher" and "Town misfit orbiting the farthest reaches of the social galaxy."

He didn't have the word for it then but he did now.

Love.

As a boy, he'd loved that bewildering, beautiful girl and lost her. Maybe this was his chance to be the man who finally got a shot at righting past wrongs.

He dug his fingers into his palms and let Annie Carson's lamp burn into him.

Chapter Three

ANNIE SQUINTED IN the not-quite-dawn light. *What's that racket?* Atticus nestled beside her, fast asleep, but not for long at this rate. Good Lord, had Grandma Kane returned to pound the front door a second time? No, wait . . . the sound came from farther off—more of a banging. Or hammering. Yes, that was it. Someone hammered out by the barn.

Her patience might stretch with salt-water taffy resiliency, but everyone had a breaking point. Annie gritted her teeth and disentangled from Atticus's sweaty body, tucking his stuffed orca under his arm to replace her presence. Her terrycloth robe hung on the door hook. She shrugged it over her Rad Mama sleeping t-shirt, knotting the tie loose at her hips.

The racket increased as she plodded down the stairs. Each pound reverberated through her throbbing skull. Her mouth tasted gross and she needed a drink of water, stat. Lesson learned—scotch was a brief, bad fling never to be repeated. Her reflection stared from the carved oak mirror at the base of the stairs. Not exactly a formidable sight. More befuddled hedgehog after ill-advised relations with an electrical socket.

Turned out pixie cuts looked cuter on Pinterest.

She eased out the back door and peered around suspiciously, but it was hard to feel menace with such a glorious sunrise unfolding. Knife-edge peaks were saturated in a golden glow, and the range's pinnacle, Mount Oh-Be-Joyful, flushed a rosy pink. She inhaled deep, savoring the hint of wild hyacinth and pine—the evocative scents conjuring long forgotten memories of braiding daisy chains with Claire or eating sun-warmed strawberries straight from the vine. Flowers sprouted in odd clumps along the dirt path, a rainbow hodgepodge of purple sage, yellow blazing stars and the last of the dusky blue lupine. Later, she'd pick a bouquet with Atticus for the dining room table like she used to as a girl. The old house had a neglected, dusty feel, too long lonely. It needed TLC, not just in the form of paint and shingles, but love and laughter.

She padded closer to the hammer strikes and each blow fractured her fledgling optimism. Grandma Kane had always seemed determined to continue the feud, hollering like a mad ox if she and Claire snuck across the ranch to go blackberry picking or hiking. Her big sister did particularly stellar impersonations of Grandma screeching, "Carrrrrrrssssooooooons, I see you, don't think I can't."

Their simple, if isolated, life complicated after Claire decided they needed to put their foot down, stop the homeschooling, and spend time at Brightwater High School, figuring out how the world operated off Five Diamonds before they turned eighteen. For the daughters of Kooky Carson, this was the equivalent to traveling to a Martian outpost, a strange environment where no one ate quinoa, listened to the Grateful Dead and Ravi Shankar, or read *The Electric Kool-Aid Acid Test*.

Claire graduated after one year, leaving Annie alone with two hundred suspicious strangers, most of them sporting the last name Kane. Honestly, that family bred like jackrabbits in the backfield, all tall, green-eyed, good-looking, and loud. So loud. A family genetically programmed to yell-talk.

Except one.

No time to entertain *that* particular line of thinking, not when rounding the corner, amped, ready to go Hatfields vs. McCoys. Grandma Kane would never pluck another feather off a Carson chicken, not on her watch. Those hens were her friends, not food. If there must be a fight, Annie would defend them to the last—

She skidded to a halt as he glanced up—not an old woman, but *him*, crouched beside the coop, hammer clutched in one big hand.

"Sawyer?" All she could do was gape, wide-eyed and breathless—too breathless. Could he tell? Hard to say as he maintained his customary faraway expression, the one that made it look as if he stepped out of a black-and-white photograph.

"Annie."

She jumped. Hearing her name on his tongue plucked something deep in her belly, a sweet aching string, the hint of a chord she only ever found in the dark with her own hand. It was impossible not to stare, and suddenly the long years disappeared, until she was that curious seventeen-year-old girl again, seeing a gorgeous boy watching her from the riverbanks, and wondering if the Earth's magnetic poles had quietly flipped.

Stop. Just say no to unwelcome physical reactions. Her body might turn traitor, but her mind wouldn't let her down. She'd fallen for this guy's good looks before, believed they mirrored a goodness inside—a mistake she wouldn't make twice. No man would ever be allowed to stand by and watch her crash again.

Never would she cry in the shower so no one could hear.

Never would she wait for her child to fall asleep so she could fall apart.

Never would she jump and blindly fall.

Sawyer removed his tan Stetson and stood. Treacherous hyperawareness raced along her spine and radiated through her hips in a slow, hot electric pulse. He clocked in over six feet, with steadfast sagebrush green eyes that gave little away. Flecks of ginger gleamed from the scruff roughing his strong jaw and lightened the dark chestnut of his short-cropped hair.

"Hey." Her cheeks warmed as any better words scampered out of reach. The mile-long "to do" list taped to the fridge didn't include squirming in front of the guy she'd nurtured a secret crush on during her teenage years. A guy who, at the sole party Annie had attended in high school, abandoned her in a hallway closet during Seven Minutes in Heaven to mothballed jackets, old leather shoes, ruthless taunts, and everlasting shame.

He reset his hat. "Did I wake you?" His voice had always appealed to her, but the subtle rough deepening was something else, as if every syllable dragged over a gravel road.

She checked her robe's tie. "Hammering at sunrise kind of has that effect on people."

He gave her a long look. His steadfast perusal didn't waver an inch below her neck, but still, as he lazily scanned each feature, she felt undressed to bare skin. Guess his old confidence hadn't faded, not a cocky manufactured arrogance, but a guy completely comfortable in his own skin.

And what ruggedly handsome, sun-bronzed skin it was, covering all sorts of interesting new muscles he hadn't sported in high school.

"Heard Grandma paid you a visit," he said at last.

Annie doused the unwelcome glow kindling in her chest with a bucket of ice-cold realism. He wasn't here to see her, merely to deal with a mess. *Hear that, hormones? Don't be stupid.* She set a hand on her hip, summoning as much dignity as she could muster with a serious case of bedhead. "Visit? Your grandma killed one of our chickens and baked it in a pie. Not exactly the welcome wagon. More like a medieval, craz—"

"Subtlety isn't one of her strong points. We had words

last night. It won't happen again." He dusted his hands on his narrow denim-clad hips and bent down.

Unf.

The hard-working folks at Wrangler deserved a medal for their service. Nothing else made a male ass look so fine. "Found this too." He lifted her forgotten bottle of scotch.

"Oh, weird." She plucked it from his grasp. "Wonder how that got out here?" Crap, too saccharine a tone, sweet but clearly false.

He raised his brows as his hooded gaze dropped a fraction. Not enough to be a leer, but definitely a look.

Her threadbare terrycloth hit mid-thigh. Here stood the hottest guy west of the Mississippi and she hadn't shaved since who-the-hell knows and sported a lop-sided bruise on her knee from yesterday's unfortunate encounter with a gopher hole.

Maybe she failed at keeping up appearances, but God as her witness, she'd maintain her posture. "About your grandma—I was two seconds from calling the cops on her last night."

"That a fact?" The corner of his wide mouth twitched. "Next time, that's exactly what you should do."

"Next time?" she sputtered, waving the bottle for emphasis. "There sure as heck better not be a next time!"

That little burst of sass earned the full force of his smile. Laugh lines crinkled at the corners of deep-set eyes that belonged nowhere but the bedroom. As a boy, he was a sight. As a man, he'd become a vision. "Why are you back? I mean, after all this time?"

My husband wanted to screw other women while I kept the house clean. "Divorce-induced homelessness." She dropped the bottle to her side, somehow managing to keep her voice steady.

Sawyer glanced to the farmhouse, jaw tightening. The place appeared even more run down in the light of day. The earlier idea of infusing the home with love and happiness seemed laughable now. Instead, it looked like work, and more work.

"The coop should hold your hens for the moment," he said at last. "But the wood's rotted. What do you say I come 'round tomorrow and replace the frame?"

More Sawyer? Desire and panic converged, churning against her lower ribs. "That's okay. I can handle it," she answered quickly—her autopilot answer for everything these days. There had to be a DIY YouTube video for hen-house repairs, right? Move along, nothing to see here. No divorcée in distress up at Five Diamonds.

"It's not a—"

"Everything's under control." It was bad enough having him here at six a.m., catching her hung-over and half dressed. No way would she become a pitiful charity case. After all, a gal had to keep a shred of pride when her life frayed.

"Okay, whatever you say." The strange light in his eyes from a moment ago—that flare . . . or spark of interest—smothered like baking soda on a grease fire. The swift change startled her even though she'd never forgotten that remote look, the way he could pack up his thoughts and retreat to God-knows-where. In fact, at seventeen, she'd squandered far too many hours sitting on sun-warmed rocks along the river, trying to decode the meaning behind his various brow quirks and private half-smiles.

"I have a question too." Looks like her brain's caffeine withdrawal prodded her to do incredibly stupid things like try to gain closure, an answer to the *why* she'd been rolling like a boulder up the back of her brain for the last decade. *Why did he invite her to that stupid party? Why did he never come to the closet?* She had gone hoping Sawyer Kane would be her first kiss. Instead, he became the first guy to break her heart.

Sawyer stilled.

A truck backfired in the distance.

A red-winged blackbird laughed from atop a wood rose.

"Go ahead then, what do you want to know?" So he still did that trick too, the one where he scoured all emotion from his tone.

She bit her inner cheek hard, the faint taste of copper flooding her mouth. Her stomach waffled. Did she really want to hear the reason he betrayed her all those years ago? It was ancient history, water under the bridge. "Never mind, I forget."

He tilted back his Stetson, running his intense gaze over her face. "You haven't changed much."

The simple statement threatened to fell her. He had no idea everything was different. The dreamy, hopeful girl she'd been, the one he'd known all those years ago, had her atoms obliterated and her soft underbelly refashioned, armored with titanium plates. She didn't run barefoot through meadows or jump blindly into rivers.

Not anymore.

"Thanks for the repair job," she said, stepping back, blinking rapidly. He'd fixed the coop, but no one could fix the cracks in her confidence and imploded self-esteem. She needed to do that—if only she knew how. Was there a *Self-esteem for Dummies*?

Then he moved. Close. Closer. Way too close. The old magnetic pull between them hadn't lost any potency. The air charged. So much so that when he reached out, cradling her cheek, she expected a zap. "I missed you, Annie Girl."

Her heart beat sideways at his use of the old nickname.

"I . . . " *missed you too. God. So much.* "I have to go." She took another step backward and then another. "And anyway, I'm not staying, at least not for long. My family's decided it's time to sell the farm."

"Sell?" His body went rigid. "But this place has been in your family forever. All your history is here. How can you let it go to a stranger?"

Who was he to come around at an ungodly hour, in those tight faded jeans that showcased his . . . everything, touching her cheek, giving her unsolicited guidance? Her chest heated. Is that why he was here—being the good cop to Grandma Kane's bad cop? "I appreciate your help with the coop, but let's not pretend you're giving impartial neighborly advice. Your family wants the property back. Trust me, I get the situation. I was raised with it, but we can get more for Five Diamonds than your grandmother could ever offer."

He dropped his chin, leveling a penetrating stare. "That's not what I meant, it's not about the feud. You know I don't care about any of that."

She used to believe that, had once fooled herself into believing they were kindred spirits. "I don't know anything about you anymore, Sawyer. Maybe I never did."

She pivoted and strode toward the house, clenching the scotch bottle. Why did he come, force her to feel things better forgotten? She was almost at the stairs when a large, powerful hand closed on her upper arm, not a grip, but a gentle touch that halted her mid-step. Her heart pounded, her belly breaking into wild flutters.

Slowly, so slowly, she turned.

He held her gaze squarely, as if daring her to look away. "You know who I am," he said.

She couldn't reply, even if she knew what to say. She couldn't blink or swallow or think. The only sound beside the wind came from their shallow breaths. She and Sawyer might be water under the bridge, but it looked like that water was churning, roiling whitewater.

But even if, purely hypothetically speaking, she still wanted him in that same heady way that threatened to consume her at seventeen, it didn't make a damn difference. She wasn't that carefree girl anymore. And what she wanted, and what she needed, were two vastly different things.

"Please, let me go." No mistaking the desperate edge to her voice.

He released her in an instant. "Annie—"

But she was already opening the back door, and when

it slammed behind her, for once she was grateful for this farmhouse, however dilapidated.

It still had walls and could keep people out.

SAWYER HELD IT together until he reached the fence. Annie rattled him more than he expected. Even with her short hair going north, south, east and west—goddamn was she a sight. The cute, awkward girl had grown up, less skin-and-bones, more womanly, but still a pixie. With baby blues that left him as tongue-tied as ever.

She'd run from him as if fleeing a ghost. He kicked a post, his boot going through the wood. More rot. He shook his head, molars grinding on reflex. Roger Carson seemed like a nice enough man, but if he were here, Sawyer wouldn't be able to account for his actions. Leaving Annie to sort out this mess wasn't kooky. It was damn irresponsible. Everywhere he looked required hard physical labor.

It didn't surprise him that she didn't want to be needy or ask favors. Not really. This was a hard country and it bred independent spirits.

Still, she needed a hand.

Annie Girl.

When he said she hadn't changed, he'd told a lie—her smile had. Her open grin had vanished. Now the shape of her sweet mouth went through the motions, but was a poor imitation. She appeared tired, worried, and a little angry.

He paused, lost in memories of long ago. He'd invited

her to a party the night of graduation, not giving two shits that Grandma considered the Carsons to be mortal enemies, and giving even less of a shit that her dad was the town weirdo. He wasn't attracted to Kooky Carson, but his youngest daughter . . . now that was a different story. There was no one else as open, pretty, perfect and fine, a little bit of an oddball. But he didn't mind the odd. The odd was cute.

By the time Annie had arrived, the kegger turned dangerous, too much beer. Too much restlessness. As she walked into the kitchen, people drew in like sharks sensing blood in the water. They hated her peasant skirts and strange tastes in music like it was a normal fact of life, as obvious as the idea cereal tasted better with milk, or Tuesday followed Monday.

Everything went down fast. Someone suggested a game of Seven Minutes in Heaven, and as the crowd drove her toward the hallway closet, another person yelled, "Aw, yeah. Sawyer's going to get some hippie ass."

What was supposed to happen in a perfect moment— his and Annie's first kiss—twisted into something ugly.

He'd set his shoulders and stalked through the mob, ready to bust into the damn closet, grab Annie and get her away. Instead, hands seized his torso, dragging him backward. He was bigger and sober, but they outnumbered him, beating him hard and fast behind the house. So-called friends, saying it was for his own good.

Inside, people cheered. He finally broke free and ran to the front, but it was too late. Annie fled down the porch steps, her eyes bright with unshed tears. "Did you set me up?" she'd whispered, as someone shouted, "Way to teach that little Carson freak a lesson, Sawyer!" through an open window.

Annie had made good on her promise never to speak to him again, at least until today. Was she serious about selling Five Diamonds, a property that had been in her family well over a century, slamming the door on Brightwater forever? The town hadn't treated her kindly in the past, but people grew up and changed.

He glanced down. There, beside his boot, a wild rose nestled half hidden in tall field grass. He'd almost stepped on the damn truth. Despite their thorny past, and whatever her recent hurts, something still bloomed between them. He squatted down and traced his thumb over the rose's delicate petals.

All he could do was see how things would grow. He didn't have anything to lose. There was no such thing as a third chance. Better make this second one count.

Chapter Four

[draft]

Musings of a Mighty Mama

Gratitude

older posts>>

*Welcome to the start of the "Mighty Mama Thirty
Days of Thankfulness." To celebrate "the little things" here
on the blog, I'm sharing snapshots that capture blessings
in my life—an opportunity to reflect on the extra in the
ordinary, to honor the perfect moment.*

Today's choice?

Soup.

*Simple. Nourishing. No frills. Nothing else nourishes
the spirit in quite the same way. My personal favorite*

is curried kale and apple—heavenly! Atticus played
sous chef and deboned the leafy greens to simmer with
chunks of onion, homemade stock, and a crème fraîche
(we concoct our own curry powder using hand-grated
turmeric, dried chiles, and organic garlic). Tasty and
affordable, what more can—

"Mo-om, what's that nasty smell?" Atticus inched
toward the stove, sticking his tongue out.

Annie glanced from her laptop to the television timer.
Her son might be her everything, but he still had twenty-
two minutes of allotted PBS Kids time. From the living
room, a cartoon character screeched at his little sister
over who deserved the last sandwich at their family
picnic. Annie gritted her teeth. This particular show
shredded her last nerve.

She'd been staring blankly at the screen for ten minutes seeing only a pair of intense green eyes. There wasn't
time for blogger's block, not with everything else going
on. She had to finish the essay. Now. Her original content
posts had dropped to a dismal twice-weekly rate since the
divorce, padded out by Instagram-filtered photographs
and product endorsements. Good, but not good enough
to get her taken seriously once they moved to San Francisco. She needed to be seen as a serious writer, not a hob-
byist.

The month of gratitude was an attempt to get back on
track. She couldn't afford to lose momentum, not after
all the progress she'd made building up a stable reader-

ship and securing sponsors. How many hours were spent every week writing posts, trialing recipes, experimenting with new craft projects, scheduling social media across Twitter, Tumblr, Pinterest, Facebook, responding to comments and emails, and figuring out techy glitches on the site?

So many.

Too many to fail. Especially when she was finally on the cusp of making it.

Come on, focus. Focus!

Okay, which photograph should accompany today's post? The shot where Atticus chopped kale turned out cute, but recently a troll had started filling her comments section with snark. Better not provide ammunition about the fact he wielded a knife and select a more generic shot featuring the simmering stockpot. The blue cast-iron was rather fetching in contrast with the soup's earthy green. Although, frick, she should include the new wooden ladle. Earthwoods Utensils was *Mighty Mama*'s newest sponsor and needed to be kept happy.

Smiling at the Sun, run by Zoe Renee, homeschooling mother of five who also managed a fourth-generation Vermont sugarhouse when not spinning wool or weaving, was the Death Star of mommy blogs. No one else came close to making motherhood look oh-so-effortlessly joyful. All Zoe's posts went viral. All Zoe's five children were daily showcased in hand-knit sweaters, happily feeding ducks, gobbling collard greens, putting on home puppet shows, or whittling chess pieces. Earthwoods also sponsored Zoe and she'd hosted a series of giveaways for the company last week. Annie couldn't copy that, but a subtle slice-of-life endorsement wouldn't go amiss.

"Ew, I don't eat puke." Atticus clutched his belly, round despite the recent five-year-old growth spurt that left his legs this side of gangly.

"We don't use that word in this house." Annie dropped her chin in her hand and stared out the window, suddenly exhausted. Imagine lying out in the grass, watching clouds drift over the range, without a camera for once, reveling in the sheer pleasure of the moment?

Sun shone on the split-rail fence that divided Five Diamonds from Hidden Rock. Sawyer had come this morning on foot. Did that mean he still lived next door? Once, okay, maybe twice, she'd searched for him on Facebook, purely out of idle curiosity, or so she told herself. He never set up an account.

"Vomit, vomit," Atticus chanted, beating a fist in time. "The soup looks like vomit."

"Come on, bud." Annie searched for serenity and came up lacking. Instead, she reached for her favorite handmade pottery mug. "You have twenty more television minutes." The coffee tasted bitter and black, but she chugged the lukewarm contents anyway.

Unlike Sawyer, Gregor never made her go all brain-mushy with longing, even in the earliest days of their courtship. She'd been more impressed with his age at first, thirty-eight to her twenty-two. He wasn't another commitment-phobic college guy swilling PBR and playing video games. The fact that he didn't hang at bars, but invited her back to his place to split a bottle of pinot noir, was intriguing. He traveled widely, wore collared shirts and read the whole paper, not just the sports section. Her own father wasn't much of a grownup and hindsight suggested maybe her marriage wasn't ever based in love, but rooted in Freudian daddy issues.

Fabulous.

Her college pals used to tease her for being an old soul. When the pill failed and she got pregnant, a city hall marriage at twenty-three felt fun, like playing at a normalcy she'd never had in her own eccentric youth.

She'd marched from a barefoot hippie childhood to a journalism degree into motherhood, and after founding *Musings of a Mighty Mama*, her world expanded with a large online community. Her recipes for pureed sweet potato and chick peas, or popular essays pondering water and electricity waste in cloth diapering leant a certain significance to what was otherwise hours of being screamed at while facing down various bodily fluids. Plus, writing was enjoyable, days passed more quickly when she put her brain to use. As college friends drifted away, she connected more to strangers through parenting forums and one-on-one messaging.

She poured another cup of coffee, her third this morning. The caffeine combined with post-Sawyer jitters set her teeth on edge.

No. Don't think about him.

So what if she focused her attention on writing posts about Atticus's food bravery (his favorite lunch—baked tofu with nutritional yeast), or making bird houses from reclaimed wood? The blog had made her feel valued when Gregor's hobby became how many times he could dismiss her at dinner parties.

For the record, she got his jokes.

How many surrealists does it take to screw in a light bulb?

A fish.

It was just that they weren't funny.

The soup bubbled and she turned off the gas before it burned. "Honey," she called to Atticus, now cannonballing off Great-Grandma Carson's rocking chair with accompanying war whoops, "if you don't want to watch a show, can you play with Lego? I'm so close to getting this post finished. Two more minutes."

"Love you, Mommy." Atticus snuck from behind and hugged her waist.

Her throat constricted. "I love you, too, little man." Atticus was all that mattered, being his mom was a privilege, what she did, what she knew, what she was more or less good at—at least around sixty-seven percent of the time.

Her darling little privilege unleashed a high-pitched noise like a humpback dying a slow death by strangulation.

Time to get out the mental shovel and dig for patience. "What are you doing?"

"Is this what bobcats sound like?" Atticus made the ear-splitting sound again.

"Please, enough, stop." She winced. "Let's investigate it later."

His dramatic sigh came from the toes of his red Converse. "I'm bored."

"You're five."

"So?"

"So, you're not allowed to use that word yet."

He marched into the center of the kitchen and crossed his arms in a huff.

"Look, why don't you run outside, poke around the old garden, go on a ladybug hunt? I can make you a snack." Maybe they could take a hike to Rainbow Falls this afternoon. Generate material for a future post. She'd written a similar one about connecting kids with nature six months ago and generated lots of traffic and pingbacks. Also, she needed to focus more on writing about the farmhouse. Despite its many—God, so many—problems, it was charming in a way, with the wonky porch step, pressed-tin kitchen ceiling, and root cellar bursting with vintage canning jars.

Just don't mention the plumbing or the roof.

Or hot neighbors.

"Hey, guess what?" Atticus brightened. "You know where food goes? Poop!"

Annie caught her grimacing reflection in the coffee. There wasn't enough dark roast in the state this morning.

Atticus flitted to a chair and grabbed the Hello Kitty t-shirt crumpled on the seat.

"Wearing that again?" Annie kept her voice neutral. Another nail in the guilt coffin. The shirt was

Margot's, Atticus's acutely missed half-sister. Annie had known Margot since she was eleven, the worst loss in the break-up.

Atticus whisked the shirt over his shoulder and banged out the back door. How many times had she requested he close, not slam, the screen during the last twenty-four hours?

Bills spilled from the wicker basket beneath the phone. Joy of joys. Another place Dad likely dropped the ball. Rather than face the wrath of the utility company or finish her post, she sat and clicked through the blogosphere, visiting virtual friends. Everything was coming up roses at *Happy Mommy*, *Three Kids and Counting*, and *Baby Steps*. Looked like *Smiling at the Sun's* family had started grinding their own wheat, bully for Zoe.

Everyone appeared in top form: the essays were thoughtfully crafted, bursting with charm, felt toys, finger weaving and homemade chore charts. Everyone projected upbeat domestic bliss that settled on Annie like a weight.

Is Annie Carson real? She recently googled her name and the first hit on the search engine popped up with that question.

Was she?

Yes and no. Some days she lived her best and worst self simultaneously, writing mothering essays that made her want to fist pump, while Atticus crawled between her legs begging for attention and dinner overcooked.

Last Easter, Annie paced the holiday grocery store aisle for fifteen minutes debating whether or not to buy box dye for the boiled eggs. It was right after the divorce papers were signed and her energy levels barely registered. In the end, she trudged to the produce section with a heavy sigh and stayed up through the night, stewing beets, purple cabbage, and kale.

She made the shit out of homemade dye.

"I am divorced," she chanted, on repeat, over her keyboard at four a.m., writing up the corresponding blog post.

Divorced.

A love failure.

I suck.

Annie didn't record how her tears infused the dye. Or share how the next day she'd screamed herself hoarse when Atticus splashed beet juice on the wool rug.

The Easter egg post received over two hundred comments. Every word of praise burned her insides like toxic ooze.

Outside, Atticus made another noise, a breathless grunt that didn't sound good. Her chair clattered to the linoleum as she tore down the back steps at lightning speed. He hunched in the open barn doorway, face puckered, cradling his wrist.

"What happened?"

"Hurts, Mama," he wailed. His hand bent at an awkward angle, one that threatened to send her breakfast across her fuzzy slippers.

"Shhhh, shhhhh. You're okay, you're okay." She scooped his light frame against her and bee-lined to the car. Thank God the keys were under the sun visor.

"No! No!" He arched his back against the booster seat.

"I'm going to make it better." She clicked the shoulder strap, gasping when his scream fired into her ear canal. Jumping into the driver's seat, she carefully navigated the gravel driveway, avoiding most, but not all, of the potholes. Each backseat whimper struck her heart like a felling axe. At the main road, she gunned it, barely registering the scenery, the wide river lined with leafy cottonwoods or the snow-capped ridgelines.

"Hurts, Mama," Atticus moaned over and over. She glanced in the rearview mirror searching for inner calm, bravery, anything, but the sight of his tears, the way his snub nose wrinkled as he held his body rigid, trying to move as little as possible, undid her. She sucked in and held a ragged breath.

If only she could siphon his pain into her own body.

If only she'd paid better attention.

If only wouldn't fix the bone in her child's arm or the guilt-laced acid dissolving her stomach.

The local Brightwater hospital wasn't big, and on a quiet Sunday morning the only other people in the emergency room were a black-eyed ranch hand who looked like he'd spent the night tangoing with an angry bull, and a grizzled man in Carhartt overalls snoring in the corner.

Great, she and Atticus were part of Derelict Hour. The more respectable Brightwater residents sat in church pews, not ushering their weeping only child into the x-ray room. She didn't miss the frown the wiry-haired nurse gave her son's Hello Kitty shirt. The woman glanced at the chart, a knowing expression crossing her features. "Carson, hmmm? Any relation to Kooky, er, Roger Carson?"

Didn't sound like she was a fan of the man with the long salt-and-pepper ponytail, left-wing political sympathies, and endless supply of tie-dyed ensembles that contrasted with the valley's usual denim and plaid uniform.

"He's my father." Annie resisted the urge to fidget. Did hospitals purposely make the seating as hard and uncomfortable as possible?

"Can I have a pink cast?" Atticus stared with a hopeful expression. His skinny legs dangled off the edge of the examination table and made him look so small and helpless. He should be wrapped in tender cotton wool, not sitting here with broken bones.

The nurse pulled a face like a camel sucking a lemon. Claire would call her a twathole, but Annie preferred to kill haters with kindness.

"Hey, no big deal." She forced a conspiratorial smile. "He likes pink and Ninja Turtles. A well-rounded kid."

Were clinic staff allowed to roll their eyes?

"How about blue?" the nurse pressed, turning to Atticus. "A big boy like you prefers blue, right?"

"But pink matches Margot's shirt," he whimpered, fresh tears coursing his blotchy cheeks.

"He said pink." Annie spoke through her teeth.

"Well, now I've seen everything," the nurse grumbled, eyeing the closed door as if mentally summoning child protective services.

Annie stood firm and Atticus got his pink cast.

"Maybe I should have chosen blue," he whispered when it was over.

"Maybe so." The nurse's sneer wiggled the thick hair on the mole beside her lip. "Tell Mommy to keep a better eye on you up there." As if Five Diamonds was seeped in pot smoke and anarchy—a hippie commune not fit for a child.

That wasn't the case, at least not anymore.

"I think we're all set here." Annie rose to her feet. No doubt Brightwater would soon buzz with tales that the kooky Carsons were back in force. She could take it, she always had. But if anyone dared say a word crosswise about her son, they'd be eating a knuckle sandwich.

Annie helped Atticus get back into the car and started home. Broken coops and broken children . . . what if she couldn't cope? Mount Oh-Be-Joyful rose up out the driver's side window. The name mocked her, and the vast size made her feel small. Insignificant. Those ancient rocks knew her for what she was, not a pioneer babe or a perfectly orchestrated photograph, nothing but fleeting entertainment, easily deleted. Her tears fell in utter silence as she returned her gaze to the empty road. She knew how to do that, had a PhD in Muted Grief.

A red light flashed in the rear view. A siren blared.

Crap.

That was a stop sign back there. She blew through the quiet crossroads without even tapping her brakes. The same way she'd been living these last days and months. Keep going, keep moving, and get through it.

She had her license and registration out by the time the officer sauntered to the driver's side window and bent down.

No freaking way. Her mouth gaped, she blinked, but yep, he was still there. Sawyer Kane dressed in a beige and green uniform, his lean hips encased by a black leather holster. A trapdoor opened in her stomach as she met his fixed gaze and prayed for a little mercy.

Chapter Five

SAWYER GAZED THROUGH the driver's window. *Aw, hell.*

"It's you." Annie removed her oversized sunglasses, her eyes suspiciously shiny. At first glance they were an ordinary blue, but look deeper and they held the same color gradient of a mountain lake, light on the outer ring with indigo encircling the center.

His ex-fiancé favored silk and lace, but Annie's Lewis and Clark College hoodie and denim cut-offs were a form of temptation all on their own. Conjured an image of lazy weekend mornings, cooking a late breakfast, sleeping in, or better yet, not sleeping at all. The thought lasted only a moment, because a skinny, bespectacled boy regarded him from a booster in the backseat—wearing a pink shirt and color-coordinated cast.

Sawyer hid his start of surprise, just. Where'd the kid come from?

"You're a cop?" Her gaze ping-ponged back and

forth from his badge to his holster. "But . . . earlier when I threatened to call the police on your grandma . . . I didn't . . . you didn't—"

"License and registration, please." Easier to stick to the rulebook while deciding how to play this. Discovering Annie Carson drove the stop sign–running purple hybrid with the bumper stickers "I'm straight, but maybe it's a phase" and "This is what a feminist looks like" threw him for a loop. Realizing the boy was her dead ringer took him on a disorienting ride around a corkscrew roller coaster. He was her son. Annie was a mother.

Guess she still had a knack for surprising him.

That was an unexpected complication he hadn't considered. He didn't know the first thing about kids.

She handed over the documents and as their fingers grazed, nerve endings tingled as his ribs contracted a good inch. She still had a knack for doing that too.

"This is my sister's car. The registration's in Claire's name. She's letting me borrow it."

He studied her license photo, refocusing. "Portland." So that was where she'd run off to. People talked, said she'd gotten a scholarship to a fancy college in the Northwest, but no one was ever sure where. If she'd been back to visit the farm, he'd never seen any evidence. "You liked living in Oregon?"

"It's greener than here. Close to the ocean." Her gaze darted in any direction that wasn't his as she drummed her thumbs on the steering wheel.

"Did you ever miss Brightwater?" he asked softly. *Me?*

She shrugged, clearly not wanting to talk more than necessary. "Should I?"

He tipped back his hat. He didn't care. He'd missed her. "This is your home."

"My home?" There was that smile again, the one that didn't reach her eyes. "This valley is beautiful and it's probably a wonderful town to settle down in if you're part of the 'in' crowd. But I wouldn't know, would I?" She shook her head. "Sorry. I shouldn't snap. It's been one heck of a morning."

"What can I do to help?"

"Nothing." She bit her lower lip, but not before it gave a tell-tale wobble.

"Annie—"

"I'm fine." She did a good job of keeping her sigh internal, but not good enough.

"I fell in a hole," the boy piped from the backseat.

"In the barn, the floor is rotted . . . " Annie burst into sudden, helpless tears.

Nothing tore him up more than a crying woman, and for that woman to be Annie?

Shit.

Gritting his teeth against a nearly physical need to provide her comfort, instinct held him back, kept him from murmuring, "Stop. Hush. Everything will be all right." Instead, she seemed to need a moment to let go, release whatever tore up her insides. He could give her that, despite the fact each hitching sob slugged his guts like a fist.

The kid peered out the window with eyes the size of dinner plates. Sawyer offered a reassuring nod.

The next minute passed as slow as an hour, but finally, her sobs lessened. He squatted down and offered the clean handkerchief from his back pocket.

"I'm sorry." She dabbed her eyes. "That was uncalled for. I'm fine and should really be—"

"Follow me."

She blinked in red-eyed confusion. "Please, don't bring me in. I'm sorry about the stop sign. If you need to write me a ticket you can—"

"I'm not taking you to the sheriff's office," he said, touching her shoulder. She tensed but didn't move away. Beneath that too-thick cotton was bare skin. The idea of being that close to her hit him like a shot of tequila in a Red Bull. "You still like hot chocolate?"

"Hot chocolate?" The boy perked. "We love hot chocolate, don't we, Mommy?"

Mommy. In ten years, Annie had become a woman, and a mother. And yet, some things never changed. She still had a weakness for chocolate. And despite everything, he still had a weakness for her.

"A new coffee shop in town opened up today," he said. "I've been told it's going to be good. The test will be if the new owner can make a mean hot chocolate."

"It must be eighty degrees out."

He rubbed his chin, already covered with scruff despite the morning's careful shave. "That never stopped the Annie Carson I knew."

That earned a glimmer of a real smile, small, but her eyes brightened. "You got me there."

He stood. "So you'll follow me?"

"But you're working. I don't want to take your time. It's fine."

"*Fine*. You keep using that word." But saying a thing didn't make it true. He knew because he'd been feeding himself the same line and still felt hungry. The bachelor life with Maverick was fine. He liked his job, had a good house, and could watch a ball game or fish whenever he wanted.

But shouldn't life be better than fine? Something full, rich, and real?

"Mommy, can we go with the sheriff? Please, please, plea—"

"Fine." She wrinkled her nose, catching herself, and glanced back to her son. "I mean, okay. Yes. After all, don't we deserve a treat?"

"I think you do." Sawyer didn't mean it to sound suggestive, but she blushed all the way to the tips of her ears. Hell, maybe he did. His reflection stared from the back window. Sometimes he hid his thoughts so well even he didn't know where to find them. That wasn't the case now. He looked like a man on a mission. Something told him Annie needed a heavy dose of sweetness.

SAWYER HELD OPEN the door to Haute Coffee.

"Cute name," Annie murmured, looking around. The

interior was cuter still, with wooden floors polished to a warm honey-gold, exposed brick walls showcasing vintage travel posters from the region, and a pressed-tin ceiling gleaming in the morning light. This was a spot where she could curl up with a good book or work on the blog. Her kind of place.

"Today is the grand opening," Sawyer said. "Looks like it's going well."

Most of the tables were full and a striking woman frothed milk behind the counter, her thick red hair held back by a paisley headband. She glanced in their direction with a distracted smile. "Welcome! Be right with you."

Annie racked her brain, but couldn't place the barista, who exuded a casual but stylish poise. She'd have remembered someone with that vivid hair color. Plus, all her freckles contributed to a unique but undeniably eye-catching look.

"Her name is Edie and she's new in town." Sawyer leaned close to whisper into her ear. "The rumor mill claims she comes from New York City."

His breath teased the side of Annie's neck, a heat that spread south, leaving her breasts full and aching. "A friend of yours?" she managed to grind out.

"Archer knows her. I'm not sure how they met, but he seems to have taken an interest of sorts."

"Your brother?" Even in his teens, Archer had a way with women. Lots of women. "Who isn't he interested in?"

"Well . . . I don't think he's made the rounds at the nursing home. Yet."

Annie was surprised to find herself smiling, a real

smile, something that seemed impossible twenty minutes ago. She gave Sawyer a grateful look. "Thank you for inviting us."

"Thanks for saying yes." His hooded gaze dropped to her mouth. "You know, smiling is a good look on you."

A delicious warmth spread through her lower belly as if she'd already drank the promised hot chocolate.

"Um . . . " Edie discretely cleared her throat. "Are you ready to order?"

"Oh, yes. Yes, indeed." Annie placed a hand on the side of her neck, her pulse pounding beneath her fingers.

"Can we have a cupcake too, Mommy?" Atticus pressed his face against the glass display case.

"A cupcake and hot chocolate? That's a lot of sugar."

"It's hazelnut with Nutella frosting," Edie said with a conspiratorial wink.

"You don't play fair." Annie's mouth dropped. "How can anyone resist?"

Edie's aloof expression disappeared with a laugh that was shy but genuine. "That's my hope."

A Mumford & Sons song came on over the sound system and Annie sighed, "Ah. This is my favorite song," right as Edie said, "Hey, I love this song."

They exchanged warm glances. How nice to meet someone new in Brightwater, a woman who didn't know her as a kooky Carson, who liked great music, good coffee, and Nutella. The tension left her shoulders as Sawyer placed their orders, adding a slice of strawberry rhubarb pie to the mix and insisting on paying despite her protests.

"I'll bring this all right out," Edie said as more people came through the front door.

"It looks like your first day in business is a success," Annie said.

"Such a relief." Edie took a deep breath. "I wasn't sure how the town would react to a new coffee shop. The Baker's Dozen has been around forever."

Annie nodded with understanding. "People here can be slow to embrace change."

"I'm learning that, but still, I'm determined to make it work."

"Well, for as long as I'm in town, plan on me being a regular customer," Annie said. "Nutella lovers need to stick together."

"That sounds like a deal." Edie giggled. "Are you here for a visit?"

Annie glanced to the booth where Atticus was laughing at some story of Sawyer's. "No. I'm selling my family farm. Then moving to San Francisco to expand my business or maybe start a new project."

"What do you do?"

"I'm a mommy blogger. I know, it sounds strange, right?" Annie added quickly.

Edie leaned forward on her elbows. "Don't undersell yourself! You are an entrepreneur."

That put a certain glamor into what was essentially working from her kitchen table in yoga pants. "I don't know about that. I haven't used my journalism degree in so long that I'm not sure it's worth the paper it's printed on."

Edie gave her a considered look, absently chewing the corner of her lip. "You know what, I should introduce you to my cousin. He's new in town too and works in media. We could all have dinner together."

The idea of dinner out in Brightwater sounded strange. She hadn't expected to come back and make friends, rather keep her head down and get out as soon as possible. But the hesitant eagerness in Edie's eyes was hard to resist. It had been a long time since she'd had a girlfriend. Someone that she wasn't simply trying to co-ordinate play dates with.

"I'd like that."

"Me too," Edie said softly. "I'll get your order going." She turned before pausing and looking back. "I'm so happy we met."

Annie walked to the booth, grinning. Sawyer and Atticus were chuckling. What did he think about the fact that she had a son? Most single guys weren't lining up around the block to date a divorced mom with a child.

Not that this was a date. Purely platonic. Possibly even a pity party.

He glanced up and—oh, whoa, his hot, hooded gaze wasn't anything pitying. She might as well be covered in Nutella with a cherry on top.

"Wh-what's so funny?" she stammered, sliding into the bench beside Atticus, rubbing her palms on her shorts.

"The sheriff told me a story about how he broke his arm as a kid. His big brother pushed him out of a tree."

"That's terrible!" Annie said, vaguely remembering Wilder. He was a big guy, quiet, broody, and a little dangerously unsettling. But she had never taken him for being an outright bully.

"Oh, I asked for it," Sawyer replied.

"I don't believe that."

"No, I literally asked for it." His laugh lines crinkled around his eyes. "Told him to push me. Guess I'd watched Superman a few too many times."

"You thought you could fly?" Atticus asked, confused.

"Yep. And found out I couldn't the hard way. Wore a cast most of the summer. The best part was getting it signed."

"Signed?" Atticus stared curiously.

"Yeah, you ask people you like to sign the cast. Collect autographs."

Atticus looked down at his cast and mumbled, "Would you sign mine?"

Sawyer glanced at Annie. "Is that okay?"

Sometimes the past and present pushed up against each other, and at the peak was a sharp unexpected sweetness, an almost unbearable beauty. She nodded slowly.

Sawyer pulled a black Sharpie from his front pocket. Atticus laid his cast on the table and Sawyer printed his name in careful, bold letters.

"Sawyer Kane," Atticus said, sounding out the words.

Sawyer gave a slow nod. "Sorry I didn't introduce myself to you earlier. Your mama is one of my oldest friends."

"She's never talked about you. She never talks about anyone here."

Sawyer gave her a long, impenetrable look. "Guess she has her reasons."

Atticus sat back in his seat and looked out over Main Street. "I like this place."

The silence dragged after that, one, two, three long seconds before Edie appeared with the tray. Three hot chocolates, a cupcake cut in half, and one slice of pie.

Saved by dessert.

"I hope you enjoy," Edie said, passing out forks. "And I'll be in touch about connecting you with my cousin. I'm looking forward to having you around. I could use a friend."

Annie smiled. "Me too."

After Edie left, Sawyer nudged her foot with his boot. "Hey, I feel like we got off on the wrong foot."

"That might be my fault," she said. "When I heard the hammering this morning, I thought Grandma—"

"That woman singlehandedly raised me and my brothers. I love her for it, but that doesn't mean she's not crazier than a sackful of raccoons."

It was hard to speak when his gaze glued to her face. Didn't he realize how stare-worthy he was? Once she started, she couldn't stop. "You were trying to set things right. I guess I'm not used to people doing nice things for no reason."

Not smart, putting herself out there like this. She'd fashioned battle armor for a reason, because she was soft, too soft, and here she went making herself vulnerable again.

"You deserve good things," he said quietly.

"Do I?" She wanted to look away, *needed* to if she hoped to draw her next breath, but his calm, steady gaze had her on lockdown.

"I think so."

Whoa, Nelly. This conversation was too deep, too quick, for two almost strangers in the middle of a coffee shop.

She'd left this town swearing she'd never think of Sawyer Kane again. And over the years that proved impossible. Every so often she'd wonder what he was up to. Had he married? Did he have kids? Perhaps yes, she oh-so-quietly rued the fact he eschewed social media in an age when most people posted everything from what random snack they ate after the gym to humblebrags to yet another invite to play freaking Candy Crush (the answer always and forever was no).

"How come you haven't settled down?" she blurted.

"I nearly did, once." He ran a hand through his hair. "Got engaged even."

The sharp pang in her chest was unfair. She couldn't be jealous. It was stupid, irrational, and yep, she totally was. "To who?"

"Ruby King."

Her heart deflated like a pinpricked balloon. Ruby had once been the Queen Bee of Brightwater High School, captain of the cheerleading squad, and her father ran the largest realty company in two counties, buying her a red convertible on her Sweet Sixteen. Everywhere that Ruby went, the boys had been sure to follow.

Face it, Ruby made sense, for Sawyer.

The sort of perfect girl the star pitcher would settle down with.

"Things didn't work out."

"Oh." She shouldn't pry but she broke out the conversational crowbar nevertheless. "Why?"

"If you're going to spend forever with someone, it's got to be the right kind of love." He cleared his throat. "The real kind of love."

"The real kind—what, no artificial flavors?" Annie kept her tone light and teasing. When in doubt, or your nerves threaten to strangle, go for a joke.

He didn't smile. Instead, he slanted closer, folding his hands on the table between them. "The kind that when you know, you know."

The way he stared, it was as if he wanted to send her a telepathic message . . . or eye fuck her. There was a charged beat. Then another. *Holy Mother of God.* How had she forgotten that look?

And that was the problem, she never had.

Chapter Six

SAWYER STRODE EAST on Main Street toward the rodeo grounds for the Brightwater Fourth of July fireworks. The lead glass over The Dirty Shame's front door still sported a bullet hole from a Kane and Carson disagreement during the Roaring Twenties. Official word stated no blood was spilled in the saloon that night, but Grandma swore Old Man Carson took buckshot in the ass.

Sawyer shoved a hand into his worn jeans, grazing the peppermint he'd grabbed when leaving Haute Coffee yesterday. Since their mid-morning date, Annie had been a near fixture in his mind. Even though his boots stayed planted to the earth, he felt himself falling hard and fast. Like it or not, he kept rewinding the details to play again in slow motion. The way she shivered when he leaned close. How her eyelids fluttered as she bit into the cupcake. Or how difficult it seemed to be for her to hold his gaze.

But when she did, something bubbled between them, an undeniable chemistry.

Opening the cellophane, he stuck the candy into his mouth and bit down. The other undeniable truth was that it had been a while. A long fucking while.

Get a grip.

There was a risk of playing mad scientist, being an overeager dickhead who'd rush his last shot with her and have everything blow up in his face.

Two other complications were also slowing him down. He chewed the peppermint and mulled the facts.

First, he was a simple man, content with a modest country life. He couldn't offer a woman a castle in the clouds, and in the end that was what Ruby had wanted. He didn't get the impression Annie coveted any sort of wild, jet-setting lifestyle, but she had made it clear her future was in San Francisco, while his roots were firmly sunk in this land.

Second, she had a son, Atticus. He liked children fine, but hadn't grown up with a father figure. He'd pet a kid's head on occasion, or throw a football around at a family picnic, but he didn't have a clue how to actually interact with one. Sure, he could tell funny stories about the crazy things he and his brothers got up to as boys. But acting as any sort of a parenting role model?

The noise from the festivity increased. He waved at a few familiar faces, always keeping one step back or forward from the clusters of people filing inside. The children's activities were in full swing, kids busy with the watermelon seed spitting contest, frog jumping, or the burlap sack race. From the stage, ancient speakers blared live music. Currently, Old Man Fred banged out a polka on his accordion. No blonde pixie in sight.

But Annie was amazing, so that made her son pretty damn amazing too. The idea of spoiling them and being part of their lives was addictive. Who knew what the future held, but he might as well find out once and for all, because, yeah, he'd wondered.

Even during the Ruby years, he'd wake with a start, chest covered in cool sweat. He'd gained whatever success guys like him were meant to achieve—a beautiful woman, a good, stable job . . . but in the quiet night, his thoughts drifted to the boy he'd been, the chance he'd lost, and regret filled his mouth like sawdust.

A splash of pink caught his attention.

A hot pink cast.

Atticus stood at the far end of the watermelon seed spitting contest. It didn't look as if he'd be turning pro any time soon. Hell, with that range, he'd never make it to the minor leagues, but the kid's heart was into it, that much was obvious. Annie must be—

"Didn't think I'd see you here, man." Archer, his youngest brother, a wrangler on a nearby dude ranch, sidled up, pointing to a flask in his hip pocket.

"Nah, I'm good."

"Come on." Archer punched his shoulder. "Stop taking life so seriously. None of us gets out of here alive.

Have you seen all the new women in town? Word to the wise, man, they've come looking for the Wild West. Give 'em a wink under that Stetson and they'll ride you like a mechanical bull."

"Easy, Slick." Sawyer held up a warning hand. The Eastern Sierras gossips were kept in business from Walker to Lake Point tracking Archer's romantic exploits.

"All I'm saying is it's no crime to end a night with a bang, big brother. Just trying to look out for you." Archer gazed into the crowd with the same single-minded focus he exhibited rounding up cattle. "Unless you have someone specific in mind?"

"What's that supposed to mean?" Sawyer muttered, but his brother only walked away, shaking his head with a sly chuckle. Then the crowd parted, Sawyer's eyes connected with a deep blue pair across the grounds, and all his thoughts flat-lined.

ANNIE KEPT HER face politely tuned to Mrs. Peasey as her old 4-H instructor rambled about a rare coin she'd found at a flea market in Carson City.

" . . . and so it turned out to be a 1943 Lincoln wartime penny, steel, not copper, and did you know there are folks getting one hundred and fifty dollars for it on the eBay? So I says to George that we should . . . "

Sawyer stood behind the funnel cake stand trying very hard to appear as if he wasn't staring. She hoped she did an equally good job pretending not to notice. *Stop fidgeting.* She dropped her hand from playing with the back of her hair and ended up settling it awkwardly on her hip.

How could Sawyer say she hadn't changed? What a ridiculous statement. Maybe he'd reconsidered, came back to his senses after their coffee shop date. No! Not a date, a thing.

Their coffee shop thing.

" . . . and so that's how we ended up picking shot out of every bite. It was the Thanksgiving turkey no less, so I says, 'George, next time you better . . .' "

Annie managed a tight smile at Mrs. Peasey, daring another quick side eye. Darn. Her stomach muscles clenched. This time he caught her out. She tugged her sunglasses off the top of her head and shoved them on. Not exactly a superhero disguise, but beggars couldn't be choosers. This way he couldn't tell where her eyes wandered.

What did he see when he looked at her? She wasn't a fresh-faced teenager anymore. The world had revealed itself to be tougher and crueler than she'd ever imagined.

Mrs. Peasey laughed, so Annie joined in, with a private prayer the older woman hadn't said something inappropriate like "And now I'll be wearing a colostomy bag forever." Because she couldn't focus on chitchat or anything except Sawyer and the way that dang tan cowboy hat offset his eyes.

Speaking of anything—how was Atticus doing? Behind Mrs. Peasey, he balanced a hard-boiled egg on a spoon, his tongue poking out as he tiptoed in careful concentration. Looked as if he was having a blast. Good.

At least one of them was.

She glanced over to the food table, where her contribution sat untouched despite the hungry crowd. Old Mr. Higsby approached her adorable "crazy daisy" vintage Pyrex bakeware, the one she'd chipped a nail to own, pounding the refresh button during a furious eBay bidding war. The stout proprietor of Higsby Hardware poised to rescue her from total potluck shaming—an unlikely hero in a John Deere mesh cap and Time to Get Star-Spangled Hammered t-shirt. He studied her little chalkboard food label with a furrowed brow.

"What the Sam Hell is avocado lime cheesecake?" Instead, he reached for the Jell-O salad.

This was how a bead of oil must feel when dropped in water, more proof positive that she didn't mix here, never had, probably never would. She glanced back to the kid games and her heart gave a queer sideways beat. The egg race finished and a burlap sack obstacle course was in progress. No sign of Atticus's towhead. She touched the base of her neck as her insides gave an uncertain flutter.

He'd been there a minute ago.

"Excuse me," she cut off Mrs. Peasey. "My son, I don't see him." She turned and strode toward the contest. She'd been directly in his line of sight. Atticus didn't wander. He was a cautious, anxious kid. If anything, he usually gripped her hand in public, burying his face in the side of her leg. Lately, he'd become a little more withdrawn. He was never as close to Gregor as she preferred, but he missed Margot, his half-sister, desperately.

Could he finally be acting out from all the stress and change related to the move? *No, no I'm overreacting.* She hastened her step, glancing this way and that. The Brightwater High School band started and the snare drum kept quick time with her pulse. He was a little towhead boy with a hot pink cast, surely he'd stand out. Where could he—

"Can I help?" Sawyer appeared on her left without warning.

She was too panicky to react to his unexpected proximity. "Atticus. I—I can't find him. He was right here a second ago."

"On it." He turned and walked into the crowd. The calm certainty in his voice calmed her jagged nerves. Still, she wouldn't settle down until her son was back in her arms.

"Atticus," she called, useless in this noise. "Atticus!"

She passed a vaguely familiar woman with pursed lips, the whisker in the mole pointing like a judgmental finger. Oh, right, the nurse at the community hospital.

Yeah, hi. Me again. This time I haven't got a broken kid. I don't have a kid at all.

Fear choked her. How could she have been so careless? Daydreaming about Sawyer and not paying careful attention to her son.

"Atticus!" More heads turned. No missing the hysterical note in her cry. She needed to calm down. Brightwater was a small town, lost in time, transported from a Norman Rockwell painting. But these weren't her people.

LAST FIRST KISS   71

She recognized many of the faces, but they didn't know anything about her, no matter what they thought.

Except they watched a disheveled, frantic mom, so maybe they had her number after all.

Mother trucker.

Anger ignited in her chest—could he have run off to scare her? The brief flash was doused quickly by a bucket of ice-cold guilt. He was five. He couldn't be responsible for remembering to wash his hands after using the bathroom. Stupid—so stupid—to have lost sight of him for even a split second.

By the time she'd lapped the rodeo grounds without a sign, she started hyperventilating. Surely he wouldn't have gone to check out the horses? Oh God, what about the bulls or the parking lot full of big trucks and drivers who could so easily miss a little guy?

What if . . . Bile burned her throat. Atticus was so gentle and trusting, a kind-seeming stranger could take him by the hand with a friendly word. She'd vaguely mentioned stranger danger, but not in a bad-guys-might-steal-you way because she didn't want him having nightmares.

Big mistake. Huge.

She should have told him the truth—the world wasn't safe, terrible things could happen and—

"Found him." She froze at the sound of Sawyer's deep voice and slowly spun around. Sawyer stood an awkward distance from Atticus, whose bottom lip quivered.

"Oh, thank God." Annie fell to her knees and pulled

her son close. She needed to hold him tight, remind herself that children were precious, and so delicate. She needed to take better care. Except a darker truth gritted against any silky sheen of optimism. Atticus needed her to be perfect, and she wasn't. She was far from it.

Chapter Seven

"COULD YOU GO for another one?" Sawyer tapped the edge of her paper plate.

Annie's eyes cut to his face. She'd been so relieved about finding Atticus, and flustered by Sawyer's proximity, that she'd stammered out an acceptance to his unexpected offer of fair food. No doubt Atticus would swing from the ceiling light after finishing his cotton candy. Her own paper plate was empty. She'd said she wasn't hungry but devoured the funnel cake in a record-setting two minutes. Desperate times called for desperate stress eating.

"I'm okay," she responded. "Thank you though."

"Would it be wrong to say you seem to like funnel cake more than Nutella?" he said teasingly. Laugh lines bracketed his deep-set gorgeous eyes, grooves that told a story. He wasn't weathered, but had seen a thing or two. His boyishness roughened to the point where he possessed that indefinable air often described as character.

Hard to find a witty comeback while busy licking the powdered sugar from her fingers. His smile faded as she withdrew one. Did she slow it down a little? Let the tip pop over her lower lip?

A little.

Maybe it was the sugar, or the endorphin rush of danger averted, but she felt good—damn good—not overthinking for a second and . . . just seeing what could happen.

"I'd forgotten about Brightwater fair food," she said. "Whatever went down with my taste buds was nothing short of sinful."

"Good. Seemed like you could use a little more sweetness." He leaned against the picnic table and kicked out his legs, half turning his narrow hips in her direction. His Western shirt stretched over a leanly muscled chest, the pearl snaps marching down a trim abdomen, disappearing into his jeans, and that simple metallic belt buckle shaped like a—

He's going to think I'm eyeing his package.

Which, come to notice, was hard to miss, the thick line evident against the denim of his inner thigh. Would something that size hurt or feel amazing? Gregor had been average on all respects. No complaints, but nothing to give pause.

Her ears heated. If she looked up now, she'd giggle and it would become painfully obvious that she perved on his manhood. "Atticus and I should go find a spot to set up before the fireworks." This had been a nice exchange. Combined with the coffee shop thing yesterday, maybe she could leave town feeling as if things between them were at peace.

She drew a star in the dust with her shoe. Yeah, she should go . . . except it was awfully nice sitting here with him.

"There's a meteor shower tonight," he rumbled.

"So you're still into astronomy?" He'd invited her to sneak out and stargaze once. She'd tiptoed from the farm after midnight, hoping "stargazing" was code for wild clandestine make-out session, her first real kiss.

When she arrived on the knoll behind the ranch, he had an actual star chart spread out. She hadn't gotten her first kiss, but had sat wrapped in a quilt, sipping hot chocolate from the thermos he brought and listening to his stories about different myths related to constellations. Under that night sky, she felt poised to turn the page from girlhood, to whatever stage happened next, and even though he never so much as held her hand, her heart felt full.

"Yeah, I still dabble in stars, nothing serious. You live far enough out you'll see a hell of a show tonight. No light pollution on Five Diamonds."

"Hidden Rock is the only light I ever see." The Kane's ranch.

He frowned. "You can't see Grandma's from your place."

"I can too, near the hill's rise."

"Nah." He rubbed the back of his neck. "That's not her."

"Who is it then?"

"Me."

"Oh." Something about the idea of seeing his home light from her bedroom window seemed rather wistful. "I saw the light come on two nights ago after your grandma paid me a visit."

"I got home late, been out looking for the first meteors. The Alpha Capricornids."

"The Alpha huh?"

"A yearly meteor shower, not very strong, only four or five in an hour, but here's the thing. They're big and bright. Good bang for your viewing buck."

"Sounds lovely." She kept trying not to stare, or at least not be obvious about it. The problem was that she started to feel like one of those paintings in Scooby-Doo, where the eyes kept moving while the face stayed still.

"Yes, lovely, indeed," he murmured. Had he leaned in, because Lord, suddenly his scent was stronger and he smelled good, all spicy aftershave and cinnamon chewing gum.

The sugar must be entering her bloodstream. Either that or he was throwing out serious signals. She just wasn't sure if she could, or more importantly, if she should, try to decipher them.

"Too bad I don't know Morse code," she burst out. "I mean, because then I could send you secret messages."

"Like what?" He scratched his denim-clad thigh, right near his, ahem, rather large—

Say something, anything, that doesn't have to do with pop cans or sausages. "Got meteors?"

He froze. "That's what you'd Morse me?"

"You have a better message?"

"Imagine I would."

"Go on, then. Let's hear this Morse magic."

"I have to be in the moment, not big on rehearsing ahead of time."

"Impromptu Morse."

"Yes."

"You're a freestyler." Was she giggling? Yeah. Crud. That was definitely a giggle. Still, being in Sawyer's company again was good. It was easy—too easy—to settle into a comfortable rhythm with him.

The corner of his mouth turned down, but his eyes danced. "You're making fun of me."

"And you're only now picking that up."

"Annie Carson, you're trouble."

"Don't smile too big. People are staring. They don't look like they notice but they're waiting."

"For what?

"Probably to see if I'm going to provide some kooky Carson excitement. Maybe go on stage and play a pan flute, or break into spoken word poetry, or announce Five Diamonds has become a nudist colony, or—"

"Annie," he said huskily.

Oh God, had she really mentioned nudity? "Mm-hm?" she said, not trusting herself to speak.

"People are staring because you're a knock out." He glared around the crowd with a look that said in no uncertain terms "mind your own fucking business."

Everyone turned away with a shrug. Guess being

sheriff had its perks, as did adding another two inches of height and twenty pounds of muscle. A sweet warmth pooled in her lower abdomen as he smiled back at her. Gregor never stared like he saw *her*, the Annie that existed deeper than her mere face, or body, and other outward manifestations of self. Not like Sawyer and his gorgeous green eyes. The effect was disorienting, but a little addictive.

"S-so," she stammered, struggling to recalibrate to this new reality, the one where Sawyer was a friend, or . . . something. "That was so great of you helping out today, finding Atticus."

"Glad I could be of assistance. You looked like you . . ."

She realized what he was going to say, and maybe she should be offended, at least a little. "Go on, get it out," she said, belly tightening.

"I didn't mean anything rude," he said.

"You wanted to say I needed help."

"Yes, but not in the way you might—"

"You know, I can't argue the facts. Maybe I need a hand."

"It must be hard, being a single mom." He nodded at the top of Atticus's head.

"He's my little buddy. His father . . ." *Wasn't around much. Didn't care about children.* Annie hadn't said a stray word about her ex in front of her son, and she could only hope that she never would. Atticus needed his father and Gregor was off doing some sort of mid-life cuddle pile party. She'd spied a flier when she was there a few days ago, picking up Atticus so they could make the drive to California with as much daylight as possible before starting. It advertised an Orgasmic Meditation course, to become a Certified Master Stroker.

Annie couldn't begin to wrap her head around what that meant. Or maybe she could, and it was that easy. Divorce to her meant soul-searching, navel-gazing, late nights alone with Joni Mitchell and Norah Jones on iTunes wondering where she went wrong. Divorce to Gregor meant finger-banging strange women in a sanctioned yoga classroom.

"His father's a good guy, but he worked a lot at the university." She cast a gaze to Atticus and back to Sawyer, silently willing him to see there was more there, a lot more, but her son didn't need to hear it.

Sawyer's mouth lost its easy angle, flicked to a more rigid shape, stern and just this side of angry. Not hard to see a sheriff in that moment. He was the quintessential strong silent type. The in-charge, don't-mess-with-me man of the law. But also the stargazing guy with an easy smile and kind word.

Who was the real Sawyer? Her feelings for him had been balled up like a crumpled piece of paper for years. They might have started to smooth things out, but creases remained. She'd never return to that innocent, reckless abandon of first love. He'd stolen that from her, on purpose or not. Maybe it was irrational. It wasn't *Sawyer* she hated; it was the fact she'd given him the power to hurt her, and his brand of kindness was its own dangerous form of seduction. Her whole body craved it like a sunflower long deprived of light.

"Okay, well, I'm sure you've got other people to visit. Atticus and I will go set up a blanket for the fireworks, and tonight I'll drive slow. Scout's honor. No stop sign will go unnoticed."

Sawyer shrugged and looked out at the crowd, spreading out across the rodeo grounds. So many people, and right now, all she wanted was his company. "What if we watch the meteor shower back up on our hill, between our places? It's owned by the National Forest, so neutral ground."

"Our own Switzerland."

"It will be quieter. We can talk better." His look was typically inscrutable, but there, just there, the flicker. That was definitely a flicker. Was it her imagination or did his gaze hold some sort of promise?

She tested out a laugh that sounded suitably breezy, even as her insides were melting faster than vanilla ice cream at noon. "Now, I've been gone a long time, but you were never known to like talking much."

He scuffed a boot heel against the ground. "I do with the right person."

And there, with six little words, he found the straps of her armor and unbuckled them with a flick.

"Excuse me, did you bake this?" Annie turned, startled, and Edie Banks stood there, holding a paper plate with a fat slice of her avocado lime cheesecake in the middle.

"Uh, guilty as charged. Sorry."

"Sorry?" Edie's eyelids closed as she put another forkful into her mouth. "This is good. And by good, I mean incredible. There's really avocado in it?"

"Yeah, I saw a few overripe ones at the Save-U-More and couldn't bear for them to go to waste. The flavor gets muted during baking but makes the texture extra creamy."

"No kidding. This is really good stuff."

"I don't think the other locals feel that way."

"Are you kidding? I snagged the last piece. That's why I came over, to bring you this cute Pyrex dish before someone walks off with it." She removed it from under her arm and passed it over. "And by someone, I mean myself, because it's adorable. Where'd you find it?"

"eBay," Annie replied, taking the dish, slightly bewildered. People were eating her pie and liking it?

"You're going to have to give me the recipe, unless it's an ancient family secret." Edie gave a conspiratorial grin. "And if that's the case, you'll have to tell me how much to bribe you for it." She took another bite and this time moaned, clapping a hand over her mouth. "Oh my goodness, look what you made me do. I sound like I'm having a moment over here."

Annie chuckled. "I'll happily share the recipe."

"That reminds me, I told my cousin about you. He is having a function at his property in a few weeks and added you to the guest list. You'll be getting an invitation soon."

"I'm flattered, but an invitation sounds kind of formal for Brightwater."

Edie gave a good-natured eye-roll. "That's Quincy. He doesn't do things by halves. He bought The Dales as a retreat from the city to relax. But if this is him relaxed, I'd hate to see him in LA. He's lovely, but an all-work no-play sort of guy."

"The Dales?" She glanced at Sawyer. "You mean—"

"The Dales Manor." Sawyer gave a nod. "It recently sold."

The Dales was Brightwater Valley's largest home, built in the late nineteenth century by a Gold Baron as a mountain lodge. Annie and Claire had always called it "the castle."

"You said your cousin worked in media?" Annie said, increasingly curious.

"Yes. Quincy Bankcroft."

Annie's jaw dropped. "Quincy Bankcroft as in the heir to the multi-million-dollar Bankcroft Media empire spanning the gamut from cable stations to newspapers?"

Edie raised her brows. "Tell him that and it will go to his head, but yes, one and the same."

Annie laughed. "I can't believe you casually suggested having lunch with Quincy Bankcroft."

"Well, to me, he's just Quincy. An older cousin, but a good friend. I owe him a lot." Edie's gaze ran to the horizon, temporarily lost in thought. "Anyway," she said as she glanced at her watch. "I need to get back to the coffee shop. Three pies are still in the oven. I wandered up to have a quick look around the festivities. I've only been living here since late-March, still getting the lay of the land."

With a quick wave, she was off.

"Looks like you two are hitting it off," Sawyer said.

"We are, aren't we? It's nice."

"I wonder if you'll hit it off with her cousin too."

Was that an undercurrent of jealousy in his voice?

She shouldn't mess with him, but she couldn't resist. The funnel cake, the friendship, and a warm summer night made her feel more herself again. The teasing old Annie, who liked to laugh and kid around.

"Haven't you seen Quincy Bankcroft yet?" she asked with studied casualness.

"Nope, I haven't had the pleasure," Sawyer said.

"Well, he's pretty famous, and oh, very handsome. If you like blond men with a bit of young Paul Newman in the face. And a lot of money. We're talking a guy who could take Scrooge McDuck money baths."

A muscle ticked in Sawyer's jaw. "Sounds like every woman's dream."

"Yes. He really does, doesn't he? Plus he was raised in England, so there's that accent."

The pop can Sawyer held audibly dented.

Time to relent.

"There is one slight problem. At least for me."

"What's that?" Sawyer rumbled. Whoa, that was actually more of a growl.

She heaved an exaggerated sigh. "He'd never be into me in a million years."

Sawyer's gaze shot to her face. "What guy in his right mind wouldn't be . . . " He broke off, realizing what he almost said.

Annie tried to play it off like she hadn't noticed the slip up, but his words were still there, rising between them like a big cartoon bubble.

"He's openly gay," she said quickly. "An outspoken GLBTQ activist as well."

"Oh, well, I mean, good. Good for him." Sawyer's shoulders dropped. "And yes, you should meet with him. You like to write, or blog, or whatever it is you do."

"Whatever it is I do?" She wasn't sure whether to laugh or be a little offended.

"I use a computer for work, when I have to. But I don't spend time on it. For fun. Not that there's anything wrong with that." He looked genuinely rattled, the effect was actually making her teeth ache with from the sweetness.

"Not at all. You don't have to read my blog. You aren't exactly my target audience."

"When are the fireworks going to start?" Atticus crawled onto Annie's lap.

"When it's dark," she said, giving him a kiss on the top of his head.

"Can we get our spot now?" Her son stared up with an apprehensive look. Fiery reds and pinks spread across the blue sky.

"Yes," she said, fingering the plaid wool blanket she'd found in the chest in the living room. The one she used to use for making blanket forts on rainy days. "Sorry, we're going to have to rain check on the meteor shower."

"Is there a spot on your blanket for one more?" Sawyer asked. "Whoa there, champ." Atticus leapt into his arms without warning. Sawyer held him a little stiffly but didn't seem to mind.

"You'll watch with us?" Atticus said.

"Sure, if your mom says it's okay."

Annie crossed one leg and then the other. Sitting in the dark and watching explosions overhead while trying not to catch fire from the sparks bursting between them? That sounded dangerous. But then, fireworks lasted only a few minutes. A lot of razzle dazzle and noise, and then poof! Everything returned to the way it was. Things had fizzled between her and Sawyer before.

The old Annie stirred inside her, the braver Annie. *Maybe after the fireworks the sky would return to a quiet, black calm. But then there were always the stars.*

"Yes," she said softly, clearing her throat and repeating the word, for him, but also for her. "Yes. That does sound good."

Chapter Eight

"Should we wake him up?" Sawyer asked Annie, staring down at Atticus's sleeping face. The kid's mouth was open slightly, and faint snores emanated from his skinny frame. Sawyer liked the way she stroked her child's hair back from his forehead. He liked most everything about Annie, but seeing her as a mother was a whole new side, something he'd never imagined and yet indescribably completed her.

"Not yet," Annie murmured, rolling back on her elbows and crossing her ankles. Her skirt was short, cut above the knee, and despite the fact she was a wisp of a woman, those were pretty legs stretching down to her sandals. "We're way past his bedtime already. He'll wake up when the show starts."

Across the rodeo grounds, Neil Diamond's "Coming to America" blared from the speakers. The quiet spreading between them wasn't strained, but companionable.

This was another thing he liked about Annie. They didn't have to fill every second with conversation. Not that he minded talking to her, he never did. But sometimes it was nice to just sit with another person. Sit and simply be.

Finally, he knew it was time. "Hey, so I have to say something," he said. Something that had been burning a hole in his chest since he saw her step away from him by the Five Diamonds chicken coop. Something that had been burning in his chest for ten long years.

Her baby blues locked on his, not flickering away as they usually did, but holding fast. The twilight had transformed to darkness. Perhaps she felt safer in the shadows. He rolled to his side, took off his hat and set it on the grass.

"That night, the party—"

"Oh, please. Let's not talk about that."

"We don't have to talk about it. But I do owe you an apology."

She fidgeted with the blanket's edge. "It was a long time ago."

"It was, but I need you to know one thing."

"Okay." She didn't actually say the word, but her mouth moved silently.

"I—you—I didn't have anything to do with what happened to you in that closet. It wasn't a joke to me. You have never been a joke to me. "I didn't want our first kiss to happen with a group of idiots outside, snickering. You're no game, you never were. I wanted it real between us, you and me and no one else's damn business."

"I waited," she whispered. "People stood outside, laughing, making fun of me, and all I could think was that it would be worth it. Once you came."

"People were drunk. They got out of hand. I couldn't get to you. I tried, but I couldn't. I failed. I failed us."

"Us." She ducked her head. "There has never been an us."

"There has to me," he said. "I know you want to leave and think moving to the city will give you—"

Boom!

Atticus bolted upright as the first fireworks exploded in gold and purple. The crowd oohed and ahhed. Another followed, and another.

"Look," Atticus said, pointing. "And look at that one, that's my favorite. And that one, that's my favorite too. And—"

Sawyer looked. But the beauty in the sky had nothing on the beauty of the woman on the opposite end of the blanket, face tilted up, bright lights reflected in her wide eyes.

She glanced over. "Aren't you going to enjoy the show?"

"I am," he replied.

She licked her lips and there went that damn muscle in his jaw twitching again.

The show could have lasted fifteen seconds, fifteen minutes, or fifteen hours. Sawyer lost all track of time. Last week, he'd have considered himself to be a happy man, or at least not unhappy. Now he realized that he'd been living around a hole, a hole that a small woman with a huge heart could fill. As good as this felt, as right and perfect, it was also scary as shit, because she'd made it clear Brightwater was a stopover on her journey, not the final destination.

This could end badly for him. Hope was dangerous. But time to know, at last, what the writing said on their wall. God hated a coward.

After the grand finale, the crowd rose in one collective motion, gathering blankets and lawn chairs and streaming for the exit.

"Think it'll be a busy law enforcement night?" Annie asked, cradling Atticus, who was already drifting back to sleep.

"Could be. Kit and Leroy are on duty tonight. There are always one or two dumb shits who drink too much and think it's a good idea to drive."

"I'll be extra careful."

"Let me walk you out."

"Oh, you don't have to."

"Maybe not, but I'd like to. Pass that little champ over here." He reached out and gathered her son. "He's heavier than he looks."

"Don't I know it," she said with a grin. "Carrying him is what passes for my workout these days."

He waited while she folded up the blanket and gathered her pie plate.

"You know, I had fun tonight." A hint of wonder tinged her voice.

Hope set down another root in his stomach. "Bright-water has plenty of good things going for it."

"Hmm" was all she said, suddenly very busy with her sandal's buckle.

They walked slowly, on the fringes. A few people waved to him, did double takes at Annie, recognizing her after a moment. Asking where'd she'd been, about her plans.

Sawyer tried not to listen to her responses, all the talk about San Francisco. It had been a long time since he'd played ball, but one reason he could throw a pitch was because he had a knack for filtering out the crowd noise. The opposite team could yell taunts and jeers but he could zero in on the batter with single-minded focus, quieting the din.

A useful trick still.

At the purple car, Annie popped the locks and opened the back door. "I can get Atticus into his seat."

"Nah, I've brought him this far." Sawyer leaned in and settled Atticus into the high-backed booster. Incredibly, he barely stirred. Imagine sleeping that soundly. He'd wake every morning feeling like a million bucks. As Sawyer clipped the chest strap, the little boy reached out, eyes still closed, and gave him a hug. Every doubt he had about not knowing what to do around kids faded under a rush of affection. Maybe he didn't know how to act around kids plural, but kids single? Atticus in particular? Yeah, he could probably figure that out fine.

He shut the door quietly and Annie was back by the trunk, putting away the blanket.

"It's nice, spending time with you again," she said, keeping her gaze averted. Her earlier contented stillness was gone, replaced by busy hands and words that couldn't come fast enough. "It's nice to be back on the farm too, actually. Dad always kept pestering me to come for a visit, but I always convinced him to fly to Portland instead. Or meet up with Claire in San Francisco. But I—"

"Annie." She stilled. Those busy hands halting, reaching up to grip the trunk door instead. The parking lot had cleared out.

"Yes?"

"Look at me."

"Um, hang on. I want to check and see if my sister keeps a spare tire in here. Some of these back roads are atrocious. It's only a matter of time until I get a flat. Maybe we should contact the local representative and—"

"Annie, look at me."

"Why?" she whispered.

"Because this." He stepped behind her and placed a gentle kiss on the nape of her neck. She smelled sweet, pretty, a little like coconut, a little like flowers and a lot like woman.

"Sawyer," she gasped. When his hands bracketed her waist she leaned back against him.

"And this." He kissed her neck, right over her pulse, deeper, more open-mouthed, adding a hint of tongue. She arched, her sweet ass driving him to the edge. Hell if he could be this close and not savor her. He couldn't help the groan. She tasted gorgeous.

"Don't forget this," he whispered, sucking the lobe

of her ear into his mouth, grazing her soft skin with his teeth until she trembled. "Good night, Annie." He whispered. "Happy Fourth of July."

Her ragged exhalation served as response.

Slowly, he turned and strode to his truck, glancing back to make sure she got inside her car okay. He waited until finally she started the engine, reversed and then left the parking lot, her rear lights disappearing into the dark. She wasn't a woman to rush and that was fine, nothing good ever came easy. But he'd made his first move and was still hard from the way she'd responded, rocking against him, those soft, hitching breaths as he sucked her sweet skin.

It wasn't until he set his head back against the cab that he spotted it, by the horizon, a single meteor.

The light wasn't showy, it didn't make any noise, but the pure, simple beauty tightened his throat.

Chapter Nine

[draft]

Musings of a Mighty Mama

Getting in the Groove

older posts>>

Dear Readers,

Day ten of the "Mighty Mama Thirty Days of Thankfulness." Today, I want to give thanks for my body. It's not perfect but it's healthy, and strong. The more I work on the farm, the more new muscles make themselves known (for better and worse). Each night, I massage in my own homemade muscle rub of jojoba infused with lavender, ginger and peppermint essential oils. Click <u>here</u>

for the recipe. Everything hurts, but it's nice to feel in my body, you know?

Being a mama is hard work. Sometimes it's oh-so-easy to feel like you are losing yourself. Here are a few tips on how to find your missing mojo:

~~1. EAT ALL THE DARK CHOCOLATE WHILE CONTEMPLATING MASTURBATING TO THE GORGEOUS COWBOY? SHERIFF? COWBOY SHERIFF NEXT DOOR WHO KISSED YOU, BUT DIDN'T, BUT KIND OF DID.~~
~~Was it a kiss?~~
~~What's a kiss, technically?~~
~~WHAT IS LIFE?~~
~~Ah forget it. Who needs kisses when there's a sale at Save-U-More on Ben & Jerry's Funky Monkey?~~

Draft Saved by <u>Mighty Mama 08:35am</u> in <u>mama mojo</u>, <u>gratitude challenge</u>, | <u>Permalink</u> | comments (0)

DURING THE NEXT two weeks, tiny miracles kept occurring around Five Diamonds. First, the screen door lost its irritating squeak, then the porch's wonky step quit wobbling. The neglected boxwood hedges along the front walkway were pruned to something approaching order and the garbage can had a funny habit of wheeling itself to the end of the driveway on trash days. Annie realized she wasn't going quietly nuts after discovering the hole in the barn floor—the one Atticus had stumbled into when he broke his arm—magically repaired. From that moment on there wasn't much point refusing the facts.

No fairy godmother bibbity-bobbity-boo'd her way around the farm. She was in the debt of a hot—and sneaky—cowboy.

How the heck did Sawyer covertly pull off these chores? She rarely left the farm and hadn't woken at dawn to any new hammer banging. And why didn't he stop by for a visit? Knowing he was around but not around drove her crazy. She hadn't felt empty since the fireworks. No, she had the opposite problem. She was too full, had to walk around carefully so as not to spill over and make a mess.

You had one job, Annie, one job.

Get Five Diamonds ready for sale. Not kiss the sexy neighbor, or whatever that was. Kissing but not lip kissing. Dear Lord, that was the hottest not lip kissing to ever go down this side of the Rockies.

Gah. High time she quit twisting her brain like a pretzel and take up an easier hobby, like studying quantum physics or the basics of thermodynamics.

For the moment, plopping down at the kitchen table for a quick check of the *Mighty Mama* blog analytics had to serve as sufficient Sawyer distraction. She opened her laptop, letting her fingers run quick and efficiently over the keyboard. Her shoulders dropped as promising stats filled the screen. *Yes, good.* The daily gratitude posts were proving popular, and all the charming shots of Brightwater's quaint Main Street and the surrounding mountains racked up page views. She'd gained three new sponsors in as many weeks and a shout out on *Huffington Post* pushed her readership to record highs.

She scrolled through the comments, past validation after validation. Strange to think so many strangers believed she had it all together, thrived in this rural adventure.

How do you do it all?

You are such an inspiration!

I could never do what you do.

Are you for real? I smell bulls and shit.

Annie's stomach flip-flopped at the last comment. Ms. Hootenanny, her daily heckler, appeared two weeks ago, and had made a hobby out of leaving unpleasant comments.

Are you for real? Annie traced her tongue along the inside of her cheek, fingers itching to respond with a truthful, "I'm a scared mother who still hasn't fixed the leak in the kitchen sink even after watching a dozen YouTube repair videos. Half my day is spent fantasizing about napping and the other half about my gorgeous neighbor."

But did the troll want truth? Fantasy Annie paid the bills, her joyful homesteading act created the foundation needed to build a viable career.

She stood, suddenly feeling trapped, and left the kitchen, tiptoeing around the Lego piles Atticus arranged in an unfathomable system across the living room floor. The sounds of his boisterous play drifted from upstairs.

"Here comes the rocket ship, look out! Pow zoom!" He unleashed a victorious cheer, defeating imaginary foes.

She'd figure out the source of the loud boom-related crash a little later; for now her limbs were restless and chest tight. Out on the front porch, a light breeze blew, carrying the invigorating fragrance of sun-warmed pine. *Mighty Mama* was never originally intended for a wide audience. She'd been struggling with a case of stay-at-home mama boredom and found herself drafting short essays during Atticus's naps. Who'd ever give two fat figs about her little corner of the world? But people did, lots of people, ones she'd never met in real life. The approval grew addictive. Strangers cheered her on as she took pride in and celebrated mothering, cherished the simple beauty found in otherwise mundane day-to-day rhythms. But lately, her compulsion to live online waned even as her readership numbers soared past her wildest dreams.

Social media had its place and purpose, but it had replaced an actual social life.

She glared at the weeds choking the front yard and marched out to pull a handful. A futile action when there were so many more. Still, she grabbed more, cursing under her breath when a thorn lodged beneath her thumbnail. Mounting exhaustion made it hard to find magical moments. The chore list overflowed with tasks like painting old weatherboards or scrubbing away years of grime. Maybe Sawyer's subtle presence should be more unsettling, but at least backup existed if the roof blew off.

And this roof looked exactly like the sort of jerky roof that would do such a thing.

She braced her hands on her lower back and stretched.

As much as she hated to admit it, all her hard work had hardly made a dent on the property. The farmhouse's frame canted to the right in an awkward lean, and more than a few shingles looked in need of immediate replacement. If next winter carried strong winds or too much snow, the whole house might well crash down. Who'd ever want to buy such a dump?

Gravel crunched behind her. She turned at the unexpected footsteps and delighted shock detonated her gloom in an instant. Her older sister stood in the driveway wearing a black maxi-dress, chic leather backpack, and mirrored aviator sunglasses.

"Surprise," Claire called, throwing her arms in a victory "v."

"Claire? Oh my God!" Annie didn't run, she flew into her big sister's arms and held on tight. Only sixteen months older, Claire transcended sibling status. Her best friend was here. You couldn't ask for better cavalry.

"You're here. I can't believe you're really here," Annie managed to gasp, ribs crushed by her sister's grip. Claire worked out at a CrossFit gym. The result was a pair of strong arms lifting Annie as if she weighed less than a sack of flour. "Hey, put me down!"

"But you're such a Lil' Bit." Claire's nickname for her.

No one would ever pick them off the street as sisters. Annie stood five feet two inches in heels, with butterscotch blond hair and fifties-style curves. Around these parts, Claire might be called a long drink of water. Her legs went on for days, as did her dark hair, the same shade as the double shot espressos she mainlined as breakfast replacements. Still, they were heart twins, laughing at all the same jokes and often sent texts right when one was thinking about the other.

"How did you get here?"

"I flew." Claire flapped her arms, looking around. "Where's my favorite nephew?"

"Defending Earth from a renegade alien invasion."

"That's my boy."

"Seriously though, how'd you get here?" Annie repeated, still stunned by the manifestation of her best friend and kickass protector at the moment of need.

"I am serious. I caught a plane from SFO to Mammoth then grabbed the one cab in the county to get out here. What can I say, I missed my baby sister. You've seemed distant on the phone."

"Oh, Claire." Guilt thickened her throat. "That must have cost more than a pretty penny."

Claire waved her hand like blowing hundreds of dollars wasn't worth the cost of words. "My financial planner isn't worried about my bank account so why should I? Toast has been good to me." A few years ago, she transformed an old Airstream into a retro food truck, The Daily Bread. She served five-dollar slices of toast and jam to dotcom millionaires, making a killing off the latest craze to sweep the Land of Food Snobs. Insanity, but Claire was a pirate, plundering opportunity with glee.

Annie gave her another hug. "Only you could turn bread into a gold mine."

"I'm a modern-day Midas. Hey, that's actually a great

name for a—holy hell!'" Claire must have finally focused on the dismal surroundings.

"I know, I know," Annie said with a cringe. "The place's a disaster, right?"

"Screw the farm." Claire pulled back and eyed Annie's threadbare yoga pants and stretched out pink t-shirt that read *Cowabunga* in a cursive font with undisclosed dismay. "What happened to my baby sister?"

Annie's stomach clenched. She loved Claire but sometimes could throat punch her. "You're saying I've gotten too comfy with frumpy?"

"Hey now," she gentled her tone. "You're as adorable as always, but, girl, those are serious dark circles under your eyes. If I tucked you into bed, you'd probably sleep for a year."

Annie slumped her shoulders. "Fixing this place up is hard work, harder than I expected."

"So why are you doing it to yourself?" Claire glanced from the wobbly roof to the overgrown flowerbeds to the uneven front path, wrinkling her nose. "What's the point?"

"You and Dad aren't volunteering to get Five Diamonds ready to sell," Annie snapped, exhaustion fraying her last nerve. Maybe the place did look like it was going to hell in a handbasket but she was doing her very best. When she'd arrived the farm was a disaster; it was at least upgraded to a hovel.

"Whoa, whoa, whoa. Don't bite my head off. I know the plan is to put the property on the market, but who ever gave you the idea to fix it up first?"

"If we're going to command a decent price point that will allow us to move close to you, the place needs to look its best, right?"

"Oh, Annie baby." Claire let out one of her annoyingly world-weary sighs. "Wrong, so, so wrong.

"Don't 'Annie baby' me. Make your point, then let's get inside and let Atticus know that his favorite person in the world after Margot is here."

Claire crossed her arms. "Knock off the renovations."

"But—"

"We want to sell to the highest bidder, right?"

"Of course."

"Do you think cashed-up folks trolling Brightwater in their fancy SUVs dreaming of a mountain vacation home are going to want to mess around with restoring a crappy farmhouse?"

Annie examined the place. *Crappy?* Fine, it was old, mildewed, and completely devoid of a straight line, but a protective instinct rose through her chest. "Let's show some respect for our ancestors who worked this land. We were born here. Mom . . ." *died here.*

Claire wrapped her arm around Annie's shoulders. "I know, Lil' Bit. Brightwater's our past and we did have some good times here. All I'm saying is that anyone who buys the place will no doubt tear it down."

"Demolish the house?" The idea sent a chill zinging down her spine.

"And the barn," Claire replied with a sage nod. "That will probably get knocked down first actually."

"But, but . . . " Annie sputtered. "Five Diamonds sold to tear down? You can't be serious."

"As a heart attack. Look around with unsentimental eyes. Whoever offers is going to replace this termite tower with a nine-thousand-square-foot estate, complete with a pool, and tennis courts, and other yuppy trappings. No way will they want to put a new roof on a rinky-dink farm."

Annie groaned, her sore muscles suddenly ten times more aching. "How have I been such an idiot? These past few weeks I've been breaking my back, and for nothing."

"You are a warrior, never apologize for that."

"That's not the word to best describe me."

Claire slung her arm around her shoulders with an affectionate squeeze. "What else is new?"

Annie had put off sharing the next piece of information as long as she could. "Um, not much. Oh, Sawyer Kane and I are back on speaking terms."

For once, she shocked her big sister into dropping her mouth open.

Annie rolled her eyes. "There's nothing to say. Don't look at me like that."

"The astronauts at the space station can see your blush."

"Stop," she giggled. "It's warm out and I've been working. Want some lemonade? I've got mason jars cooling in the freezer, so they'll be all frosty and delicious—"

"Oh. My. God." Claire followed her into the house. "You want to see, don't you?"

"I haven't a clue what you're talking about."

"Sawyer Kane. You've never gotten over that eighteen-year-old dumbass Casanova who treated you like dirt at that party."

"It's been over ten years."

"Did his brain grow with the rest of him?"

"He's Brightwater's sheriff."

Claire burst out laughing. "Priceless."

"He wants to serve his community." Annie bristled opening the front door. "I don't see what's so funny about—"

"Handcuffs?" Claire winked. "That does it for you? A little good cop, bad cop."

"You're nuts."

"Admit it. You've always held a candle for the guy."

"Shhhhhh." Annie shoved a warning finger against Claire's mouth. "Quiet. Atticus has uncanny hearing."

"Fine." Claire dropped her voice to a whisper. "I think it's a great idea, by the way, a little fling with Sawyer. Get it out of your system."

"You don't understand."

"Enlighten me."

How to explain that if Sawyer penetrated any deeper into her system, she'd never be able to willingly walk away, at least not without a wrench that would leave part of her heart behind.

No thinking of Sawyer and penetration in the same sentence.

"He isn't fling material."

"Then what is—" Claire couldn't finish her sentence because Atticus flew into her arms with a delighted shriek that deafened anyone in a mile radius not wearing personal protective equipment. Annie left them to their happy reunion, headed to the kitchen, opened the fridge, took out the lemonade and two mason jars from the freezer. The temperature was heating up, and she needed a cool drink before a headache set in.

"So back to Sawyer," Claire said as she entered the kitchen, her raised eyebrows vanishing beneath her thick bangs.

Annie sighed. "It's complicated."

"Maybe stop fighting yourself on this. Bury the hatchet."

"It sounds like you mean that as a gross metaphor."

Claire spied the mini blueberry muffins cooling on the counter and crammed one into her mouth. "Oh man, that's delicious, and yes, I do, but in a good way."

"Gross and good are two vastly separate things."

"How did you two love birds reconnect?"

"It's not like that." *At least we're not mouth kissing.* "He's been helping out around here is all. Odd jobs. Fix-it-up stuff like repairing broken boards in the barn floor and the like."

"Aw." Claire crinkled her nose. "That's adorable."

"It's kind."

"Have you thanked him properly? For all that hard manual labor?" More suggestive eyebrow waggling.

Annie propped a hand on her hip, hoping to appear the picture of moral outrage. "Hey, I'm not going to thank him by—"

"Whoa, whoa, don't get your panties in a knot. All I'm suggesting is to fix him a plate of those delicious muffins and pay a friendly neighborly visit."

"Muffins?"

"Trust me, food is the way to a man's heart."

"I'm not sure I want into his heart."

"His pants then."

"Claire!"

Her sister unleashed a devious chuckle.

Well, he had done so much. "Okay, okay, I'll do it," Annie said, taking a bracing swig of lemonade and nearly choking on an ice cube. Was she really going to face him down after all those neck kisses? It would be a way to clear the air. "Okay, I'll fix him a plate as a thank you. After all, who doesn't like muffins?"

"No one of sound mind. Do it right now. Go pay a baked goods delivery house call and I'll discuss the ins and outs of Pokémon with my favorite nephew in the whole wide world."

Annie opened the cupboard and stared at all the different plates, the patterns and colors. Would Sawyer like the green one with white trim, or the pale yellow one covered in strawberries? Easier than deciding whether she and Sawyer were back to being friends, or whatever two people were who didn't kiss on the mouth but did other stuff.

She settled on the strawberry plate. Everything else was simply too overwhelming to consider.

"Oh, and Lil' Bit?" Claire paused in the doorway.

"Yeah?" Annie gripped the plate as a powerful urge rose inside to drop it. Let the ceramic hit the old wood floorboards and shatter into a hundred pieces.

"Before you go . . . " Claire delicately cleared her throat. "Maybe you want to, I don't know, wash your face? Comb your hair? Switch shirts?"

"Are you saying I look bad?"

"You'd be a fetching doll baby in a burlap sack and lederhosen."

"I don't think that combo actually works."

"My point is you're Annie. That means you are lovable and gorgeous no matter what. But you've . . . "

"Let myself go." No point sugar coating the facts. She managed to say the words as if they didn't matter, but inside, she missed that part of her that used to care. Not that she needed to be vain or obsessed with looks, but wanting to brush hair or change into outfits beyond yoga pants and hoodies on occasion might not be a bad idea. She used to sew, copy cute styles she saw in Claire's magazines.

"You used to make all those sweet dresses, and remember your vintage shoe collection? You were the only one who could fit into Grandma Carson's cute kitten heels.

Who has time to worry about that stuff? "They are packed away. Those get me through most days fine." Annie cocked her chin at the Dansko Mary Janes propping the back door.

"You've got it going on, sister, so might as well use it."

"Whatever," Annie responded. Worst retort ever. On

the inside, her mental cogs turned. Fine, so she had let herself go a little, and some neighborly flirtation might be the ticket to finding out where she went.

"You used to be so . . . so . . . joyful. I miss that part of you."

Joy? Ain't nobody got time for that. Still, spending more time with Sawyer didn't have to be all overthinking and serious. "You're right. I do need a little pick-me-up."

Claire snapped her fingers. "Yes, and something tells me that Sawyer might be the man to lend a helping hand . . . down your pants." She left the room with a cackle.

Even as Annie eye-rolled, she grinned at the sounds of the joyful aunt and nephew whooping it up in the living room before turning a gaze to the muffins.

Deep breath. Okay, one more. She could do this. She could cross the fence and approach Sawyer on his home turf. This was happening. She wrapped up the plate, taking extra special care to make it look pretty. Would a ribbon be nice or too much? *Too much.* Sawyer wasn't the fussy type.

Her blue dress hung on the clothesline. The soft jersey clung in the right places, but didn't scream trying too hard.

She walked outside, set the muffin plate on a log, shimmied out of her work clothing and walked to the water pump in her bra and undies. For a second she panicked, glancing around for a sign of Sawyer appearing in time to catch an eyeful, but the coast was clear. It was fun to pump the water, cup it as it came from the earth, toss it on her face and the back of her neck. Then, yanking the clean dress on, she ran her hand through her hair hoping the pixie cut looked edgy and modern, rather than sadly disheveled.

Just because she wasn't settling in Brightwater didn't mean she couldn't try to track down her old, more free-spirited self.

Maybe a little harmless neighborly flirtation would provide the key to the map.

Chapter Ten

ALL SAWYER WANTED was a cold beer and an hour to catch the end of the ball game. It had been a long day, a routine traffic stop leading to a drug bust. He startled at the movement in the corner of his darkened living room. "What the hell—"

"I saw you this morning." Grandma gripped the handles of the recliner. Her shadowed jowls resembled Marlon Brando's Don from *The Godfather*.

"What do I owe the pleasure of this visit?" He shot Maverick a look. *Couldn't you have alerted me with a warning whine?*

His trusty guard dog responded with a yawn and curled on the hand-braided rug.

"You aren't fooling me, Sneaky Britches," she snapped. "Nothing stirs so much as a feather on this ranch without me knowing. I saw you."

"Doing what?"

"Climbing over the fence."

He said nothing, learned a long time ago that the less he said, the more others talked, and that was the way to acquire useful information.

"You're helping the Carson girl, aren't you?" she growled.

He should have anticipated this outcome. Grandma kept binoculars on the window ledge above her kitchen sink and patrolled Hidden Rock with the tenacity of a Cold War soldier.

"I keep talking myself blue in the face about how it's not natural for a man of your age to live without a woman. You have needs and it's high time you start a family."

Had he pissed off karma? He'd done things he wasn't proud of in life, but in no way, shape, or form did that warrant a lecture on his "needs" from Grandma.

"I've made a list." She briskly plucked a piece of paper from her shirt pocket and opened it, clearing her throat. "Let's see, what about Marigold Flint? She never married and owns The Baker's Dozen. At least you won't go hungry."

Goldie's real specialty wasn't baking, it was spreading scandalous rumors under the guise of *Now, I can't say this for an absolute fact but . . .* "I wouldn't date that blabbermouth if she was the last one on earth."

"Oh, pshaw, men always say things like that, but trust me, if you and she were the last two people on earth you'd—"

"I said no. Can we please quit?"

"Fine. Her coffee is always burnt anyway." She tapped

her finger on her lower lip. "The new librarian is one of the Higsby clan. They are good, honest folks. Not the brightest bulbs in the box, mind, but loyal, long-lived, fertile."

He couldn't restrain a snort. "The trifecta of marital happiness?"

Grandma cast him a sharp-eyed gaze. "Don't gamble on your future, boy, there's no sense in that. Marry for like. Love only brings heartache."

Sawyer wanted to point out that most Kanes with the exception of himself, and his older brother, visited Vegas at least once a year. Gambling was in their blood, a family passion, but he held his tongue. Grandma had a far-off look in her eye, as if remembering her own short-lived marriage.

"With all due respect, please don't manage my life," he said gently.

"Anyway, you're barking up the wrong tree." Grandma blew out an annoyed breath. "She's fixing to sell up."

Sawyer didn't need to be told who *she* was. Annie.

Grandma coughed. "What she should do is return what's ours."

"The Carsons have owned that property over a hundred years, made improvements—"

"Improvements? Hah. Imagine planting an orchard in this climate? What's the sense in that? They've always been kooky."

Sawyer had to chalk one up to Grandma. The orchard was stunted, the fruit unable to grow well in this climate.

"The land can't go to an outsider," Grandma said, steel in her voice. "It's rightly ours."

"Well, the law's clear that it's not."

"Law, shaw."

A car door slammed. Maverick growled. Sawyer cocked his head.

Now what?

A low grumble rose from deep in Maverick's throat as his ears folded back. Strange. He once encountered a mountain lion on a hike and all the dog did was give a high-spirited tail wag.

Someone knocked on the front door.

"Expecting company?" Grandma twiddled her thumbs. "A woman?"

"Jesus," he muttered.

"You know how I feel about blasphemy, boy."

He gritted his teeth and turned the doorknob, and the Earth shifted underfoot.

"Boy?" Ruby King set a hand on her hip, tossing her long platinum hair over one shoulder. "Well, you are a big boy."

Grandma actually gasped. Talk about being between a rock and a hard place, except he wasn't hard for his ex-fiancée anymore.

Grandma rose to her feet. "You have some nerve showing your face on my land."

"Afternoon, Mrs. Kane." The white veneers on Ruby's teeth were blinding.

Grandma clenched a hand as if mentally reaching for

her trusted BB gun. No doubt Ruby fell under her defini-
tion of a common varmint.

"Grandma, why don't you go on and take Maverick
back to your house?" he said, stepping between them.
"Give him one of those bones he likes so much."

Maverick kept up a low growl that matched Grandma's rumble.

No one budged.

Finally, Ruby entered, and stepped over Maverick,
who caught Sawyer's eye. Sawyer shook his head once.
No biting.

Maverick woofed, rose with his tail between his legs,
and padded to the front door.

Grandma looked like she might do the biting instead.

"I'll come and fetch him soon," Sawyer said quietly.

Grandma kept her posture ramrod straight, but he
sensed her relenting on the inside. Affection licked him.
She might be crazy, but she was his crazy, on his team,
ready to guard his back through thick and thin. Not that
he needed a team against Ruby. He had this handled.

"God, I thought she'd never leave," Ruby drawled
after Grandma slammed the door with a little too much
force. She picked an imaginary split end and frowned
at his L-shaped sectional couch. "Is there dog hair on
that?"

"Probably."

He didn't offer her a seat. This wasn't going to take
long. "Why are you here?"

She smirked and strutted to his fireplace, setting one

hand against the mantle, thrusting her shoulders back and showing off her twin assets.

His heart didn't quicken. Nothing like the gallop when Annie tromped out of her house in that short pink bathrobe, eyes sleepy and hair wild, or how she looked in a simple pair of cut-off jean shorts. The thing was she was impossible not to like. She infused the air she moved through with a warm glow, even now, after all this time apart. With Ruby, physical desire was all well and good, but he'd grown old enough, and wise enough, to have learned true chemistry had an indefinable extra spark, that thing where after burning up the sheets you can agree what to watch on Netflix or wander out for a midnight stargaze.

"It's time we have a little chat, Moose," she purred. Chatting to Ruby meant dirty talk, and he was over that particular conversation, at least with her.

"You're married, Ruby," he said tightly. "Congratulations."

She rolled her eyes. "In name only, dummy." Her lips pursed with smug satisfaction as she noted his obvious confusion. "Buck's my husband, but not my *husband husband*."

"I knew things were different in Hollywood, but what you're saying doesn't make sense."

"He's batting for the other team, Moose. Your team."

"What?" He was so confused he let her old nickname for him slide. Of all the things he imagined Ruby saying this was nowhere on the list.

"I'm a beard, baby."

Ruby hated body hair. "A beard?"

"Buck's gay, but he makes his living playing big, macho men on screen. Guys who get the girl, not the guy. He wants to keep up appearances, and that's where I come in," she said with a smug smile.

"Are you shitting me?"

"It's a business decision. Buck can offer me a lifestyle second to none. He's a great guy, brings home great guys, and it's all a lot of fun. But I'm lonely and a girl needs to have a good time."

"Your marriage was a business decision?" he repeated, stunned.

"Buck gets that silly 'heterosexual' label, which is good for his career, and I get my foot in the door in Hollywood." She gave a one-shouldered shrug. "Buck made me sign all these legal papers and promise to be discreet while he promoted *Tumbleweeds*. With all the reporters poking around Brightwater after it won the Oscar, the risk of someone discovering our arrangement was too high. But now the hype's died down, and I miss you, Moosey."

"Don't." She'd called him that in bed. Once she'd gotten out a ruler and he'd let her measure it. He thought it was a bit of fun until she bragged about the size to all her friends. "Don't ever call me that again."

"You're so mean." She gave her trademark pout.

"Let me get this straight." Sawyer's insides churned. "You didn't want my ring on your finger, but still want me between your sheets?"

Ruby clapped her hands. "Yes, that's it exactly." She

sauntered forward, hips swinging and expression confident. "See how perfect it is? You and me can still be, well, you and me. Do what we do best." She stroked his chest, let her fingertips drag suggestively down his ribs.

He couldn't move. Not from lust, but shock.

It wasn't until she cupped his cock that he jumped. "Whoa," she laughed. "Been a while?"

He stepped back and held a warning hand. "Whatever you came here for isn't happening."

"Oh, really, Sawyer, don't be a prude." She arched a brow. "Unless you want to play hard to get? Hmmmm. Roleplaying could be fun."

"No games, just straight talk. You and I are finished. There's no epilogue."

"Now that's your pride talking. Buck and I have a house in Beverly Hills and the Hamptons and a yacht in the Bahamas. I told him I wanted a place here too, in my hometown. A little love nest for us, Moose." She reached behind her and there was the faint metal grind of a zipper before her dress puddled at her ankles. She'd come in battle armor, black lace push up and a barely-there thong. Every inch of her was *Maxim*-grade hotness, but repelled him like an opposing magnet. Not because her husband was gay, he didn't care about that, but because she thought he'd agree to be used. The path to his heart wasn't between his legs.

"Ruby, come on, let it go," he said, soft but insistent.

A spark of doubt appeared in her eyes. This was a woman who sought approval like air. The secret vulnerability was what originally drew him to her, until he'd realized it was insatiable. She was a human flytrap, would catch people and suck them dry to fill herself.

"I'm not letting you go." Steel replaced the momentary insecurity. "There's no point resisting. You know I always get my way." She molded her hands around her breasts. "I need a little Oscar Mayer. My favorite bologna has a first name, it's M-O-O-S—"

Glass shattered behind him and Sawyer turned with a muffled curse. *Damn it to hell.*

Annie blinked in the doorway, a broken plate and scattered muffins at her feet. Her pretty blue dress matched her eyes, like the August sky, so warm and deep it seemed impossible winter could ever come. She looked cute, vaguely different than the last few times he'd seen her. Good. Maybe the chores he kept doing were lessoning her workload. She'd been working too hard, with no time to take care of herself.

"Sorry, I'm interrupting," she mumbled.

"Yes," said Ruby, just as Sawyer answered, "No, you aren't."

He bent and grabbed Ruby's silk dress. "She's leaving."

"No, that's fine. Keep singing, Ruby," Annie said, before disappearing the way she came, flying down the steps, running from him again. Fuck. Would anything ever go right between them?

"Moose," Ruby screeched as he stormed out of the house. "Stop! We aren't finished here, not by a long shot."

He turned and lifted a warning finger. "If you aren't off my property by the time I get back, I'll arrest you for trespassing and indecent exposure."

He ignored her outraged gasp and chased Annie into the gathering dusk. She ran like wildfire, but he caught her near the fence, barely.

"Annie," he said breathing hard. "Wait. Please."

She pulled up short at the "please," but kept her back to him.

"I didn't know you were coming over."

"Clearly," she said flatly. "Jesus, I'll never be able to look at bologna the same way again."

"I didn't know Ruby was coming over."

"You're a busy man." Her hands balled into fists. "It was an imposition for me to show up unannounced. A stupid impulse. I don't know what I was thinking."

"Turn around. Look at me."

Annie's shoulders hitched with one long heavy sigh. She slowly pivoted. The unshed tears in her eyes made him want to kick his own ass for causing her even inadvertent pain.

"I know this doesn't sound right, but none of that with Ruby was what it looked like."

"Okay."

He started. "Okay?"

"Well . . ." She rocked her head back and regarded the sky. "First, it's not my business. But secondly, yeah. I believe you." She kept her gaze away from his face. "Because if you wanted to be with her, you'd be there now."

Raw emotion clogged his throat. "Annie—"

"All I wanted to do is say thanks for helping around the property."

"You're welcome."

"So guess we're all done." She executed a slow one-hundred-and-eighty-degree turn.

He stepped toward her back, aching to take her into his arms. "Do we have to be?"

"I meant for now." She hugged herself tight. "You've probably had enough excitement for one afternoon."

His chest hurt and head throbbed. How the hell could he breach the gulf between them? All he could think to do was stick out his hand. "Friends at least."

She regarded it as the silence between them thickened. What he wouldn't give to see the thoughts cranking through her head.

"Sure." She took his hand and he couldn't tell if the scent filling his senses came from the meadow grass or her. "Friends. At least to a point."

"Nah, it doesn't work that way." His voice came out husky and intense. Good. Let her know she affected the fuck out of him. He pulled her close, pressing his forehead against hers. "We're either friends or we aren't."

She seemed to consider her response carefully, but gently pushed him away regardless. "Friends then. Don't want to be on the sheriff's bad side." She forced a laugh and tugged free, swinging a leg over the fence. Her dress exposed her up to mid-thigh, but he kept his face trained on hers.

"Annie . . . since the fireworks, you're all I can—"

"See you around." And all she left him with was the view of her cute ass disappearing into the gathering shadows. He was an idiot to stand there, watching her go, pining so hard he'd create his own damn forest.

She dipped down the hill, the last sign of her vanishing from sight before he tore off his hat and hit the side of his leg with the brim. Part of him wanted to forget common sense, hurdle the fence, take her into his arms, and show her how right they could be, if they'd only give each other a chance. But he didn't want their first kiss to come under the shadow of Ruby. It had to be special, a moment that was theirs and theirs alone. After all, he wanted it to be her last first kiss.

Chapter Eleven

[draft]

Musings of a Mighty Mama

Sister, Sister

older posts>>

Dear Readers,
Today is the eleventh day of the Mighty Mama
gratitude challenge. Let's talk about family ~~can't kill them~~
~~so might as well love them~~*. In particular, let's chat about*
sisters. I'm going to go all Christmas in July and quote
my favorite holiday movie, White Christmas (can I get a
What? What? For the dapper swoon that is Bing Crosby?).
If you've seen the flick, you know the two heroines are
sisters, famous for a singing act where they croon about

their devotion to each other, as long as the other doesn't get in the way of their man. Now, my favorite person in the whole world is currently at Five Diamonds, my big sister, Claire. While we don't share the same taste in guys ~~*she has a thing for bad ass bikers and I trend toward confusing cowboy sheriffs,*~~ *, we do have a lot of fun* ~~*fighting*~~*. I think you can truly say there have never been such devoted sisters* ~~*devoted in the art of driving the other bonkers*~~*.*

Draft Saved by <u>Mighty Mama 04:45pm</u> in <u>family life</u>, <u>summer fun</u> | <u>Permalink</u> | comments (0)

"Shut your pie hole and shimmy into this dress, Annabelle Carson!"

The only thing preventing Annie from snarling at her bossy sister was the fact Atticus stood in the doorway, hands pressed over his ears. She loved Claire. She truly did. But her sister drove her to Crazy Town with that know-it-all attitude. She'd built an empire selling overpriced toast to suckers, but apparently power had gone to her head because she appeared more than justified ordering Annie to attend the gala at The Dales once the invitation arrived.

"I really, really, really don't want to go." Annie hugged her towel closer. The party seemed fun in theory, but now that it was actually here, why go out when she could stay home and obsess over the memory she'd played on repeat the last few weeks, that moment in the parking lot when Sawyer's lips pressed warm against her neck. Her hands and heart had been so long empty, and for those brief seconds she'd been filled. Every few hours she'd find herself paused, mid-task, idly touching her mouth, lost in longing.

Claire shook the flapper dress, snapping her back to the present. "And I really, really, really don't care."

"Why can't I stay home with you?" Annie wheedled. The yoga pants splayed across her bed looked so cozy and inviting. "We can go for a river walk with Atticus, then bake something for the blog and eat it out of the pan while watching a rom com on Netflix. You love *When Harry Met Sally.*"

"Annie."

"Okay, how about this. Two words. Paul Rudd."

Claire stamped her foot. "Annie."

"Do you ever miss it?" Annie asked suddenly.

"What?"

"Living here at Five Diamonds? Being back in Brightwater?"

"Yes."

"Really?" Annie was startled by Claire's simple admission.

"Of course I miss it. We have fun here, you and I. Sometimes I see kids playing in the city playgrounds and I feel bad for them. We didn't have a little scrap of play space. We free-ranged across thousands of acres. Explored whatever we felt like. Growing up here made me who I am, you too."

"You're kind of right," Annie said.

"Kind of? I'm absolutely right. As always."

Annie glanced down at herself again. "I wish I hadn't told Edie that I'd go. I feel bad flaking."

"You want to miss the chance for a night of fun to sit around the house, watch old movies you've seen five billion times, and show off online for strangers who don't give two cents about you?"

"Ouch. Tell me how you really feel."

"I'm not saying you're not good at your job, because you are. Hey, I subscribe to the *Mighty Mama* feed. Your voice, your style, your photos, they're fab, but you're so much more than the sum total of that blog." Claire went for the jugular like a cheetah on the savannah.

"It's part of me," she retorted weakly.

From the expression on Claire's face, Annie was about to go down faster than a sick gazelle. "If the best part of you is a fictional supermother creation for the benefit of the Internet, then you've got serious life choices to make. Now quit whining and stick on this fabulous dress because I hunted to hell and back unearthing the iron. And don't forget the headdress. I mean, talk about fate, here's a jazz party and you have a flapper dress and twenties-era headband."

"I like vintage."

"There are no coincidences. This is fate, Lil' Bit. Your night to shine." She held up Annie's bright red t-strap pumps. "And can we talk about these shoes? I covet them. The color is absolutely delicious."

"I don't feel like I have any business wearing heels. I'm just a . . . " *Mommy.* The beloved word suddenly felt like an excuse. Had she been hiding behind motherhood, using it as an excuse to avoid uncomfortable truths like the fact her self-esteem had fallen and couldn't get up? "Fine, I'll go, but what if no one talks to me? Quincy Bankcroft is huge and I'm not even a minnow, more like a tadpole."

"Then hang out at the dessert table. When in doubt, trust in chocolate."

Annie let out an exasperated sigh and tugged the dress over her head, smoothing out the lace, beading, and fringe. Claire might be a holy terror but she was also one wise woman. A night out might be the ticket to grown-up, sexy, independent woman land. She needed to find that person. She loved being a mother, but she needed to remember to leave some love for herself too, find better balance, and be the kind of person who said yes to a night out that required lipstick and blow-dried hair.

ANNIE STARED DOWN the snarling lion's head door-knocker of The Dales historic mansion. Laughter and jazz poured from the open windows while behind her a coyote yipped, no doubt prowling the perimeter of the manicured lawn for free-ranging peacocks. Who allowed unattended ornamental fowl to free range at dusk in the mountains? Seemed like such an obvious no-no.

She fingered the invitation, tracing her thumb over the engraved words. *Cordially invited. Costume gala. Live auction.* Edie had come through on the invitation, but she was going to be busy catering in the kitchen. Annie wanted to network. After all, that was what she planned to do in San Francisco and there should be lots of media types here. But the urge to retreat, backpedal to the car, and lead-foot it home to Five Diamonds slithered through her, whispering sweet temptations. It would be so easy to scuttle away, drive home and tell Claire she had a headache.

Okay, maybe not easy. Claire would bust four different blood vessels, but it was oh-so-tempting. After all, the comfort zone was such a cozy place. Plus, she wanted to spend time with Atticus because in a few days he'd be heading off to Disneyland with his father and Margot for a quick weekend vacation.

No, stop with the excuses. You can do this. How bad can it be?

Annie adjusted her rhinestone-encrusted flapper headband and gave a hard knock. *Here goes nothing.*

It took less than five minutes to regret not trusting her initial instincts. She sipped champagne, nodded to the band's beat, and pretended to ignore the three-foot space around her. Polished, well-coiffed guests laughed and mingled, everyone seeming as if they knew everyone else. Here and there were a few familiar faces but the locals present clung together on the fringes and didn't see willing to make room for a kooky Carson.

Inhale. Exhale. She was more than her past. She was a mother, a semi-famous Internet somebody.

Wanda Higsby, or Kane now, she'd apparently married one of them, walked by and then slowed. "Why, Annabelle Carson, is that you? I heard you got married, where's your husband?" Her smug smile revealed she damn well knew about the divorce.

Inhale. Exhale. The pang in Annie's chest intensified. What she wouldn't give to be back at home, happily tapping on her computer.

"Excuse me?" A friendly, deep voice spoke on her left. *Who now?* She tried not to flinch.

"Dessert?" A waiter waved a tray of bite-sized delights under her nose. "Let's see, we've got hazelnut macaroons, huckleberry tartlets with vanilla bean cream, some kind of chocolate Kahlúa cake pops, or . . . "

"Yes, all of those." Wait, eating her feelings might not help Operation Mojo recovery. Ah, screw it. "What's in the shot glasses?"

"Tiramisu."

"Yum."

The waiter gave her an approving wink.

"That too, please." If she was going to be noticed tonight, let it not be for being the prodigal daughter of a strange family, but for consuming her weight in miniature sweets.

Someone approached on her left. She caught the black and white tuxedo in her peripheral vision. Another waiter. "One more of those please," she said, brandishing a clean-licked stick.

"I can attend to the cake pops, Daisy, but I'd prefer to make your acquaintance." A faint British accent clung to his words.

This wasn't a waiter, but a slim, ash-blond man, with a close-cropped goatee and keenly intelligent eyes peering from beneath a silk top hat.

"Sorry, I thought you were—oh. Oh God. Quincy.

You're Quincy Bankcroft." He was shorter than he appeared in photographs, not much taller than her.

He spread out his arms in welcome. "And you are Daisy."

"No, I'm—"

"Allow me a little F. Scott fantasy. *The Great Gatsby* is the book of my heart. Look at you, you're a living, breathing incarnation of Daisy Buchanan. Great shoes, by the way." He gave her t-straps an admiring once over.

"Thank you. They aren't actual period. Neither is the dress to be honest, but my bag and headpiece are."

"Annie Carson, is it?"

"Yes, how did you know?"

Quincy raised his champagne flute. "My cousin filled me in on the details of your charming blog."

"What?" The idea of Quincy Bankcroft having an idea *Musings of a Mighty Mama* existed made her want to put her head between her legs and hyperventilate into a brown paper bag.

"Edie insists I take a peek soon. You are putting this place on the map," he said after a sip.

"Jeez, I hope not. Look at the town's reaction to the *Tumbleweeds* movie."

Quincy placed a hand over his heart. "Buck Williams's backside deserved its own award."

"I'll give you that," she said with a shaky laugh. "But people around here wish it never happened." Almost every local truck in the valley besides Sawyer's sported a *Love Brightwater? Then Go Home!* bumper sticker.

Quincy waved a dismissive hand. "Change happens, like it or not."

"Um, you know this is Brightwater, right?" She smothered most but not all of her bitterness. "No one around here ever gets over anything."

He inclined his head with a polite nod. "If my sources are correct, your own family is embroiled in quite the little Hatfield and McCoy drama, am I right?"

"An old vendetta, it's dying but not dead, I'm afraid," she said with a sigh. "Anyway, I'm looking to move to San Francisco."

"Not too quickly, I hope." He kept his curious gaze trained on her face as if considering . . . something. "You're looking at the new owner of *The Brightwater Bugle*."

"The local paper?" Annie raised her brows, intrigued. "Isn't that small potatoes for someone like you?" Quincy Bankcroft owned *Nation Today*, one of the country's largest papers, plus one or two cable networks.

"It was struggling financially and about to go under. Small towns like this deserve a paper, but I have ideas about ramping the online presence, increasing features, and expanding the Western lifestyle component. I'd rather hoped to pick your brain."

Hold the presses. He wanted her advice? How much champagne had this man consumed? "Wow, I'm flattered, but—"

"No buts. We should spend more time together. I'm at Haute Coffee most weekday mornings. Do come see me."

"That would be lovely." Sipping cappuccinos with a media tycoon who appeared to be an excellent human? If the rest of the night went bust, it was still a slam-dunk win.

"Edie bakes chocolate chip scones that hover between miraculous and divine. These are her creations you are sampling tonight."

"She's amazing," Annie replied with sincerely. The Baker's Dozen could use some competition, and if these desserts were any indication, Edie Banks had brought her A game to Brightwater.

Quincy gave a private smile. "She is, and is a lovely person. I'm glad you are making friends." He clapped his hands. "Now if you'll please excuse me—"

"Go! Go!" She waved a flustered hand. "I'm sorry to have monopolized so much of your time."

"Absolutely not," he said firmly. "I'd rather stay and get better acquainted, but time to be a good host. I'll find you later."

"I'll see you soon." She met a few cool, disinterested stares before examining the marble tiles. Definitely not her crowd. "Probably time I head home."

"But you haven't seen the library yet."

"Oh, that's okay—"

"I'm going to insist you take a look. You do know the library's secret?"

"The passages?" The Dales was meant to have secret passages, but they were often dismissed as rumor.

His whisper deepened with dramatic conspiratorial flair. "There's a shelf behind the desk with a row of red-leather bound books. Pull the third one from the right."

"You've piqued my interest." She licked the frosting from her fingers, heartened by the sugar buzz and excuse to escape. A quick peek at the mysterious passage and then she'd go home.

At least her home for now.

THE WORST PART of Sawyer's job as Brightwater's sheriff was putting in public appearances at Brightwater social events. The only reason he'd accepted the invitation was because he had a sneaking suspicion Annie would be here, and the sight of her purple car in the valet parking confirmed it. He glanced at the crowded dance floor, but there wasn't a sign of her.

Most everyone here was a newcomer, but a few locals rubbed elbows with the high flyers. Guests decked out in jazz wear swiveled their heads in his direction. Some subtle. Others? Appraising. Sawyer hadn't played dress up, figured his uniform was good enough.

"Liquid refreshment, sir?"

"Arch? Who the hell let you weasel through the front gate?" His brother was almost unrecognizable out of blue jeans and square-toed boots that served as his daily dude ranch uniform. At some point his little brother would have to stop showing off for tourists and grow up. He didn't know why Archer didn't have a chat with Grandma, request more responsibility at Hidden Rock. The two of them had long butted heads, but it seemed a sensible, responsible course of action. Then again, those were two words no one ever applied to his brother.

Archer shrugged. "A new friend landed the catering contract and got me on the guest list. What's your excuse?"

"The sheriff gets invited to everything, even fancy shindigs, it seems." Sawyer plucked a bottle off a silver tray and took a swig, rolling his eyes toward the oil-painted cherubs frescoed on the drawing room's ceiling. Fat babies weren't his go-to decorating choice but the ale was perfectly chilled and dark, exactly how he liked it.

Archer's eyes danced. "Looking for anyone special?"

"Why do you ask?"

"Now I don't fancy myself a private investigator, but you're scanning the crowd like it's your job. The way I see it, you've come here to either take someone down or get lucky."

"Just minding my own business," Sawyer muttered to his brother's back as he swaggered away. Outside the floor-to-ceiling bay windows, the snow-capped pinnacle—Mount Oh-Be-Joyful—turned rosy from the sunset's lingering flush.

Watch check. What he wouldn't give to convince Annie to blow this Popsicle stand and head back to his cabin for a drink while watching the sunset. He stalked the room's perimeter. Gilded framed paintings hung from crimson wallpaper while beaded lamps brightened even the darkest corner. The Dales looked the best it had in years. Decades of neglect had allowed the historic mansion to fall into disrepair. The new owner must have sunk a small fortune into returning the crumbling estate to its former glory.

The folks shooting him curious side eyes were from the new crowd, the ones who drove the Land Rover and Mercedes Benz SUVs. Sawyer's old '73 Ford F-100 stood out like a sore thumb in the circular driveway. He liked it that way.

This set acted out elaborate cowboy fantasies on their multi-million-dollar ranches on prime cattle land, hopping private jets when they got sick of playing country. Sawyer didn't begrudge success, but Brightwater was his home, born and raised. These days, you couldn't get a pot to piss in around the quiet, mountain-ringed valley for less than half a mil. He made a good sight less than that. The wealth these people had, it was so far out of reach he'd need a telescope to see it.

And there, right in the thick of it—surprise, surprise— stood Ruby. Smiling, with those blood-red lips, the same shade she used to smear on his collar, his chest, his cock.

Sawyer didn't feel a twitch when their gazes caught. His body knew she was bad medicine. She jutted a hip, and that smoldering look could set hell ablaze.

Did she think he'd saunter over and play nice? Apologize for leaving her half-dressed in his house last week? Or better yet, sneak her into an upstairs room and give her multiple orgasms for old time's sake?

Sorry, sweetheart. I'm not your plaything.

Just because trouble came visiting didn't mean you

had to offer it a place to sit down. He looked through her before striding to the corridor. Big band music and raucous laughter retreated the farther he walked.

Where was Annie?

He peered through open doors. A music salon, followed by a personal home theater, and finally the library. She wasn't anywhere to be found.

"Moose?" Ruby's whisper echoed up the corridor, clearly on the prowl.

Shit. The last thing he wanted was to deal with her games. With any luck, the rumor of this old house would prove true. He stepped forward, seeking out a red-leather-bound account of the Lewis and Clark expedition. Found it. He yanked the book forward, and the wall gave a low grinding sound before the bookshelf swung open, revealing a narrow but well-lit hall.

He rocked on his heels, deciding. Grandma had ingrained in his thick head a few steadfast rules. The first was don't let your yearnings get ahead of your earnings. The second? Never go in if you don't know the way out.

"Moose?" Ruby was close, mere heels clicks away from discovering his ass.

Sawyer plowed into the passageway.

Rules, like hearts, were meant to be broken.

Chapter Twelve

"HOLY SMOKES," ANNIE muttered. She'd pulled the book as per Quincy's directions and the shelf swung open to reveal a secret passageway. Be still her Nancy Drew–loving heart—the rumors were true.

She stepped inside, a floorboard depressed under her weight, and the door slammed closed. The blood pounding through her ears increased to a Niagara Falls–level roar. She pushed on the wall. No budging. Maybe if she'd paid more attention in yoga she'd remember a helpful tip or two for calm, centering breaths. She resisted full-blown Stage Five freak-out hand flailing only because the corridor was well lit. Music from the party played ahead. If she could hear the piano and horns, people would hear screams for help. Right?

She started walking and realized her initial claustro-phobic fears were overblown. A door tucked away in an alcove ahead, one with an actual knob that turned, leading back into the world. She cracked it open and peeked into the bustling kitchen. Staff in starched white chef coats scurried in every different direction under Edie's calm supervision. The pretty redhead stood in the center looking remarkably unruffled. Relief shot through her. She wasn't trapped, instead she could go back to embracing her inner sleuth.

The hall veered in a sharp corner, widening into an antechamber. The walls were peppered by holes. *Ooooooh, perfect for spying!* She peeked through one. Two women leaned on the other side.

" . . . surprised she got an invite."

"I'm more surprised she turned up presentable, no tie-dye in sight."

"The question is should she sell Five Diamonds? Look around. With all these newcomers, maybe we'd be better off sticking with the kooky Carsons."

"True, good point. Better the devil we know."

She gripped her champagne flute tighter. These women were talking about her.

Jesus God, why did she bother going anywhere in this town? The band started up the Charleston and trumpets drowned the mean-girling. Annie drained the rest of her champagne, set the glass against the wall, and swayed to the beat. She threw up one hand and flipped the bird to the wall before spinning around and narrowly avoiding a big male body.

"Ack," she squeaked. *Sawyer?* How'd he manage to sneak stealthily behind her? And what was he doing in here?

The air changed, infused with coffee and cinnamon. She wanted to breathe deeper, but being a creeper who went around sniffing local law enforcement wasn't going to improve the situation.

"I frightened you." His husky voice snapped her back into the moment. He removed his ever-present tan Stetson. Dormant nerves started firing. Stupid, as Sawyer was just a friend. They'd shaken on it after he'd chased her through the meadow.

But who stared at a good buddy like that? Did the flare in his eyes mean he . . . that he . . . oh God, more neck kissing seemed imminent. She searched for words to string together a semblance of a sentence, but they were all in hiding.

He idly stroked the scruff shadowing his chin with a big, broad hand. He did work with those hands. She had an impulse to touch one, or let it touch her in soft places, regions that could use a little roughening up.

She cleared her throat, resisting the urge to face-fan. Sawyer regarded her gravely.

"How did you find your way in here?" she asked.

"I have my ways."

Maybe it was the champagne, the dancing, or the fact she hadn't been touched in far too long, but a giddy restlessness took hold, as if the bubbles she'd consumed migrated into her bloodstream.

He stared at her as if she was something he'd never seen.

"You here alone?" She made a show of looking around. "No half-naked women throwing themselves at you?"

His mouth crooked in one corner. "Not unless you're planning to drop that dress and make my night."

"Excuse me?"

"Relax, Annie." The skin around his eyes crinkled. "I'm yanking your chain. Got to say, you make it easy."

Was he flirting? He really sounded like he was flirting. "I'm not easy." *Unless you start in with those neck kisses.*

"I know that. You take effort, like that toy you have to twist around to make all the colors line up, I forget the name, had one as a kid."

"A Rubik's Cube?" she asked with a laugh, unsure whether to be offended or flattered.

"Yeah, that." He regarded her steadily. "Those things take patience, but I'm a patient man."

"Really, because Ruby doesn't seem like the kind of woman who'd keep a man waiting." Ugh. Listen to herself. "I'm sorry. That was out of line. Women are entitled to live their lives any way they choose."

"They are indeed. But so are men. And me and Ruby, well that's the thing, see, there is no me and Ruby. I got lucky with her—lucky I got out before I made the worst mistake of my life. I mistook fool's gold for the real thing, and it's an error I don't plan on making twice."

She nodded slowly. Gregor gave her Atticus, but that was the only reason she didn't regret their marriage. "Yeah, I know what you mean."

His face softened. "I'm sorry you've had a hard time. I know I've said it before, but smiling is a good look on you."

"Do you dance?" she blurted. His "smiling is a good

look" line churned her brains better than her trusty KitchenAid mixer.

"No," he answered, too quickly.

"Spoilsport." The champagne must have loosened her inhibitions. "I bet I'll get you to dance with me someday." What was she thinking talking about the future? She'd be out of Brightwater soon.

His eyes widened before a chuckle broke free from deep within his ribs. He leaned against the opposite wall, crossing his arms. His shirtsleeves rode up, revealing a line of lean muscle. Someone won the genetic lottery.

Why did he stare at her like that? Did she have tiramisu on her face?

"Why are you so quiet?" She casually brushed her cheeks. No crumbs seemed evident.

"I say something if it requires saying." His eyes dropped a fraction, checking her out. Either that or she'd spilled cake pop crumbs down her front.

"Maybe I could show you a move or two," she said, because this moment didn't count. A chance encounter in a secret passage wasn't real. It was a hall pass.

Those big hands. How often had she fantasized about them the past few weeks? Her ability to perform long multiplication in her head didn't go that high. She took one hand into her own. It was rough, with calluses etched across the palm, and she fought a sudden urge to suck his index finger into her mouth. His breath came a little more uneven, as if he could read her thoughts.

"I told you"—his words were a rumble—"I don't dance."

"Who said anything about dancing?" Her fingers looked absurdly small next to his. "I'm going to tell your fortune."

"You are?"

You are? Her subconscious added a silent, "You know I know what you're doing."

But she needed this, she craved a few stolen moments of fun. The Fourth of July had made her remember how it used to be with them, and she wanted more. More everything.

"You seek something." She traced her nail down the centerline in his palm. This one fanged like a fork in a river and she chose the path that ran deep toward his inner wrist. "And this tells me you have a strong sense of passion."

"Does it?" He sounded amused.

"Hands never lie." She was talking straight out her ass. She didn't have the first clue how to distinguish a life line from a love line. Nothing was going on here but pure, awkward wish fulfillment. If it didn't work, it didn't matter. She'd leave and fake a sudden case of amnesia.

"Interesting." She circled the pad beneath his thumb. "It says here that you want to kiss me," she whispered, raising her gaze, but not quite daring to meet those guarded green eyes.

He leaned in, fingers tangling in her hair. As he tilted her head back, his whisper brushed hot against her skin. "I do, more than anything."

GOD HELP HIM, Sawyer wanted his mouth on Annie's since he'd woken her up that first morning on the farm. He knew what would happen if he did this. He'd burn. And a long-forgotten part of him hurled toward the blaze like it wanted nothing more than to feel the sweet hurt.

She settled her red lips at the join between his fingers, and when the warmth of her tongue licked his skin, the last grasp on his self-control snapped.

He grabbed her hips. Her ass was curvier than expected. The low-waist dress hid interesting dips and swells. Such a crime. When she nestled against him, the fit was perfect, like she'd always belonged there. He hadn't messed around for a good long while. But he'd never been so goddamn hard, because this was Annie in his arms, the culmination of his boyhood dreams.

Cool it. She'd feel his need.

She rubbed against him, her belly teasing against his thick cock.

Yeah, she felt it.

He crushed his mouth against hers and tasted a champagne tartness followed by a deeper richness, close to hazelnut, and another flavor lingering behind, alluring and elusive, like the woman herself. He devoured her whimper as his hands connected at the back of her dress, tugging up the fabric and grazing—what the hell? Sweet Jesus—garter belts.

Another moan followed, and this time it came from him. He flipped her around and pinned her with his own body against the rough wooden wall. She arched when his lips fastened to her throat, tracing her pulse with the flat of his tongue. Strong. Vital. Her fingers fumbled behind her, searching out his buckle, while his slid to the satin of her panties. His thumb skimmed along the elastic hugging her inner thigh, catching a hint of warm, wet arousal.

"And supposedly they kept the moonshine stored in these alcoves." A nasally voice echoed from around a corner ahead. His quicksilver melted from his grasp. Annie stared, her chest heaving in ragged breaths.

"I—"

"We have to get out of here." She grabbed his hand and tugged him away from the direction of the voices.

What else could he say? *No. I want more.*

"Here, this way." She yanked a door knob and hurtled them through the exit. They stood, blinking, in a busy industrial-sized bright kitchen.

"Sawyer!" He turned instinctively at Archer's shout.

He glanced back to help Annie navigate through the activity but all he saw was her dress glint as she ducked through a swinging door into the party.

His brother held up a beer across the kitchen, questioning. *Want another?*

He shook his head and pushed into the hall. Annie wanted him, he could taste it in her kiss, but their connection ran deeper than pure physical desire. She could run away all she wanted, but when his mouth was on hers, damn if she couldn't get closer.

At last he'd found the one bet he'd be willing to make. He'd gamble his heart on Annie. Time to find out if there'd be a payout.

Chapter Thirteen

SAWYER DIDN'T SLEEP a wink after the party. Eventually, he threw on a pair of grey sweats, brewed some coffee, and stood in his front doorway, watching the stars disappear from the sky one by one as dawn returned to the world. His mind worked slow, turned things over at its own steady speed. All he knew for certain was that he wanted Annie, and everything that entailed, including her son. The idea should scare the shit out of him, but there wasn't uncertainty inside him, only a growing confidence.

He could do this. He could figure out a way to convince her to stay.

He went on rural patrol to have time to think, and Kit was happy enough to hold down the office fort. As Sawyer left Main Street, he got the unshakeable feeling he was being followed, but didn't know for sure until he passed the city limits. A car gained speed and closed in, kicking dust high in the air. Sawyer tracked its progress in his review mirror, the color jolting him like a third coffee. Purple. Annie's car. He frowned. Where was she going at twice the speed limit? She flashed her lights and beeped the horn.

Hopefully nothing was wrong. He flipped the siren and pulled over at the turn out, flushing a rafter of wild turkeys from the underbrush. They broke into frantic gobbles as he leapt out and tore to her car. He leaned in the driver's side window and . . . not Annie.

The older sister. Claire.

"Can I help you, ma'am?" He switched to all business, willing his heart rate to slow.

She winked a blue eye the same color as her sister's, except if Annie was sweetness, this one was spice. He preferred the former.

"My sister's the one who needs help."

"Not sure I'm following," he deadpanned.

"I heard about all the kisses." She dropped her voice to a theatrically seductive tone. "You're quite the Don Juan, Sheriff."

He stepped away and scratched the back of his neck. "Ms. Carson—"

"Please, call me Claire. We're neighbors. Besides, you've got the hots for my baby sister."

Jesus Christ, he wasn't going to stand here addressing his love life with this woman. "Look, I'm on the clock."

"And this is a bona fide emergency, Sheriff. Tick tock. Tick tock."

He arched a skeptical brow, doubt darting through him. "Is Annie in some sort of trouble?"

"Yep. Big trouble."

He frowned, the doubt turning into a piranha, gnawing his gut. "What the hell happened?"

"Her morale got steamrolled by her douchebag ex-husband." Claire jabbed a finger against her steering wheel. "If that's not an emergency, then you tell me what is."

Relief and annoyance duked it out. "Listen, I need to—"

"No, you listen. My sister is the best, sweetest person in the whole world. I left her behind, stuck in Bright-water High School, where kids couldn't handle anyone marching to the beat of a different drummer. Except you. I heard all about it one night when I went to visit her in Portland, at Lewis and Clark, fresh man year. She downed one too many Jell-O shots and talked all about you, and what happened at that stupid graduation party."

The memory of Annie's broken, tear-streaked face that awful, fucking night still haunted him. "I didn't have anything to do with—"

"Maybe not, but what bonehead brings her on a first date to the lion's den? She's strong, Sawyer, stronger than she knows, but she's sensitive. She hates admitting it, but she needs back-up. Everybody does."

He couldn't argue there. "What would you have me do?"

"Turn up at Five Diamonds tonight. When are you off work?"

"Six o' clock."

"Perfect. Wear a nice shirt. Bring a bottle of wine. Red

is her favorite. You're a handsome guy, got that whole brawny mountain man thing going in your favor. She needs a hero, Sawyer, and there's something about you that makes me believe you're hero material."

"Thanks for the vote of confidence."

She ignored his sarcasm. "I'm taking the kid camping tonight. I've got a spot near Juniper Lake reserved. Atticus and I will swim, fish, and eat too many toasted marshmallows. You? You're going to figure out how to woo my sister."

"Are you always this bossy?" She reminded him of his older brother. Who'd win in a cage match between Claire and Wilder?

"I haven't even warmed up," she quipped.

"You should be a general."

She shoved the key into the ignition. "I make toast, Sheriff, not war. Six o'clock. Don't be late." And with that Claire drove off. He had no idea what she was talking about, but buried in all the nonsense was common sense.

As he walked back to the car, he thought of seeing Annie for dinner and whistled Hank Williams "Hey, Good Lookin'."

ANNIE GAVE A final pound to the "Happy Hen Eggs $3.50 a dozen" sign and stepped back to admire her handiwork. She'd whitewashed old barn wood and stenciled the lettering in cheerful turquoise acrylic rummaged from her old art supplies. One could find only so many creative uses for all the eggs. She'd be sick if she so much as looked at another quiche, and her butt didn't need baked goods for breakfast, second breakfast, lunch, and dinner.

A cloud of dust kicked rose up the road. She wiped her brow and straightened, prepared to offer a friendly wave to the passing driver. Her heart kicked up a gear as a beat-up orange Ford truck came into view. Sawyer's truck.

No need to overreact. Last night was a kiss, nothing but two mouths touching, and a little tongue. Okay, a lot of tongue. Still, no big deal. *Shake it off.* It wasn't as if either of them had never kissed before. An earth-shatteringly delicious kiss she still could taste. She'd come close to finding her missing black box when he skimmed her panties last night. She'd come close to seeing God himself. Okay, maybe brushing off her dress and fluffing her hair would be sensible. Maybe even squeezing her cheeks a la Scarlett O'Hara. Besides, a flirty little wave was preferable to dive-bombing in the front hedge, especially when he slowed down.

She raised a hand in greeting as he put the truck in park and swung open the door. Worn denim hugged his long, muscular legs. Made it kind of hard to notice the stunning vista behind him.

He nodded at the sign. "Happy hens, huh?"

"As long as your grandma isn't issuing them a one-way ticket to the coop in the sky."

He snorted. "The, uh, the lettering looks good. Real good."

"Thanks." She took irrational joy in his small talk. "How was work?"

"The usual. Spent the afternoon in the office taking care of business."

Oh, I have some business you can take care of, Sheriff, in a very official capacity.

Stop. Just stop. Otherwise her ovaries would explode.

"What are you cooking?" he asked.

She coughed. "Excuse me?" Were these dirty thoughts stamped on her face?

"For dinner?"

"Nothing special." Her brows knit. What was he hinting at? First it seemed like flirting, but now—no idea. "Probably leftovers." Or standing up and eating yogurt from the carton in front of the fridge. "Claire took Atticus camping for the night."

A puzzled expression skimmed his features, vanishing in an instant. Still, she didn't miss it. "What's going on?"

"Oh." He cleared his throat. "Nothing."

She'd been so distracted by his jeans that she'd missed the bottle of red wine clutched in his hand.

They both stared at it.

"Your sister . . . "

"My sister . . . "

In retrospect, Claire had given a particularly evil giggle as she drove away.

Annie envisioned an evening spent soaking in the bath, or maybe slaking her frustrated lust with an ubernaughty romance novel, but apparently her sister arranged for actual romance to be on the menu.

"You didn't have any idea about dinner, did you?"

Sawyer thrust his free hand into his hip pocket and held perfectly still.

She used to be able to do that, in the hills behind Five Diamonds, become a human statue and watch deer, quail, bobcats, and once a prowling mountain lion high on the ridgeline. These days, her hands always moved, adjusting, fixing, like little apologies constantly making reparations with the greater world. *Is it okay for me to be here? To take up space? Please let it be allowed.*

"No! No. I'm sorry." She remembered her manners after the longest pause in recorded history. "Of course I knew you were coming."

He pressed his lips together, the craggy skin around his eyes losing its tightness. "Annabelle Carson, permission to speak plain?"

Her stomach flipped. "Permission granted."

"You are the single-worst liar in the entire state of California."

"I'm not lying." Wait a second—was that a giggle? It sounded an awful lot like a giggle.

"I might amend the statement to include Nevada and Oregon, the tri-state area."

"Fine. I wasn't exactly privy to the evening's plan, but I'd be glad for your company." *The key word being "your."* Her flirting skills were as rusty as the old milk cans at the end of the driveway, the ones she'd filled with potting soil and now held black-eyed Susans.

He appeared to let out a breath. "Would you?"

"Yes, I . . . I haven't spent a night alone in some time." God, she sounded like a child. As much as the idea of

Sawyer sharing a meal with her in an empty house was unsettling, it was better than being alone wondering who she was when she lost the identity of being Atticus's mom. When the wind picked up after sunset, she didn't want to imagine her Carson ancestors lined up at the edge of her bed, staring in judgment. She was the weakest link. They had invested sweat, blood, and tears into Five Diamonds, and she was letting it all go, letting them down.

She smoothed her hair, pointless as she could feel the stubborn waves sticking up in back. "Do you want to come up?"

"That all depends," he replied evenly.

"On?"

"How much you want me to?" His voice, the way he dropped it low, was undeniably sexy, and not only because of the timbre. It was the assurance. Like he was able to infuse every vowel with a sense of "This might be a bad idea, but it also might be the best one you've ever had."

"Come for dinner." Saying the word "come" gave her a naughty shiver, followed by a shiver shiver. Would this blow up in her face? The old Annie would jump without looking, but she'd learned that sometimes there are big rocks below. Kisses might feel magical, but falling hurts.

"Just dinner."

"You've got yourself a deal." Even as she stuck out her hand to shake she knew that it wasn't going to be just dinner. No way could she prepare him a meal, alone in her kitchen, and call it good. Her heart accelerated, the same way it used to when she stared into the river from the top of a cliff. She missed this—having a rush.

"Come on, I'll drive you to the house."

The wind picked up a little as she followed him to his truck, the cool mountain air kissing the back of her neck, sliding up her skirt. Overhead a red-tailed hawk turned in lazy circles, and it looked exactly how she wanted to feel.

Free.

Chapter Fourteen

SAWYER PARKED THE truck in front of Annie's ramshackle farmhouse. The gear box separated them, but despite the distance, her sweet lavender scent and glimpse of lacy white bra strap peeking out beneath her sleeveless dress, compelled him to breathe deeper. Last night's kiss was like discovering a treasure he didn't know he sought. Neither of them mentioned what happened in The Dale's secret passage, although from the way he stared at her mouth, and she at his, it was on both their minds. Good God, her lips were put on Earth to tease him with their softness, and the way she boldly slid her tongue over his—

"Here we are." She moved to open the door.

"No, wait. I got that." He leapt out and rounded the front of the cab. She'd been married for a couple years at least. Guess her ex wasn't the kind of guy who opened doors for his woman. *Jackhole.*

If she ever became his, he'd make it so good that she'd never have a reason to leave. Her being his, that sounded good. He'd never been a commitment-phobe, like Archer, but after the Ruby debacle he hadn't craved another relationship. But since Annie got back in town, all bets were off, and this unexpected direction felt exactly right.

"Um, you know I'm perfectly equipped to do that, right?" she said as he lifted the passenger door handle.

"That's not the point." Her short cotton print dress hitched up her legs as she slid out. A memory struck him of her, naked, on the cliffs when they first met. When she stood, the distance between them was mere inches, and he swallowed hard. "I want to open your doors because I respect you, not the opposite."

She pressed the back of her hand against her cheek. "I'm not sure what to say."

"A simple thank you works."

She blinked. "Of course, right. Thank you. I'm not really used to that sort of thing."

"What?" His stomach hardened as he eyed the falling-down house Roger Carson had dumped on her to handle. "Men taking care of you?"

The frown struck her face, vanishing quick as lightning. "Hey, mind if we go around back? I need to return the mallet to the barn."

"Sure thing," he answered, watching her hips sway as she walked away. She'd worked hard to fix things around the place. As much as Annie insisted that she didn't want to stick around Brightwater a day longer than necessary, the work she'd put in around Five Diamonds had been done with love. That much was clear.

"I wasn't married to a monster," she said, pausing near the barn door. "I don't want to give that impression."

"Never thought that," he replied. *Just a dumbass.*

"It was more . . . I don't know. Gregor and I got together when I was so young, barely an adult. I think that was the big attraction for him, my youth. He was quite a bit older. The trouble is, I grew up."

"He's an idiot," Sawyer muttered and Annie turned with a half-shrug.

"I'm serious."

"So am I."

"Look, I'm done defending Gregor, but you've got to admit that he's not unusual. Lots of guys want to be with the youngest, prettiest thing they see. It makes them feel young themselves, I guess."

"I don't want to go back in time."

"You don't?" She searched his face.

"I'm a little older now, but I'm wiser."

"That's nice. I just feel older." She gave a little laugh, one he didn't respond to. She needed to hear these words. What he had to say.

"When I was a kid, I had dreams," he said softly.

Her smile tilted from her face as she caught the quiet intensity of his words. "Me too."

"Have yours come true?" Emotion deepened his voice. She was close, so close, his hands itched to reach for her, but instincts said not yet—not quite.

She pressed her lips together and shook her head.

"Me neither, not all of them anyway. Not the ones that count the most. When I was a kid, I thought wanting something would be enough to get it. I've learned if you want a dream bad enough, you have to go out and make it happen."

Her lips parted, her pupils dilating. "And what do you want?"

"The same thing I wanted when I was eighteen, but was too stupid to—"

A hen must have laid because the whole coop behind Annie broke out in wild clucking, and she startled before bursting out laughing.

"Calm down, girls," she said. "Why do they always feel the need to broadcast their eggs? You'd think they'd be used to it."

And just like that, his moment was lost to a bunch of damn squawking.

"Those do sound like some happy hens," he muttered, knocking his boot against an exposed field stone. Right now, he'd love to take a page out of Grandma's playbook and wring their cock-blocking necks.

"Thanks to you repairing the coop. You're like their hero or something."

"All it took was a bit of wire and a few nails." He kept his gaze steady. He meant to get the girl. Maybe he'd lost this particular battle, but he was nowhere near defeated.

She blinked first. "Okay, I'll go hang up the mallet and be out in two seconds. In the meantime, would you mind gathering a few eggs? I'm sick of quiche and omelets but could whip us up a halfway decent carbonara."

He didn't have a clue what that was, but she could offer him cardboard and he'd probably like it if it meant looking at her over dinner.

Sawyer strode over to the coop and opened the brooder boxes. The Carsons kept different varieties, so the eggs weren't uniform in size or color. He selected the pale greenish blue ones for no other reason than that they were the same shade as the tiny flowers dotting the dress Annie wore. He didn't know how the woman managed to look so prim and yet earthy. She came out of the barn, and he used his half-hidden vantage to study her.

She still went about barefoot, and that pretty dress had at least a dozen buttons running down the front. Hell, a man could have some fun with that get up, take his time, open each one slowly, like a secret that needs answering.

He stood and cleared his throat. "Six enough?" He held three in each hand.

She laughed. "I don't know why I put that sign out front. I could probably give the extras to you. You'd devour three eggs in a sitting no problem."

"Try five." He thought of his weekend omelets.

"Where do you put it all?" Her gaze roved his build. Normally, he didn't wonder about women. They seemed to like him fine, but this was Annie, and a flicker of uncertainty licked his heart. His size made him clumsy next to her dainty grace. What thoughts spun behind that impenetrable gaze? He wasn't a city boy. His hair had never seen gel, nor did he pay attention to fashion. When he wasn't in his sheriff's uniform, he wore his other uniform—blue jeans and a flannel shirt. Plain Hanes t-shirts on hot days. That was it. Tonight he'd made extra effort, dug out his best church shirt, the checkered navy and white one he wore to weddings and funerals.

Annie broke her silent assessment and called back to the coop, "Thank you, Constance, Shy, and Petunia."

"You name all those birds?"

"Oh sure. Constance, Shy, and Petunia are the Araucanas over there." She pointed to the three white hens with impressive feathery ear tufts. "They're the only ones that lay those pretty blue eggs. Over in the far corner are the Rhode Island Reds: Bixby, Big Mama, Miss Thing, Chatterbox, Honey, and Crazy. Then scratching in the back is Feather Foot, because, well, that's obvious, and . . . what? Are you laughing at me?"

"You name your chickens." God, she really was too fucking adorable for her own good.

"What, Mr. Funny—if you had a coop, you're saying you wouldn't name yours?"

"Sure I would." He gave a shrug. "I'd call them all the same thing."

"Oh yeah? What's that? Chicken?"

"Dinner."

Her lips twitched even as she sniffed. "That's so not funny."

"It's a little funny."

"Must be that Kane humor. I'm genetically immune."

He fell in step behind her going into the house. He reached up and pulled open the back door, resting his hand on the small of her back.

He wasn't such a good guy, despite his status as

Chicken Savior. He'd take any excuse to touch her. The dress had a slight softness, like the cotton had been well worn and well loved. His thumb brushed over the base of her spine, and he swore she gave a slight shiver.

"Annie."

She half-turned, sensing the seriousness undercutting his light tone.

"Tonight, I'm going to ask you to make me a promise."

She frowned. "These days I never promise anything without knowing the stakes first."

"That's fine. I'll tell you. I don't want to give the past a place at the table. Can we get back to how we used to, back before . . . "

"Everything."

"I know you need to take your time, but while I might be patient, I'm also greedy. I want you, and I'll wait, but when we happen—and we will happen—I want all of you."

Shit, the way she froze and stared. "I—wow . . . I wasn't expecting you to lay things out like that."

He took a deep breath. "Like what?"

"So straightforward."

"I don't know how to tell you any other way. Back in the day, I fooled myself that if I wanted something bad enough, it would work out, without me putting in the effort. Life doesn't work that way."

"I had to learn that lesson too," she whispered.

"We had something, didn't we?"

She blushed. "We were kids."

"But it was real. I'm not making it up in my head here.

Say the word if I am and I'll leave it alone. I'll eat my carbo-whatever-you-call-it, and still help out around your place as much as I can. But I'll never bother you on the subject again."

"We had something," she whispered.

His next heartbeat came extra hard, the pound vibrated through his stomach. "Do we still?"

"That's the million-dollar question." She forced a smile and turned to a cupboard, rising on her tiptoes. He wanted her against him in his bathtub, facing him, those pretty toes between his hands. If no one had the decency to open doors for her, no way would she have ever gotten a damn fine foot rub. He wanted to show her all the ways a man could treat a woman right. Make her see that she didn't have to settle for less than being treated like a queen.

Unless the humble kingdom he had to offer wasn't the one she wanted.

Still, if he walked away from this shot, he'd kick his own ass for the rest of his life. "Annie, I'm not a betting man—"

"The only Kane who could make that claim," she said, arching one brow.

"But I would bet on us."

Her silence lasted so long that he wasn't sure if she heard him, or if she'd decided to give a blow off after all. At last she turned and murmured, "What are the stakes?"

If he said *the rest of our lives* she'd probably run screaming for the door. Those were words huge to think, let alone say out loud. Still, she didn't deserve the runaround, not from him. "For you? I'm willing to go all in."

Her eyes widened. "How can you say that? You don't even know me anymore."

He wouldn't win points by telling her she was wrong. But she was the best, strongest, most fascinating person he'd ever known. "Guess that's why it's called a gamble." For a second he understood why his family loved risks. There was an inherent thrill activating inside him, as if his very DNA craved the excitement of the unknown.

"What if we lose?" she asked.

He took her hand and held it between his. "What if we win?"

Chapter Fifteen

DINNER WENT BETTER than fine. Sawyer proved himself an eager sous chef, rolling up his plaid shirtsleeves to reveal powerful forearm muscles that flexed as he diced. Despite his height and powerful build, he moved around her kitchen with surprising grace, happy to take direction. His willingness to trust her was as sexy as his Wrangler-clad ass, and that was really saying something. Gregor always second-guessed her choices; confident he'd improve upon them. Sawyer didn't flinch when she requested that he separate the egg yolks, stir them into the creamy Parmesan cheese mixture, and then pour the whole concoction over the linguini.

"The raw eggs cook on the hot pasta," she explained, coming up behind him to sprinkle in parsley, just so he'd be reassured a semblance of a plan existed. "I omitted the pancetta, hope that's okay."

"Sounds good," he said offhandedly, sucking cream off his fingertip.

Her breath audibly hitched. If she said the word, he'd lick her with that tongue, touch her with those fingers. She'd forgotten the way desire created a free-falling, vertigo sensation, as if the bottom dropped from her own personal Gravitron.

It felt good. God, it felt good. Part of her was terrified, and another part wanted to throw her head back and laugh with sheer dizzy glee.

The meal held a few awkward silences, but the wine and long looks smoothed everything over, even if all the crossing and uncrossing of her legs made it impossible to eat much.

After dinner, he rose to clean up.

"No, no," she said as she waved her hands. "Sit."

He shook his head. "I've got this covered. Your job is to relax and finish that glass."

She took a sip of the pinot. He hadn't brought over a fancy bottle. The Brightwater Save-U-More only carried the big, mainstream brands. Gregor would scoff at it, but the flavor was perfect, deliciously robust and strong, like the man washing her dishes.

After he finished drying, again at his insistence, she invited him to the back porch swing to enjoy a mason jar of homemade lemonade. "It's made with agave," she said.

"What's that?"

"A succulent that creates a syrup that's sweet like honey."

His brows knit. "Why not use regular honey? You've got the apiary for it, down in the far west corner."

"Is that still there?" She hadn't even ventured to that part of the property yet.

"Sure is. We'll go visit it soon."

The swing's chain creaked slightly as they watched the moon rise over the range. Her bare knee grazed his thigh as he rocked them back and forth. The denim roughed her skin, soft and worn, like he was a man who worked hard.

And played harder.

A mosquito buzzed and she reflexively slapped the side of her neck. "Dang, it bit me."

"Here, let me help," Sawyer reached into his jar, plucked an ice cube, and ran it over her neck. A bead of water trailed down her skin, disappearing under her collar. The cold tightened her nipples and his Adam's apple bobbed. "Better?"

"Does that really help?"

"Depends how badly you need to scratch an itch."

The cold wasn't the only thing making her tremble. "We are talking about mosquito bites, right?"

"Sure." He raised his brows in mock innocence, sliding his arm around the back of the swing, loosely draping her shoulders.

She tilted against him laughing, hands bracing his chest, and just like that, she fell into those deep green eyes. Sanctuary. He was sanctuary. She could be safe here, in the dark, with his heart hammering against her palm. Slowly, her clutch transformed into a tug as some mysterious devil pushed her forward until her lips grazed his. The ice cube clattered to the porch as he wrapped cool fingers around the back of her neck, holding her in place.

This couldn't even be called kissing. It was inhaling, vital as oxygen. Every part of her body craved contact. She swung a leg over his waist, drew herself on his lap as the swing creaked. His hands were everywhere, all at once, tangling in her hair, running down her back, molding to her ass, and hauling her closer.

She dragged her cheek over his light scruff. His hands locked firm on her hips while she burrowed into his neck, sucked the side of his throat, the thick tendon that disappeared under his collar. His stomach flexed against hers when she kissed each of his eyelids and nipped the tip of his nose. When she licked the seam of his lips, he braced her face.

"My turn." His kisses came slow, lazy, tart with a fresh lemon bite and underlying hint of sweetness. His gruff groan shook straight to her core and she ground harder, drove herself against him, determined to hear him make that sound again. Which he did.

"So good, Annie, God, you're sweet," he rasped in her ear. "How are you so fucking sweet?"

The shiver that ran through his body entered hers. "Must be all that agave." The swing's creaking grew rhythmic and they laughed softly into each other's mouths.

Then he stood, locking her against him, fingers clasping her bottom.

"Where are we going?" she murmured drunkenly. She'd had only two glasses of pinot but buzzed like she'd gulped the whole bottle.

"Got to look at you."

Look? Her stomach ached like she'd done a hundred crunches. Looking meant seeing, and what would he notice?

He opened the back door without breaking the rhythm of their kiss, sitting her on the edge of the kitchen table before kneeling to unbuckle her strappy sandals. "On second thought, these are better on." He rose, settled her onto her back, and undid the first button of her mini dress.

Can't the lights be off? More buttons opened. Should she find a sexy angle? *Do I have a sexy angle? Okay. Okay. Forget the sexy angle. Try to relax.* At least she wore a lace bra today, in a small, private nod to mojo.

"Pretty." Sawyer grazed the freckles smattering her clavicle with the back of his knuckles. The light gesture twisted her core to a maddening, impatient ache. "They look like Orion's belt."

She sucked in when her exposed belly button hit the night air.

"A tattoo?" He bent and traced the small black birds spiraling up her hip with the tip of his tongue.

Her back arched. "I got it after Atticus was born." When she'd wanted to fly away with her baby, leave the nest that felt more and more like a cage. Instead, she'd inked wings on her body and hoped for the best, but best never showed up.

She squeezed her eyes as his finger traveled the silvery stretch marks across her lower abdomen. She'd used cocoa butter, drank water, and popped Vitamin E like candy, but despite valiant efforts, her third trimester pregnant belly cracked like an egg.

She instinctively tugged her dress closed.

"No." He caught her wrists, keeping her open, urging her to be exposed.

"Please, stop," she gasped. "I—I—I don't like them."

"Why?" His eyes were serious.

"They . . . " She wished she had a better reason than the truth. "They aren't very pretty."

"Annie Girl?" He released her wrists to open her legs, placing each one on the outside of his narrow hips before bending to lace their fingers together. "You're right." He pressed his forehead into hers. "They aren't pretty."

She bit her top lip. Of course, he was only repeating what she herself knew, but the words still hurt.

"They are beautiful," he said with a sharp inhale.

She averted her face and her reflection stared wide-eyed from the kitchen window. How in the world did she end up here, spread out like a Thanksgiving feast, with this gorgeous man above her?

He nuzzled between her breasts. "They're real." He nipped her nipple through the demi-cup's lace. "Your body had to change, stretch, to hold life. Each of those little marks is a love line."

Hot tears heated the corners of her eyes.

"And your arms." He drew thumbs over her biceps. "They are strong."

"I carry a five-year-old when he refuses to walk."

"You're bothered by this." He stood, staring intensely. "Me, looking at you."

She blinked first. "It's almost too much."

He grabbed her hips and hooked his thumbs into her underwear's waistband. Her bra was Victoria's Secret, but her panties were one hundred percent boring white cotton.

"I like these," he murmured. "They are cute, like you."

"Oh God, that word." She covered her face with her hands, peeping through her fingers. "Cute is the Easter Bunny."

He snorted. "Nah, I'd never go down on the Easter Bunny."

Her rib cage compressed. *If you don't breathe you'll pass out.* "Go down?"

He blew on her stomach and eased her boycut underwear over her thighs, trembling knees, until they were off. Then more looking, and if she'd felt exposed before, this was like being in an x-ray machine.

Why did he want to look down there? This wasn't what she was used to. Gregor liked it doggie style and always turned out the light. She'd fake it, afraid less that he'd feel inadequate and more that she was somehow deficient, like his relentless pounding should do it for her. Afterward, she'd finish alone with her vibrator or fingers. That was their routine, simple and predictable.

This was anything but. Sawyer quit staring. He was, good Lord, down on his knees and about to . . . "Oh. Oh, no. You don't have to." She half-sat, digging her fingers into his thick chestnut hair and tilting his head back to make eye contact. "Don't do anything you don't want to."

His green irises darkened to a near hazel. "Oh, I want. But what about you, Annie? What do you want?"

"I don't know." *Liar.* She knew. She just didn't have a clue how to ask.

He planted a kiss against the softest part of her thigh, not breaking their gaze. "Well, why don't we figure it out?" He kissed her other thigh. Gently, he opened her up and kissed, there, once, slow, gentle, reverently between her legs. His tongue rolled over her sensitive flesh, light, teasing with the promise of what he could offer.

Her body made a confession, saying *yes, please, that's exactly it*, melting into his mouth. *Jesus, Lord, and an army of saints.* He alternated between using the flat of his tongue to tickling with the tip. Not only did he take her breath, she was sure she'd never find it again.

He spread her knees wider and someone cried out; it took a few dazed seconds to realize it was her. Each slick glide hit her senses with a sudden ferocity akin to pain. Her pelvis coiled into hot desperate pleasure. Garbled words tore from her mouth, and incredibly, he understood exactly and took her there, to the place she desperately needed to go.

She gripped the top of his head with one hand and leaned back on the other, going from wet to wetter, her shoulders thrust back, shaking from the force of his approving growl.

That was what was different. He enjoyed this, took his time, did it right, and everything that would normally be okay, or pretty good, transformed into a whole lot of awe-some. She traveled inward to the part of herself that held on tight and saw she wasn't ready to let all the way go, but she could loosen her grip. When he reached and palmed her breast, lightly pinched her nipple through the lace, the double touch of his hands and mouth vaulted her to sweet disorder, seeking mercy and hoping never to find it.

When it was over, she fell exhausted against the table, incrementally returning to her senses. He stood above her, utterly still, watching. Always watching.

No bolt of self-consciousness struck. She wasn't sure what to make of that, or the serious erection tenting his jeans.

"Thank you." A little weird to say, but that was where she was at. What he'd just done, what he'd given her—all she had was gratitude.

The words changed his features from serious to privately amused. "My pleasure."

She crossed her legs and did up her dress. Her undies lay crumpled on the linoleum like a parachute. Time to invest in new pairs that were more "Hey, I can be sexy. For real, I can."

"What?" He stepped closer and tilted her chin.

"Excuse me?"

"You've gone somewhere."

"I was wondering." She stroked the inside of his wrist. "Now what do we do?"

"Thought we did pretty well for starters."

Her answering laugh was unfamiliar, husky, sexy even. "That, a minute ago, was amazing. You're amazing.

Want to go to the living room? I'll figure out a way to return the favor."

And there she went, making a perfect moment totally awkward. She dug her nails into her palms. He'd given her the best orgasm of her life and now she'd reduced lovemaking to something to be haggled over. What was she going to say next? *I'll do hand jobs but not penetration. Or maybe penetration. Are we there now? At the sex point?* Probably. They weren't teenagers anymore. Single guys didn't do heavy petting in their late twenties, right?

Crap. She had no idea.

"I don't want anything in return," he said hoarsely.

She knit her brows. "You don't?" His massive hard-on begged to differ.

"Trust me, Annie Girl. Getting you off is its own reward."

"Um, you're all"—she waved her hand at the boner situation—"that way."

"I'm patient."

"What are you waiting for?"

"You. I want you. Always have." He ran a hand through his hair and it stood up a little wildly in the back. "But I can also see you're still balancing on that back foot of yours. Let me know if you change your mind. Jump, and I'll catch you with both hands, but I won't push."

She took a deep breath. "I'm sorry. It's hard to let go and trust after everything that's happened to me."

"I know." He pulled her close and held on tight.

He was a good guy, a great one even.

What was she doing?

Surely she didn't belong here, in Brightwater, the very place she'd spent her adult life—and a small fortune in therapy bills—trying to forget. She needed to figure out a stable career path to provide for Atticus. And her son deserved a place to grow up where he'd be happy, not picked on or bullied for wearing pink or having an active imagination.

The trouble was, Sawyer's strong arms felt a heck of a lot like home.

Chapter Sixteen

SAWYER SHUDDERED AS the icy shower spray pelted his bare chest. Staying the night at Five Diamonds wasn't an option, even though every cell in his body fought the idea of leaving. Annie needed to know he sought more than sex or a rebound from his disastrous engagement, and that meant shifting to the slow lane. After he carried her upstairs and got her tucked into bed, that drowsy smile nailed his boots to the floorboards.

There it was, at last, the old Annie smile.

"Aren't you going to stay?" she'd murmured.

He'd shoved his hands into his pockets with a prayer for self-control. The idea of undressing, crawling into those clean yellow sheets, spooning his body against Annie, and falling asleep with his face burrowed into the side of her neck was as close as he'd get to heaven on Earth.

He scrubbed his face, fingers growing numb even as

his heart burned. No. One night wouldn't be enough. He wanted forever, but if he spoke all the words rattling around his brain, she'd spook.

He slid his hand down over his rigid abdomen with a resigned sigh, flinching as he gripped the base of his cock. The sensation sucked his breath away. He had it so fucking bad.

The water warmed, relaxing his tense muscles as his groan echoed through the bathroom. His shaft slanted in his hand and he slowed the strokes, took his time, savoring the night's details. How she cried out. The hunger in her kiss. The way her thighs quivered as she came in his mouth. He leaned into his fist, squeezing hard enough it hurt, but so did his whole body for not being buried inside her. This woman wasn't a kooky Carson, or Annabelle, or even his Annie. He cradled his cock, surrendering to the powerful, primitive urgency, releasing in a thick spurt while pounding the tile with his free fist.

That woman, she was home.

Even now, as his hard-on ebbed in his hand, his body didn't feel anything approaching relief. His needs transcended simple physical desire. He flicked off the tap, toweled dry, and crawled into his king-sized four-poster bed. But sleep proved elusive. Instead, he tossed and turned until dawn pinkened the sky. He threw on a well-worn pair of jeans and padded into the kitchen, brewed a pot of black coffee, and carried the mug out to the porch. Venus hung in the sky, and not long after another light appeared, on the second story of Five Diamonds. With a half-smile, he walked to the front door, popped it open and inched his hand inside. Hitting the light switch, he flicked it on and off a few times. Then he turned and his smile broadened as her light flashed back.

He went to his room, changed into grey sweats and a hoodie, and went for a five-mile run with Maverick. Kicked it in hard on the hills, pounding the trail until every muscle in his legs screamed for relief. Good, he needed to beat his body into submission. Later today, he'd spend time with Annie, and he wanted to make sure he worked out some of his restlessness. Afterward, he cleaned out Grandma's barn, changed the oil in his truck, and gave everything a quick tune up.

Finally, chores done and body suitably tired, he left the house, giving his chin a musing rub. *Shit. Forgot to shave.* Hopefully Annie didn't mind five o'clock shadows. Wildflowers bloomed in vivid patches around the yard. He impulsively picked a bouquet and set it beside him in his truck.

His phone buzzed as he started the engine. Ruby. Probably looking for a booty call. Christ, hopefully she'd get over the idea of buying a Brightwater vacation home soon. If she missed the mountains, the Himalayas were supposed to be nice. If she didn't leave him alone, he'd block this number. Her bed might be a lonely one, but she'd made it. Not his problem. There was a world of difference between being a hero and being a chump.

As a kid, he often played cops and robbers with his brothers around Hidden Rock. They'd get annoyed at his absolute refusal to ever play the villain. All he ever wanted to do was run around behind the wheel of an imaginary squad car, making sirens sounds with his mouth and defending the ranch from harm, being the good guy.

He imagined his parents, wherever they were, watched over on him, and he was determined to make them proud.

In high school, his desire refocused on baseball, and as the starting pitcher, he played his guts out to help his team. Now, as sheriff, the town counted on him and responsibility rested easily on his shoulders. He kept peace, maintained safety, and if need be, protected the innocent from the bad guys.

The only person he'd ever failed was Annie. And he was determined to never let her down again.

ANNIE'S STOMACH FLIP-FLOPPED as Sawyer's truck bounced up her driveway. What would a life be like with him? Bumping down backcountry roads, country music blaring on the radio, Atticus wedged comfortably between them, Maverick in the back, nose to the wind?

No. Stop it. Zero point mooning over a vision of a future she wouldn't have. This wasn't home, the house was about to be listed, and it was time to look forward to a new life on the coast.

What had happened between them last night was unquestionably amazing. Sawyer made her feel beautiful, as if her imperfections were to be cherished, something that made her unique as opposed to a collection of flaws. That was a feeling she could get used to. Somehow being around him made her feel more like herself. Gregor's cheating and lying had struck deep at her core fears of being unworthy and unlovable, but she was done with being bitter and angry. She wasn't magically healed or anything, but something shifted inside her.

Dad believed that to make something happen, you should ask the universe and all would be provided. How comforting to imagine Fate as a cheerfully frazzled short-order cook saying, "Better paying salary? Improved body image? Multiple orgasms? No problemo, coming right up."

In her case, maybe all she needed was to open herself up to possibilities again. Start to connect back to the real Annie, the one who hid behind *Mighty Mama*, scared, so scared, of people glimpsing all her messy truths.

Atticus tiptoed behind her, only home from his camping trip an hour. She'd so far averted any of Claire's attempts to drag out what happened last night, no easy feat.

"Why's the sheriff here?" her son whispered, loudly. "Does he want to take us to jail?"

"Don't know—you been doing something bad?" Sawyer answered, hearing the question as he climbed from the truck.

Atticus ducked his chin and shook his head. Seeing Sawyer around town was one thing, but for him to turn up here at Five Diamonds must be confusing.

Sawyer pulled up short, looking a little stiff, uncomfortable, wildflowers gripped in his hand. "That was supposed to be a joke."

Annie ruffled her son's hair. "He's just trying to figure out people dynamics, aren't you, honey?"

No response. Sawyer didn't offer the flowers and Atticus poked the dirt with his sneaker. The three of them stood for an uncomfortable moment before she gestured to the front door. "Want to come in?"

"Yeah, sure." They walked inside as Claire skipped down the stairs.

"Aw, those for me?" she said, eyeing the bouquet with a cheeky smile.

"Oh, sorry, no. Uh, they're for Annie." He held them out, and as she took them, the realization that the stems were slightly damp quickened her heart. Was Sawyer as nervous as she was?

The trouble was deciding whether the fact was relieving or terrifying.

"Would you like a cup of coffee?" she asked shyly, trying to ignore the dagger eyes Claire sent him, an obvious warning not to mess up.

"Sounds great," he said quickly.

And it was. She made a strong brew, and the four of them sat around the kitchen table. While Sawyer didn't excel at small talk with people he didn't know, Claire chatted incessantly, doing impressions of the regulars who frequented her food truck and the big fish Atticus caught camping last night at Juniper Lake.

"Fish?" Sawyer gave Atticus a grin. "What kind?"

"Rainbow trout," Atticus replied offhandedly, even as his scrawny chest puffed with pride. "About this big." He spread his arms wide.

"Impressive." Sawyer stared solemnly.

"Maybe even bigger."

"Well," Sawyer said as he lifted his mug. "Here's a

toast to you, champ. You've already figured out that the most important part of fishing is the story afterward."

Annie found herself giggling as their eyes locked. Good Lord, the look he gave her, it caused a stirring that shouldn't happen before noon on a Sunday.

After the cups were emptied and loaded into the sink, Claire slid back her chair. "Come on, kiddo," she said to Atticus. "Let's see if I can whoop your cute butt in checkers."

"I always win," Atticus retorted.

"Confidence breeds complacency," Claire said with a wave of the hand.

"What does that mean, Auntie?" Atticus asked, puzzled.

"Come along, squirt, and I'll teach you." Claire took his hand and led him from the room without a backward glance.

"Walk with me?" Sawyer said after a moment. "The morning was beautiful and the afternoon is shaping up to be even better."

"Okay." Annie fluffed her hand through her hair and rose to her feet. Her laptop sat on the kitchen bench and she frowned slightly.

"Is something bothering you?"

How was he so tuned to her feelings, as if he dialed into her emotional frequency?

"No big deal." Hopefully her shrug passed as nonchalant. "I got a strange email this morning."

His eyes narrowed. "From who?"

"On my blog there's a troll who's been leaving mean comments for a while. That's one of the downsides of social media. There's nobody standing there to have a conversation with. Instead, they can say something nasty and run away. The strange thing is, this particular person has upped the ante and taken to sending emails."

"What do they write?" He looked troubled.

That no matter what I'm doing, I'm doing it wrong.

Annie shook her head. "Today is too beautiful to worry about any of that. Mind if we go to a destination I have in mind?"

He opened the back door and held it. "Lead the way."

They walked through the back fields in silence. When he reached for her hand, the fit felt natural, as if they'd been doing this for years. Their quiet was comfortable. In many ways it was enough, to be here, together in the moment.

She cleared her throat. "Thank you, for being so great with Atticus. He really likes you."

"He's a good kid." A little shy, but he'd been too at that age.

"I can't really do the 'boy stuff' with him, you know? He needs male role models."

"You're doing a fantastic job."

"I wouldn't say that, but I try my best. Still, to grow to be a good man, doesn't he need to be around good men?" She gave him an uncertain look. "Sorry, I'm not trying to freak you out—make you a baby daddy or anything."

He stopped. This was important. "Annie, you and Atticus are a package deal. I get that. It doesn't freak me out." Maybe it had a little at first, but not now. In fact, the idea only got better the more he thought about it.

She blinked, almost as if she might cry. He waited, and instead she shook her head, walking again, arms folded against her. "So, this morning I walked the perimeter of the farm and found the apiaries. Maybe I should order some equipment and try to harvest the honey."

He didn't want to change the subject, but she wasn't ready. He swallowed, and his throat felt full of ground glass, the next words coming out in a gruff choke. "Let's head out and see how things stand."

This summer wouldn't last forever. How was he supposed to balance her need to go slow against a ticking clock?

They reached the hives five minutes later, the buzzing audible before the boxes came into view. Annie wanted to say something to clear the air. After she'd changed the subject from her and Atticus, he'd retreated and she wasn't sure how to bring him back, or if she should.

What am I doing?

He released her hand to circle the apiaries with a concentrated look. "I want to try something," he said. "You hungry?"

"A little," Annie replied distractedly, and then snapped, "No! Stop!" when Sawyer threw open the box and reached inside as bees rose around him in a buzzing swarm.

Instead of hollering from a hundred stings, he stood magically unharmed. "Bees never bother me." He withdrew a thick comb, sticky golden liquid running between his thumb and forefinger. "It's been a while, but the honey is still sweet."

She bit down the inside of her lip. How in the world did he manage that? "What are you? A bee whisperer?"

He chuckled, coming close and extending his hand. The world distilled to his honey-coated thumb.

"Go on." His voice was just above a murmur. "Give it a try."

Hold the phone—was he talking about the honey, or something more?

"It'll be good, promise."

She didn't doubt it, the question was would it be too good? That was the trouble with delicious things—you developed cravings. This man could become her own personal addiction.

He stepped forward, clearly meaning business. No way could she refuse without making a scene. She took a hesitant bite, careful for it not to be too much, she didn't want to look like a pig, but the minute the comb crumbled between her teeth her eyes closed involuntarily, the moan was out before she had a chance to rein it in.

"Oh," she whispered, "that's really—"

"Amazing."

She opened her eyes and there he was, only the span of a breath separating them.

"Yes."

"Told you." He dropped the rest of the comb into the tall grass, his mouth slanting over hers. She parted her lips and his tongue slid forward, teasing out the lingering sweetness. She kissed back until she forgot the day of the week or how to breathe. When her body finally fought for an instinctive inhalation she drew it straight from his mouth.

Buzzing grew in her ears. Was it the bees or her own zinging nervous system?

She grabbed his shirt in two fistfuls, feeling the hard muscle beneath, and when she rose on tiptoe, another kind of hardness jabbed into her belly.

He crushed her to him and swore. "Shit, sorry."

"Why?" she whispered. God, his mouth was like a country she never grew tired of exploring.

"The honey, I got your back sticky."

"It will wash." She bit him then, right on the fleshiest part of his lower lip, not hard enough to hurt, but enough to take him by surprise. "You'll be sorrier if you stop doing whatever it is you're doing."

"You're trouble."

"So what are you going to do, arrest me?" She slid her fingers slow over his ribs to the hard expanse of his abdomen as he shuddered with a muffled groan.

"Ticklish much?" She teased her fingers over his skin and he flinched, burying his face in the top of her neck with a strangled choke.

"Keep that up and I will lock you up and throw away the key."

"Really?"

"Except there will be a problem."

"Yes?"

"I'm locking myself in there with you." He scooped

her up and she fastened her hips to his waist as he sat her on a stump, the height of it putting her face-to-face with him. "God, Annie. Every day I look out across this valley and think I've seen all the beauty this world has to offer. Then you come back and I realize I haven't seen anything."

"Oh, come on." She slapped his chest.

He bracketed her face with his hands. "You are my best friend, but it's more than that. Having you back here makes me realize why it's never worked out with anyone else." He nuzzled the base of her neck, dragged his face lower to caress his cheek over the swell of her breast as she arched her back. "Let go."

"Haven't I?" She removed one of his hands, raising it to her lips and licking the sticky sweetness clean. This was falling from thirty thousand feet without a parachute.

"Damn." He pushed a hand up the inside of her softly curving thigh, under her dress, parting her legs. "Your pretty dresses do a number on me."

She gasped as he slipped a thumb into her underwear, and then any other sound was impossible.

"Look at me," he ordered softly.

She forced her gaze to his face as he pulled and plunged his fingers in a sweet, slow, torturous rhythm. She swallowed hard, throat sore with all the things she wasn't saying because she didn't know which words were right when Sawyer stroked her to a place beyond logic.

She started to come apart and a tear escaped, trickling down her cheek. Another joined, and the whole time he kept his gaze fixed on her. She came slow and hard, taking in everything: the bold slash of his brow, the divot above his lip she longed to visit with the tip of her tongue, the chickenpox scar on his chin. He leaned close, fingers hooked inside her, and kissed the corner of her eye.

"These sad or happy?" he murmured, removing his hand, her body shuddering as he left, missing the fullness he gave her.

"Both." Because this right here was everything she hoped for, she knew it now. That thing she'd been missing for years was a Sawyer-shaped hole. She couldn't regret where she'd been, or what had happened, because her choices gave her Atticus. But now, between her and Sawyer burned a fire she could either add tinder to or blow out. God knew she'd been so cold, but what if her life blazed into something unrecognizable?

She pushed back a lock of hair from his forehead. "What are you thinking?" How could he do that? Keep his features so distant? His thoughts were secreted away while she was an open book. It wasn't fair.

She reached as he stepped back, catching him by the belt loops. "Not so fast."

"Annie," he said, his eyes darkening. "Wait."

"Why?" she replied, suddenly angry. "Why can you push me off the edge but I can't do the same?" She ground down the zipper and he responded with a short, sharp rasp as she gripped the thick root. Her fingers didn't tremble even if her voice did. "It's always been you, Sawyer. Always."

"Same." His breath grew ragged as she worked him

up and down. Good. Let her touch take him to the same places that tortured her with sweet promise.

His hands formed fists and he raised them to the side of his head, the furrow between his brows becoming a chasm. She kept the pace until he seized her shoulders, burying his face in the top of her head, coming while grinding out her name in a hoarse whisper.

She rested her forehead on his shoulder, her own gasp as shuddering and shaky as his. She was a big girl; shouldn't she know by now what she wanted?

Yeah, she really should. She really, really should. But she didn't.

Staying here after selling Five Diamonds wouldn't work. At the moment it sounded good, easy even, but that was an illusion, created from the lust juju Sawyer weaved with bee magic and heart-stopping kisses. He was handy, but she wasn't something to be fixed. Only she could do that for herself. And there was no denying that if she wanted to advance her career in the long-term, a city would be better, offer so much more opportunity. She didn't want to rely on a man to provide for her again.

But this wasn't a random hypothetical man. This was Sawyer.

There were no clear-cut answers. As she hurled to invisible crossroads, everything curled into a question. *Which way will I turn?*

Chapter Seventeen

SAWYER LEFT AFTER they returned from the old apiary. He'd kissed her deep and sure before nipping her earlobe in a way that made her shiver.

"What did you do that for?" She leaned into his chest and inhaled sage soap and cinnamon chewing gum.

He smoothed her hair off her face. "To make it as hard for you to say goodbye as it is for me."

"I'm not making this situation easy." *Understatement of the year.*

"The best things never are," he murmured into the top of her hair.

So many things were up in the air, and it was tempting to say screw it and let him kiss her again, because goodbyes were practically impossible when the taste of honey lingered on his tongue.

"I don't know a lot." He gave her a slow smile. "But I do know I want you and Atticus to come over to my place for dinner."

She took a slow, deliberate breath. "Are you asking me on a date, Sawyer Kane?"

"Indeed I am, Miss Carson." He'd leaned and pressed his mouth against her ear, his hot breath sending a jolt of heat up her thighs. "And you know something else, I'm never going to look at honey the same way again." He patted her bottom before turning away. She felt a stare and glanced over one shoulder. Claire stood on the porch, giving a thumbs-up.

Annie waved as Sawyer backed out, ignored her sister and headed to the old barn for a moment of breathing space. What happened at the apiary was private, amazing, and nothing she wanted to gossip about. The door was open. Atticus must have been playing in Dad's studio again. She stepped inside and pressed her back against the old wood, sweat pooling in her bra. Hard to know if it was from the unusual humidity or her own spiking body temperature.

Outside, clouds gathered on the range, thunderheads building, while inside—what a mess. No two ways about it, her father's studio was a serious disaster, straight from an episode of *Hoarders*. How would she know what to throw out among all this junk? Dad hadn't left any specific instructions. She had no idea what was important and what wasn't.

She rubbed her temples. Wasn't that the trick to everything? Trying to decide what to keep in life and what to throw away?

A furtive noise drew her attention to the back of the barn. *Please don't let it be a rat.* Instead, a small golden head poked around the corner, giving a tentative whine.

Annie sank to her knees and held out a hand to the shy dog. "Hello, where did you come from?" She must have snuck in through the open door.

The dog scampered forward a few steps, paused and whined again. She was clearly a mutt, possibly a combination of a retriever and dachshund.

"It's okay, girl," she coaxed. "It's okay."

The dog took another tentative step, tail wagging, then dropped her snout and sniffed the floorboards.

Annie crawled forward to give the sweet little mutt a gentle pat when the wood floor gave a creak. A flash of blue caught her eye through the boards and she pulled a loose plank, gasping to see a metal Pac-Man lunchbox hidden beneath. Stuck to the lid was a strip of masking tape on which was printed, "Do Not Open Until the Year 3000."

"Oh my God," she whispered. "The time capsule."

When she was a kid, she had gone through a phase where she was obsessed with building a time machine. Dad hadn't discouraged her, even allowed precious studio space for the project, but product development had never gotten farther than a plastic lawn chair twined with copper wire, connected to a broken car battery. Instead, she downgraded the plan, creating a top-secret time capsule instead.

She opened the latches and peered inside, lifting the carefully folded piece of tissue paper. Inside was a tiny white egg, cracked at the top. The hummingbird egg she'd discovered in an abandoned nest while climbing trees in the orchard. Then there was a beanie baby, a Mariah Carey *Butterfly* CD, her junior ranger badge, a photo of her standing beneath Rainbow Falls, and a torn-out magazine picture of Jonathan Taylor Thomas. Oh, and look, a dog-eared copy of *Island of the Blue Dolphins*. She'd spent hours pretending to be Karana, roaming her island, hunting for edible roots, fashioning spears and building pretend canoes down by the river.

At the bottom was an envelope. She opened it with shaking hands, recognizing her own childish handwriting.

> *Hello People From the Future!*
> *My name is Annabelle Margaret Carson, but everyone calls me Annie, unless I'm in trouble. I live on Five Diamonds Farm in Brightwater, California, and it's the best place in the world. Over a hundred years ago, my great-great-great-grandparents were real pioneers and traveled here in a covered wagon. A wheel from the wagon is in the attic, and one time Dad took me and my sister, Claire, up to see it. Claire is my best friend even though she's bossy and always thinks she's right (even when she's not). Our favorite things to do are going for hikes, sewing, and listening to music. She's afraid of heights, so my other favorite thing to do is just mine, cliff jumping.*

*I don't know what will happen in the future, but I
know that I hope to always live here with my sister. I
don't know what I want to be. I like writing, though,
and reading. I don't know what life is like a thousand
years from now. Do robots do all your chores? I'd like
that. The only chore I enjoy is feeding the chickens.
People probably live on Mars now, huh? I guess that's
where pioneers in the future would go. But I hope my
future great-great-million-times-great-grandkids live
right here.*

Love,
Annie

And here she was, almost two decades later, ready to
let it all go. But the fact was, even if she wanted to stay,
and she wasn't positive if she did, Five Diamonds wasn't
hers to keep. Claire and her dad were both on the deed,
and they said sell.

She glanced to the strange little dog, but it was gone,
having disappeared without a sound. They'd have to keep
an eye out. It could be lost, or a stray, or maybe a wan-
derer from one of the surrounding properties.

She closed the lid and tucked it back beneath the
board, then walked to the house under an invisible
weight. When wistfulness knotted her throat, she swallowed it away.

She was a mom and couldn't dream young Annie's
impossible dreams, not anymore. She wasn't the free-
spirited girl who ran around this farm in tutus and yellow

rubber boots, but a grown woman with a practical plan to move her son closer to family and focus on growing her career.

She walked into the kitchen as Claire hung up the phone. "That was Hank over at King Realty."

"Oh yeah?" Annie folded her arms. How much did her sister miss their life here, the simple way things used to be, before adulthood had complicated everything?

"Good news. The house isn't officially listed and already they have eight expressions of interest. We stand to make a fortune."

"Sounds great." Annie walked to the cookie jar and peered inside. Crud. Only crumbs remained. At least she could do some baking for distraction.

"Good walk earlier?" Claire said, unable to keep a straight face.

Annie's cheeks warmed. "Yeah, it was nice."

"Nice?" Claire snickered, hoisting herself up onto one of the counters. "You looked like you'd been with a one-eyed trouser snake."

"Claire—Jesus!" Annie burst out laughing despite herself. "I am going to miss you. Can't you stay longer?"

"I wish. I'll miss you too, Lil' Bit." Claire's face turned serious. "But promise me this—once Atticus is off on his little adventure, you won't wallow."

Atticus? Annie started. Claire was right. In forty-eight hours her son would depart for a Disneyland vacation with Gregor and Margot. Annie had never spent more than a day without him. Didn't have the first idea how she'd pass the time. Maybe researching San Francisco real estate? Writing a resume?

Her former self would be aghast that they were selling the farm. Maybe she'd gotten older, but had she really grown any wiser?

ANNIE PULLED IN front of the small regional airport. "You sure we can't get out and walk you in?"

"No way, this is easier. I hate goodbyes." Claire turned and blew a kiss to Atticus. "Be cool, little man."

He pretended to catch the kiss and flashed a thumbs-up.

"You know, I've been thinking—about Brightwater," Claire said, pushing open the car door. "It's getting pretty cool, isn't it?"

"There are a bunch of cute new shops popping up around Main Street," Annie replied cautiously, not sure where her sister was going with the conversation.

"You seem at home here."

"I do?" Annie pushed up her sunglasses.

"I know we're selling and everything, but I don't know . . . "

"What?" Annie demanded. "What don't you know?"

"This trip has given me a lot to think about." Claire banged the roof of the car. "I'll see you around, sister."

"Wait, but our plan still stands right? Atticus and I moving to San Francisco? Be neighbors? You'll dominate the world of food trucks, while I take on the Internet?"

Claire made her feel safe in the way only a best girlfriend/sister/ninja could.

"Life is what happens while you're busy making plans, Lil' Bit." Claire threw her arms over her head. "Remember, take some time to find your joy."

Annie shook her head. "Call me when you land, okay?"

"Will do. Love you."

"You too." Annie blew her a kiss, laughing, and drove out of the airport, making her way back toward Brightwater. She passed a ramshackle roadhouse, dry volcanic landscape, and seemingly unscalable mountains.

How could Claire say Annie seemed at home in this wild, harsh climate? And as for Sawyer, a summer fling was one thing, but seasons had a funny way of always changing.

A siren sounded and she looked up. Lights flashed behind her.

What the heck? She'd been going the speed limit, under actually, and obeying all traffic laws—*oh my*. . .

Sawyer climbed out of the patrol car and she knocked the back of her head against the seat. *Objects in the rearview are closer than they appear* and he looked close enough to lick. She glanced beside her. The Five Diamonds real estate advertisement from King Realty lay on the passenger seat. On impulse, she flipped the page over before Sawyer reached her window.

"Mama, why are you shaking your wrists?" Atticus piped up from the backseat.

Shoot, she was actually wringing her hands. It wasn't that selling the property was a big state secret. Sawyer knew her plan. The problem was, the two of them were also playing make-believe, as if there wasn't a clock counting down above them, and she wasn't ready to quit that game.

The gravel crunch grew louder and then there he was. His aviator glasses hid his gaze as he peered into her driver's side window, scruffy jaw and all.

"Sheriff," she croaked, less sultry than she'd prefer.

"Miss Carson." Sawyer's mouth crooked as he ran a thumb under her chin. "You're under arrest for being too damn cute."

"Hey, do you carry a gun?" Atticus called out.

She sucked in a breath, trying to recalibrate as he said, "Yeah, I do."

"For killing bad guys?"

"Atticus," Annie said, turning around. "That's a little bloodthirsty, don't you—"

"No, I haven't killed any bad guys."

"Maybe one?" Atticus sounded hopeful.

"Not even one." He glanced between them. "So, about my dinner invite. I was wondering if you'd both like to come around to my place this evening?"

"Your place." Everywhere she looked would be Sawyer. Sawyer smells. Things Sawyer liked.

"Yeah, it ain't fancy, but it's home."

"What will you make?" Atticus cut to the chase.

"What do you like?" Sawyer responded.

"Not kale soup."

"Kale what?" Sawyer squashed his brow in confusion, dismay, or maybe a combination of both.

"Puke soup."

Annie pursed her lips. "He's not a fan."

"Can't say I blame him." He cocked his head at Atticus. "How about a burger?"

"A hamburger. Or . . . or . . . one with cheese?"

"However you like it, champ. I'll even throw in fries."

"Yes!" Atticus kicked out his feet in delight.

"Sound good?" he said to her, expression quizzical.

"I . . . " She fiddled with the radio dial. "I actually don't eat meat."

"Really?" Sawyer kept his voice neutral. How Switzerland of him. "What about fish?"

She pointed at her face. "Nothing that has one of these."

He shook his head with a low, rumbling chuckle. "I'll figure it out."

"Do you have a time in mind?"

"Any time is Annie Time."

Why did that phrase swell her heart like helium? "Six, then?"

"Sounds good." He gave her a quick kiss on the cheek before walking back to the car.

"Mommy?" Atticus asked, jamming his foot into the back of her seat as she resumed driving.

"Yes?"

"Do you love Sheriff Sawyer?"

The engine revved and she eased her foot off the clutch. "What makes you ask that?"

"Whenever you see him you smile."

"Do I?" She mentally raced through explanations and arrived at the most simple. "I guess he makes me happy."

"That's good. I like you happy." He fell back into silence, absorbed in the comic he'd brought along for the car ride.

Annie's whisper was quiet. Only for herself really. "I like me happy too."

Chapter Eighteen

THE BLOCK OF tofu sat on the counter. After he washed his hands he'd poked it once, and the damn thing quivered. How the hell was he supposed to cook this? The grill was his kingdom, where he reigned as lord and master. That pale beige cube threatened to bring him to his knees.

But this was what Annie ate, what she liked. And he needed to show her he could make space for her in his life.

He reached for his phone and tapped in "best easy tofu recipe." The first hit was from a blog. If it ranked that high, it must be good. He clicked on the link and then froze. Annie's face stared back at him.

Musings of a Mighty Mama?

This must be her blog, the one she made offhand references to. He sat in a stool in his kitchen and read. And read. Until he realized the clock was closer to six than five and he had to fix things quickly.

A LIGHT RAIN fell as Annie walked up the front path, gripping Atticus's hand. Sawyer's house was strong and simple, like the man himself. All the lines looked exact, the kind of place that stayed cool in summer and snug in winter, with a roof that would never tilt in strange and unexpected directions.

"Welcome," he said, opening the door in anticipation of their arrival. Maverick stuck his head out and gave a friendly bark in greeting.

Atticus covered his ears with his hands, cowering behind her legs. "No dogs!"

She gave Sawyer an apologetic look. "He's afraid of dogs."

"Righto." Sawyer looked between the boy and the dog before giving a low whistle. "You stay upstairs for now, boy."

"I'm sorry," Annie said. Atticus never said why he didn't like dogs, and he only ever shrugged if she asked.

"Not a problem." The dog followed Sawyer obediently from the room.

Low fiddle music played on surround-sound speakers and the stone fireplace was dark on account of summer, but those large overstuffed couches before it would be cozy come winter.

Sawyer returned. "Make yourself at home."

Funny, she already felt that way. "Your house is lovely."

"I should give you the tour. Still have bits and pieces to finish off but it's come around."

"You built this place?"

"I had help here and there, but the work's mostly mine."

"That's impressive." *And so hot.* A threaded needle stabbed through her heart, drawing the broken pieces together. Here was a guy who knew how to build, to pull things together, and to grow, creating beauty in the process.

"First, I need to check on dinner."

"Smells good," she said, following him into the kitchen. Atticus stayed behind to play with a wooden kaleidoscope positioned on the coffee table.

"I hope so." The way he looked, moving around the kitchen . . . He was such a man, there was no other way to describe it. Testosterone practically wafted off him, but yet he wore a purple oven mitt with—wait, what did that say?

Kiss the cook.

He must have heard her chuckle. "What is it?"

"Admiring your glove."

He glanced down at it, his cheeks reddening. "I won it in a raffle last year. The color's not my favorite, but I'm confident in my manhood."

You said "manhood." Apparently she was a dirty-minded seventh-grader.

"Mind if I use your bathroom?" she asked.

"Sure thing, down the hall on the right."

She got in and shut the door, leaning against it while fanning her face. This room wasn't going to do wonders for her nerves either. The claw-foot tub promised all sorts of wicked delights.

She went to the sink, running water over her wrists to try to cool down. *You are fine. You are fine. Don't explode.*

She walked out and froze in the kitchen doorway as he withdrew a baking pan from the oven. "Is that—"

"Tofu."

"Wait." Was she hallucinating? "You? Sawyer Kane? Baked tofu?"

He shrugged. "Don't get excited until you see how it tastes."

"Okay, sorry, but for real, that's so . . . cute."

He threw her a side glance, tilting his head a fraction. "Soy cute?"

"Oh my God, stop." She leaned back, resting her elbows on the counter. "It's not fair if you're punny too." Just like that the panic subsided. How could she be nervous around this guy? It was Sawyer. Her Sawyer. The guy she'd known for forever and a day.

He picked up a fork and cut a piece, spearing it on the tines. "Tell me how it tastes. No way could I put that in my mouth."

"You're missing out."

He advanced, holding out the fork. "I'll live vicariously."

She opened her mouth and he paused, lifting it to his lips and blowing softly. "There, better," he said, offering it to her.

She took the cooled bite and chewed. "Good, really good."

He tugged her hips flush to him and kissed her forehead. "Remind you of anything?"

The flavor was familiar. "Actually, it tastes like something I make a lot."

He gave a satisfied grin. "Means I did it right."

"I don't understand."

"*Musings of a Mighty Mama*. I never knew anyone who wrote about their life for strangers." He kept her against him. "Don't wiggle, you. I'm not judging, I'm trying to understand. You're a good writer."

She quit trying to get away. "You think so?"

"Hell yes. Me? I can barely string two sentences together."

"You do fine with me."

"I know, that's the thing of it."

"What?"

"With you, hard things come easy." He kissed her forehead, his lips fastening against the wrinkles in her brow, smoothing away the worry. "I liked your blog. It's you, at least in part."

She sighed. Where'd that come from? The sound came heavy, weighted with worry.

"Why don't you take this wine and sit." He handed her a glass. "I'll call in Atticus and fix the plates."

"I don't know how I'll ever let you go." She meant it as a joke, but it didn't feel anywhere close to funny.

He flashed a private smile, grabbing a stack of dishes. "When I built this house, I took my time and my patience paid off."

The honeyed wood, the balance of airy floorplan and cozy mountain cottage—yeah, he'd made a perfect home. "I agree."

"I'm starving." Atticus wandered into the kitchen as Sawyer finished setting the table.

"Grab a seat, I'll serve you right up," he said.

When was the last time someone had done this? Made her dinner with wine and bright flowers?

The answer, never, didn't hurt like it should, because now someone had.

"So . . . champ, what's the deal between you and dogs?" Sawyer asked after Atticus demolished half his burger.

He ducked his head. "One chased me."

"When?" Annie asked, surprised. She'd never seen a dog go after Atticus.

"At the playground by our old house," Atticus muttered. "Dad was on the phone and one ran after me. I climbed up the slide, but it barked so loud. It wanted to bite my head off."

"Oh, honey—" Annie set her fork down, her heart squeezing.

"Would you mind meeting my friend, Maverick?" Sawyer asked in his easy way. "He looks big, but the only thing he ever wants to bite is a bone."

Atticus giggled even though his features remained tense. "I don't know."

"How about this," Sawyer said. "I'll put him on a leash, and he can show you his tricks."

"Your dog can do tricks?"

"A few."

"Okay," Atticus said, looking more curious than afraid.

Sawyer gave Annie a wink and left the room, returning a minute later with the German Shepherd on a leash.

"Why don't you tell Maverick to have good manners at the table and sit. Use a strong voice."

"Sit," Atticus ordered, and Maverick immediately obeyed.

"Nice job." Sawyer gave an approving nod. "Now, Maverick hasn't gotten a chance to meet you yet. How about you ask him to shake your hand?"

Atticus giggled before saying, "Shake." The dog lifted his paw, and Annie pressed a hand over her heart when Atticus slowly reached out and brushed it, only for a second, but still. Her little guy faced down his fear with Sawyer's help.

The rest of dinner went smoothly. Sawyer caught on that asking questions opened Atticus up.

"You like the Giants?"

"They aren't real," Atticus said automatically, giving Annie an uncertain glance. "Right?"

"I meant the baseball team," Sawyer said.

Annie shrugged with a rueful laugh. "Apparently the rule is teach them what you know. Baseball doesn't fit in my wheelhouse."

Sawyer sat back in his chair. "Looks like I'm going to need to stage an intervention. So, you've never thrown the ball around?"

"Nope."

"Do you own a glove or bat?"

Atticus shook his head, hiding his bashful smile behind a sip of his water.

"You disapprove?" Annie asked Sawyer.

"No," he said after swallowing. "But I think I could help out this situation."

And as Annie glanced between Sawyer to Atticus, currently staring at the man with open fascination, something told her he could do exactly that.

Chapter Nineteen

"WENT FOR A ride?" Archer sauntered into the barn as Sawyer removed Ranger's saddle, giving the stock horse an affectionate pat on the haunches. His younger brother had a bachelor pad apartment upstairs, but he wasn't home much.

"Looks like it." Sawyer took off the saddle blanket. What was Archer up to? Usually he was too busy hanging at the bar with friends or chasing skirts to spend time at Hidden Rock.

"Okay, smart ass." Archer leaned against the wall, uncorking a flask.

"Drinking before noon is one thing," Sawyer said, furrowing his brow as he checked the horse's hooves. His brother needed to start taking life more seriously. It wasn't one big party. "Drinking before nine is another animal all together."

Archer raised it up. "It's water. I don't have another bottle."

"Really? That's a surprise," Sawyer muttered, glancing up when Archer kicked a hay bale with sudden force.

"Everyone thinks they know me, but no one ever takes the time to see who I really am."

Sawyer straightened at that, tilting back his hat to wipe his forehead. "What the hell do you think I see?"

"A screwup," Archer snapped defensively. "Only good for having fun."

Sawyer hooked his thumbs under his belt. "Not true." That was all his brother did, but he was smart, had a good head for figures and the natural charisma of a leader. He could do anything he put his mind to, if he'd only try.

"Hey, I know where I fit in the Kane brother pecking order. Wilder, he's the bad ass. And you? Well, shit. You're you."

"What's that supposed to mean?"

"The good guy." Archer hooked a hand around the back of his neck. "Aw hell. Look, I'm not trying to dump my crap on you."

"Hey, I'm family, means you have a year-round dumping license."

"Nah. It's all good." He took another slug of water.

"I do think you like fun." Sawyer weighed his words carefully. His brother hadn't ever approached him for any sort of heart to heart before. He didn't want to squander the opportunity. "But I also think you want to stay in the shallows, that you're afraid of going out deeper."

"I'm not afraid of anything." Archer bristled.

Something had crawled up his ass, but what?

"Suit yourself." Sawyer hung the saddle on the peg. "I'm afraid of lots of things." If he wanted Arch to be honest, he'd best be honest too.

"You?" Archer braced his hand on a stable door. "What are you afraid of, Big Man?"

"Women, mostly," Sawyer said wryly. One tiny, pixie-haired woman in particular.

"That's the truth." Archer gave him a tentative glance. "I've got one that scares the shit out of me."

"That right?" Archer had never looked this shaken up over anyone from the opposite sex.

Archer shook his head. "Enough about me. What's the story with you and Annie Carson?"

Sawyer stilled. "What do you mean?"

"So it's true then?" Archer whistled low. "When I first saw her back in town, I wondered if you'd make a move. Took Grandma to confirm it. She's got one hell of a bee in her bonnet this morning."

Shit. "So she knows?"

"I guess she watched Annie and her little boy leave last night."

Sawyer resisted the urge to face-palm. Grandma had spied on him? Why should that be a surprise? Of course she did.

"Got to say," Archer said, "I'm not seeing great things coming from this situation."

"The feud stops with me," Sawyer responded firmly. "And if you say a thing about Kooky—"

"I'm not talking about any of that. You know I don't give a shit."

"I invited a neighbor to dinner. Her son has never ridden a horse, he's never even thrown a ball around, Arch."

"So that's it then, you're going to play daddy? Be the hero?" Archer looked skeptical.

Sawyer made a warning note in the back of his throat. "You can talk out your ass with your friends all you want, but don't ever say a fucking word sideways about Annie or her son."

"I'm not." Archer threw up his hands. "Jesus, man, listen to yourself. I might like the shallows, but you're in over your head."

Sawyer watered the horse. Archer had no idea how deep he'd gone.

He hadn't made love to Annie yet, even though the wait might actually kill him. On more than a few occasions in life he'd sported a pair of blue balls, but never this bad, to where it caused physical pain and kept him on the sweet edge of anticipation.

Sure, he'd had plenty of sex, even sex he'd thought was love. But that was a pale imitation, a shadow on the wall, flickering but not real.

"Remember she's leaving." Archer's cautionary tone returned Sawyer to the present.

He hated his brother's words. They hit him with a sudden wallop, the way the truth often does. "Maybe. Maybe not."

The whole reason he held off taking their relationship more physical was for the same reason Archer said. Annie had never given an indication she'd stay. But—

"I saw her yesterday." Archer gave a sad smile. "Downtown at King Realty. After I left Haute Coffee, Five Diamonds was listed in the window. For a pretty price too."

Sawyer swallowed thickly, saying nothing. It was all he had at the moment so it seemed about right. He wasn't making any headway in convincing Annie to stay, and time was running out. What would happen if he failed? San Francisco wasn't on the other side of the country. Still, seven hours by car was serious long-distance.

"You've had it bad for that girl a long time. Maybe—"

"Don't." Sawyer held a warning hand. "Don't tell me to have fun with her."

"I wasn't going to," Archer said, eyes darkening. "If you want her to stay, lay it all on the line. But be careful, okay? As much as I'd like to see you get the girl, I don't want you getting hurt either."

Sawyer swung out his hand and Archer clasped it back.

"Thanks, man," he said, pulling back, but not before giving Archer a playful cuff on the chin. "When did you get wise?"

"By learning from my mistakes," Archer said with a sheepish smile. He turned, walking out with a whistle.

ANNIE MADE YET another trip to the small Mammoth airport. This time, Atticus was off to meet Gregor and

Margot. They'd go to Disneyland and then visit Gregor's mother in San Diego, a stoic Czech woman who never really acknowledged Annie and would probably never notice she wasn't there.

"Are you getting excited, honey?" Annie asked, kneeling in front of her son, already holding the flight attendant's hand, his pink cast covered in black scribbles. "Ninja marks" he called them.

"Will Ursula be there?" he asked again nervously.

All he knew about Disney was *The Little Mermaid* DVD she'd found in her old bedroom. She tried sharing it with him and he nearly had a stroke when the sea witch sang about poor unfortunate souls.

"Nah, you'll meet Mickey and Minnie."

"Those are the big mice," he repeated, liking everything categorized. Ordered.

He was so different than she'd been at his age, more cautious, wanting to label things.

Maybe she'd been a bad influence, too much helicopter parenting when he should be out climbing trees, chasing garter snakes, and going fishing in the big hole along the river. Instead he stayed close to home. She felt better having him near, but also guilty that she wasn't letting him free range. He didn't ask to roam because he knew what she'd say. "Let me come with you."

And now, here she was doing an action that felt unnatural to her core. Letting him get on a plane, alone with strangers, and fly to Los Angeles where his father would meet him.

"All right, big boy, we've got to get up in the sky," the stewardess said.

The yellow button pinned to his t-shirt read, "Unaccompanied Minor."

Maybe she should go back to the ticketing desk. She didn't have much money but could fly with him and then hop a plane home.

"Your first time doing this, Mama?" the flight attendant asked with a friendly smile.

Annie nodded. Why couldn't she return the smile? Probably because her heart was breaking.

"Don't worry, we'll take good care of him. You like apple juice, big man?"

"Uh . . . " He glanced at Annie. "I'm not allowed to drink juice."

"Go ahead, it's a special occasion." Annie ignored the strange look from the flight attendant. Juice was basically sugar water, but maybe the kid could have a taste once in a blue moon. It wasn't as if he survived on Wonder Bread and gummy bears.

"Love you, Mommy."

She kissed her two fingers and held them out to him.

"I love you more."

And then the flight attendant led him up the gangway and he was gone.

Annie stood there alone, the crazy crying lady in the airport. She collapsed in a hard plastic chair and watched the plane push back from the gate. She didn't move until the buzzing engine faded over the mountains.

When she left the airport there was no one to hold hands with. When she crossed the street she didn't have to remind anyone to look both ways. When she got to the car no one needed buckling up.

She adjusted the review mirror and stared at herself. This was the first time in five years she'd been alone. Who was she if she wasn't a mother?

"Hi, Annie," she said, looking at the stranger. "I'm Annie."

And she didn't know the first thing to do with herself.

Chapter Twenty

[draft]

Musings of a Mighty Mama

Home Alone

older posts>>

Dear Readers,
Atticus is in Disneyland for the week and that means I'm pulling a Macaulay Culkin. Home alone! Wow! Since my son's birth, we've never been apart from each other for more than a single night, and that was only recently ~~when my sexy hot cowboy sheriff neighbor came over for dinner but had me on the kitchen table instead.~~

The house feels ~~overwhelming~~ silent. I ~~am terrified~~

love the idea that for the next few days I can do whatever I want. ~~Likely host a private Richard Armitage film festival, wash windows in my underwear and eat cereal from the box.~~ This will be good, a chance to find myself ~~where the heck did I go?~~. Figure out a few things ~~what am I doing?~~.

ANNIE THUMPED HER laptop lid closed and ignored the ceramic pig cookie jar's judgmental look as she grabbed the third cookie in as many minutes. Her Realtor had a full day of visits scheduled tomorrow and wanted her out of the house. Maybe she'd drive up for a visit to Bodie Ghost Town or work from Haute Coffee.

She should be thrilled the interest in Five Diamonds was huge. There would likely be a bidding war, the farm commanding top dollar, enough to get her and Atticus into a cute place in a laid-back San Francisco family neighborhood like Noe Valley. A bright, shiny new future hovered on the horizon, perfect in its promise. So why did she want to cram a fourth snickerdoodle into her mouth, add some Kahlua to her milk, and build a blanket fort under the kitchen table?

Sawyer.

He'd gotten under her skin and carved his name in secret places. As much as she wanted to admit otherwise, leaving him would be near impossible. And that was all the more reason to do so. Of course she wanted to lean on him. His quiet strength was addictive, and he stood ready to carry her burdens. He was a great guy, and for some lucky local girl, he'd make a wonderful husband. She buried her face in her hands.

Sawyer would never leave Brightwater.

Everything had gotten so complicated. Her old rule was broken in two. *Don't fall head over cowgirl boots for the cute guy from a ranch.*

But how did a woman resist Sawyer Kane?

Kind and strong? Check.

Turned you on like a sudden light in the dark? Check.

Had a sense of humor? Check.

Could snap someone in two if they messed with you? Check.

Was sweet to your son? Check.

Checkmate.

She was screwed.

But when she left, while there might be tears, there couldn't be regret. The past felt mighty close the last few weeks, but once she left, she'd have breathing room again.

Right?

How many times could she repeat "this is all for the best" before believing it. The line was like one of those Tootsie Roll pops, keep licking and eventually you'll reach the sweet center, right? *Please, God, let selling the house be a good decision.* Atticus was a gentle soul. Growing up in Brightwater, being teased as a kooky Carson, could be too hard on him—the same way it had been for her. He'd love living close to Claire. And the city had professional opportunities. She kept repeating those facts like a broken record, but they weren't making her feel any better.

A knock came at the door.

Sawyer.

How did she know he was outside? Hard to say. Maybe it was the way something intangible shifted in the air. Her body going into hyperdrive. As much as she wanted to cling to common sense, there were parts of her eager to get into the rapids, craving lust, passion, and lo—*no, not the l-word*. Had to draw the daydream line somewhere.

She opened the door, still holding half a cookie.

He stared as she licked sugar from her fingertips.

"How're you doing without Atticus? He left this morning, right?" Sawyer rocked on his boots. "I came to check on you."

Of course he did. That was Sawyer, what he did. He made sure you didn't need anything, totally unaware his mere presence made her need all the things—hard, fast, slow, and soft.

"Are you okay?" He looked closer. "You're flushed."

"I'm great. Here, take a bite." She slid the cookie between his lips and he bit down, a crumb sticking to the corner of his lip. Reaching up she brushed it away, and he caught her wrist, biting the fleshy part of her thumb.

She gasped and then he kissed her, in the center of her forehead, with the way he had that was exquisitely gentle and possessive, as if he made his claim but also treasured it.

"I want you—"

"Yes," she said, as he finished with "to come somewhere with me."

If she glanced at her toes right now, even they would be beet red.

Two mischievous little lines bracketed the corners of his mouth.

There was no way out of this awkward situation but straight through it. "I do want you. I can't stop."

"Come here." He crushed her against him, resting his chin on top of her head.

She breathed in sawdust, laundry soap, and the faintest spicy trace of aftershave. "Where are we going?"

"It's a surprise." He mimed zipping his lips. "You'll need to pack a few things. A bathing suit and some warm clothes. I've got the rest covered."

"Let me get this straight—you came over here asking if I'd go away to a mysterious place, and you already packed in the affirmative as if you knew my answer."

"That a problem?"

"I should be more annoyed but can't muster the strength. Your country charm works voodoo on me."

"I can increase the charm."

"I have no doubt of that." She bit the inside of her cheek. "But I wish I wasn't so easy to predict."

"Trust me on this one," Sawyer said, slinging an arm around her waist and nuzzling her neck. "There isn't anyone else like you."

"I'm pretty sure frazzled single moms are a dime a dozen."

"You mean pixie dazzlers who know how to kiss?"

"I'm a good kisser?"

He chuckled. "I've kissed plenty of girls in my time, but never any like you."

"Hrumph." She gave his chest a pretend slap. "Bet you tell all those many girls the same line."

"Lines? I don't have lines, only the truth." He reached out and bracketed her waist, rubbing the arc of her hip bones with his thumbs. "I see here a woman who needs to be kissed long and hard by a guy who knows what he's doing."

"And you know what you're doing, huh?" she murmured.

"Unless you're telling me otherwise." He leaned in and his mouth covered hers.

"Annabelle?" Another man cleared his throat and spoke her name a little louder. "Annabelle Carson?"

She froze mid-kiss, realizing she'd lost track of the last few minutes, that her shirt was unbuttoned two buttons below seemly and Sawyer's other hand had found a home holding the back of her thigh.

"I'm parked down on the road. Wanted to let you know that I'll be setting up the open-house sign." Her Realtor's cheerful smile evaporated. "Sheriff," he said stiffly.

"Hank." Sawyer gave a tight nod.

The Realtor cleared his throat and clapped his hands. "Doesn't look like this is the best time, so, uh, I'll get busy doing what I need to do and be back tomorrow. You're heading out?"

"Yes." She glanced at Sawyer. "It appears I have plans."

After a few long uncomfortable seconds, her Realtor forced a bland smile and walked back the way he came.

"You two have history?" she whispered.

"Hank King and I? Yeah, suppose we've had our share of differences. Mostly about his daughter."

"Of course, Ruby." No escaping small-town drama. Although Annie wondered if Hank knew her married daughter sang about another man's bologna.

"Still committed to selling?" he asked evenly, as if this wasn't a thin-ice topic.

"Sawyer, I—"

"You know what?" He shook his head, a determined look crossing his face. "Let's not talk about the future, or the past, for the rest of the day. The next twenty-four hours are about the present. Me and you, right here, right now."

No yesterday and no tomorrow? Sign her up. "I'll grab my things," she said, turning back into the house.

Each of Hank's distant hammer strikes hit Sawyer worse than a fist. Annie was determined to leave, convinced from this distance that San Francisco looked perfect. But she wasn't stopping to see what grew here, good and strong, right under her feet.

He went around to the back of his truck and checked on the supplies. A bottle of red wine, tea lights, enough food to feed a small country, and a large quilt waiting to be opened and spread out beneath the stars.

This was his last chance to get her to see he wasn't part of the problem, that running away wasn't going to give her anything better than what they could have here, together.

Chapter Twenty-One

ANNIE AND SAWYER wandered beneath twisted white-bark, towering red fir, and mountain hemlock. The rich, tangy aroma of sap infused the air as insects hummed in the undergrowth. Sawyer laced his fingers with hers as they descended a nearly unmarked trail to the river. It had been a long time since she'd been here, but as soon as he parked, she'd known. They were headed to their old swimming hollow. Down the slope, water bubbled and purled over boulders, the wild rush complementing her internal turbulence.

Sawyer promised to catch her if she jumped, and yeah, his hands were big and steady, but falling for a guy like this would be the equivalent of dropping from a plane while holding a bowling ball. She'd squish him like a pancake. He had no idea what he wanted to sign up for.

Her baggage brought its own carryon luggage.

The world didn't have a surplus of good guys, especially those who picked wildflowers but dirty-talked a woman dizzy. She sensed Ruby had put him through the wringer, and the last thing Annie wanted to do was inflict further damage.

"Whoops, there you go." He steadied her stumble. It was pretty near impossible to withstand his grin, the memory of that mouth, how it felt against—she tripped again.

"Sorry, klutz alert," she mumbled—big mistake to glance from his face to his well-defined forearms. Underneath, veins subtly ran against the muscle. An urge seized her to travel the path of one, with her tongue, to where his shirtsleeves rolled at the elbows.

"You seem distracted," he said. "Tired? We can stop for a rest, have a sip of water."

"No!" she said, a little too loud. Stopping was a terrible idea. She wanted to drag him beside the creek and bare herself again, offer her body for a taste of the beauty she felt in his arms. "I'm okay," she amended when his brow furrowed. "Just ready to get there."

Sawyer shoved his hands into his hip pockets, his face shifting from humor to intensely observant, an expression those craggy features seemed designed for. This guy had big appetites, for food, for life, for women. Scratch that, not all women. He wasn't a player, which was odd, because the entire single-female population of Brightwater, and some not-so-single, would no doubt happily play him like an old-timey banjo.

Why her? That was the mystery. One she didn't long

ponder because the trail leveled and disappeared into a grassy meadow fringed by willows.

"Wow," she whispered. "It's been a long time."

"I used to come here from time to time." He set down his bag in the clearing. "But quit eventually. Wasn't the same without you."

Tears threatened. Where had they come from? Her gaze shot to the cliffs across the water. They were taller than she remembered. It was incredible that she used to fling herself off them without a care of what might be lurking below the surface.

"Hey, why don't you get in for a quick dip? It'll be dark soon and I want to set up. The weather report says no rain tonight. How do you feel about sleeping under the stars?"

There was zero chance she'd sleep a wink beside Sawyer, but best to attempt an enthusiastic nod regardless. "Sounds great."

"Going to be another meteor shower tonight."

"Of course there is. You conjure them at will, don't you?"

"Nah, it's summer. The right time."

The river reflected the soft violet of twilight. "I'll find a spot to change."

There was an uncomfortable silence. "Into what?"

"My bathing suit?" She glanced up from her bag. "You said to pack one."

"I did, didn't I? Well, uh . . . " He blinked. "I didn't bring mine."

"Oh." The towel slipped from her grasp.

"That a problem?" He sat back and his shirt strained

his broad chest. All that muscle would soon be out for public consumption. Oh, wait, make that her own personal consumption.

"No, no. Of course not." Her comfort zone retreated into the distance, waving farewell with a lace handkerchief.

"Well, here's hoping you like what you see." That wink did things to her, throbbing, ache-filled things.

As a kid, she skinny-dipped all the time. Dad didn't care. She doubted he noticed. Claire was the one who had decided they needed to get it together and had purchased subscriptions to magazines, discussed fashion and hairstyles. After arriving in Portland, Annie made an effort, at least tried to wear clothes more or less in style. But once they became covered in baby food and sticky fingers, it didn't seem worth the annoyance. She wanted Atticus to crawl over her, not be shooed off because he might mess up a cute outfit. Still, she missed getting dolled up on occasion. And she missed being that girl in underwear, muddy knees, and yellow rain boots.

In the end, the swimsuit won out. First, it was emerald, cut in the style of a '50s vintage pinup girl. Second, maybe leaving a few things to the imagination would be wise. This place held a strange sort of magic, and she didn't want to rush, even when—scratch that, especially when—her hormones coursed like the creek.

She walked toward the banks, a little self-conscious of his watchful eyes. No need to turn and confirm, his gaze warmed the skin between her shoulder blades. Silly that she wore anything really, because this man opened her up, made her want to believe that fairytales were possible. The good stuff that seemed to happen to others waited around the bend for her to gather the courage to continue.

She dipped her toe in the water, still warm from the summer heat, and yes. Oh, goodness, yes. The temperature was perfect, a balance of hot on the surface and cooler below. She sank to the sandy bottom and rocked her head against a boulder.

Sawyer approached, face lit from the two candles he carried, flames dancing in the light breeze. His expression was half-hidden in the growing dark, but the light caught the edge of his strong chin, the angles sharply defined.

And there was his mouth.

Oh, that mouth.

"Can I hand these to you?" he asked. She moved forward and plucked the candles from his grasp, settling them on two rocks. The flickering reflected on the water, lit the deep rich green of her swimsuit. The river worked its magic, turning her into something wild and mythic, a dryad.

He kicked off his boots and set them against the tree in the same slow, purposeful way he did everything. She couldn't look anywhere else.

"You going to watch me strip?" Beneath his hat she caught a hint of a smile.

She folded her hands and rested her chin atop them. "It's hard to resist the show."

"Guess I better make it worth your while."

She laughed, and somewhere not far off, an owl called. The night arrived in earnest, and over the sound of the rushing water came a subtle metal snap. He'd tugged out his cowboy shirt and now popped open the pearl buttons, one by one.

Sweet Jesus.

He flicked back his shoulders and the shirt opened, revealing a powerful chest, thick slabs of muscle without an ounce of fat. His hands slid to his buckle. Was it a trick of the shadows or did he tremble? His jeans opened, and down they tumbled, boxer briefs and all. There he was, Sawyer, naked, wading toward her.

He didn't move in a way that hid or seemed embarrassed. In fact, he appeared at home here in this place, in this world. He was as much a part of the landscape as the trees and water.

"Hey, you." He smoothed back a damp lock from her forehead as he sank beside her, making a low noise of pleasure as he stretched his shoulders. Lord knew what her hair looked like in this wet humidity, but who cared, because he stared as if he liked what he saw, and the thing about Sawyer was his honesty. If she could trust anyone, he would be it.

And she wanted to, oh how she wanted to.

"You look like you need to ask me a question," he murmured, tilting her chin.

"Will you be careful with me?"

He cocked his head, watchful as always. "Are you frightened?"

"*You* don't scare me, but maybe I scare myself."

"Why?"

"Wanting. It's not easy, at least for me." He said nothing, but listened, so she kept talking. "I'm afraid if I name what I want, it will become real, and if I don't get it, it will hurt more."

"But, Annie Girl, what if you do get it? What if you say the word and it all just"—he scooped a handful of water and let the silky wetness course down her chest, trickle into the valley between her breasts—"falls into place."

She giggled, nervously. "That would be good."

"You and me." He took her hand and lowered it under the surface, resting her palm on his big, broad and very bare thigh. "Think we could be good?"

The air went out of her lungs. "I've wondered," she murmured dizzily.

"Have you?" He worked his thumb slowly around her knuckles.

"Haven't you?"

"I used to wonder how you kissed, and now I know. But that makes me wonder other things."

She could drown in his sexy smile. "Like what?"

"How you'd move in my arms, for one." He pulled her close. Her nipples skimmed his chest. "Would you wiggle like a slippery fish or go all slow and soft?"

She gasped. "I'd probably explode."

"Explode?" He cocked a brow. "And what will happen if you do?"

"Things will get messy." Better he knew it now. Her track record in relationships was dismally bad.

He cupped more water and this time poured it down her shoulders. "Then I'll clean you up."

How could he remain so unperturbed about the fact she was damaged goods, that her heart was dented and had lost its innocent shine? "Why are you so good to me?"

"I've got a lot of lost time to make up." He kept his voice slow, steady. "We have history, a whole lot of history, that we didn't write, and that doesn't make it easy."

"No, no it doesn't."

"But as I get older, things that once seemed too hard now feel possible." He leaned in, and it wasn't so much a kiss as a promise of one, a barely there graze against her lower lip. He came in closer and grazed her jaw with his teeth, slid all the way to her earlobe and groaned a little. "Got to say, these little things turn me on so much."

"My ears?" She giggled, and his answering smile pressed against her skin.

"They make me want to do dirty deeds."

"Like what?" She could barely get the words out.

"How bad do you want me to show you?"

In this wet, dark space, with her bones melting from longing, he wasn't playing fair.

"You want me to say I'll stay, before we take things farther."

He nodded slowly. "Seems like a better than decent idea."

"I—I want you, but I honestly don't know about Brightwater." She trailed her finger through the water, making small ripples.

"Me and this town go together." It was impossible to get a good read on his tone.

"I know, just like me and Atticus are a package deal. And I'm not sure if this is the best place for him, for us."

"You aren't sure this is enough." A sliver of tension cut through his impassiveness.

"Sawyer." Her stomach plummeted at the idea of hurting him. "I can't possibly know that."

"Why?"

"I'm a mother and need to act like a grown up. Make a list of pros and cons. San Francisco has a lot going for it."

He leaned back and regarded her. "Like what?"

Her mouth tugged in the corner. "You want to talk this out, naked in a swimming hole?"

He pressed his lips tight and then returned her smile. "No, Annie Girl." He tugged her bathing suit strap and planted a kiss on her shoulder. "Right now I want to love you until all you're saying is my name."

Pleasure drew itself into a tight hot knot between her legs. This guy might not say much, but when he did it was golden. "I know you want me all in, but maybe, tonight, you can meet me halfway?"

He pulled back and faced her. "I'm listening."

"You're a lot of things."

"I'm simple. My wants are simple."

"All you want is everything." She gave a rueful giggle and he responded with a soft laugh.

"Maybe."

"I don't make a promise I can't keep. You say you want

honesty, and that's the truth. I never thought about living in Brightwater until recently. And this thing with you, I hadn't thought about that in a long time either."

"Okay."

"Fine." She let out a sigh and pressed her forehead to his. "That's a lie. A big fat lie. I thought about you."

"I thought about you too."

"I—one time—I looked for you on Facebook, when I was going through my divorce," she whispered, the words ragged in her throat.

"I don't do any of that."

"*I know.* I even knew you wouldn't, but still I looked. I tried to tell myself I was bored, looking to catch up with old friends. But I knew that wasn't the truth. I missed you and felt lost. I've been lost for a long time."

He held out a hand. "Jump with me."

"Jump?" She glanced to the rocks, bathed in moonlight. "I don't think—"

"No thinking." He kissed the side of her neck. "Let's do it."

Her last functioning brain cell fell like the drop of water from the hair dangling over the edge of his forehead. Longing wrapped around her with frail tendrils. If she squinted maybe she could see herself there on the rocks, a ghost of her teenage self, holding hands with the ghost of young Sawyer, their laughter echoing through the forest.

He gave her a gentle tug. "The Eastern Sierras are a hard place, surrounded by high desert, higher mountains, cold winters, and far from big cities. It's not fair to ask you to jump in and make this decision lightly. I can back off a little on that. But not this. We need to jump."

"Okay." The word was out before she could snatch it back. God help her she'd do this crazy stunt. "But we have to go now, before I change my mind and think about submerged logs, or water snakes, or broken necks or—"

"Up you get." He stood, and his abs were interesting, and so was the thick dark line running beneath his navel to all . . . that.

"You're thinking again." He dove, reemerging a moment later, sending a splash in her direction. "Race you."

And that was all it took to send her off like a shot. Her arms sliced through the water, her legs kicking hard. How long had it been since she'd swam? She used to be as at home in this place as a river otter.

"I won," she crowed, hit the opposite side a stroke before Sawyer.

"You always did."

A thought occurred to her. "Is that because you let me?"

He chuckled. "I should say yes to sound manly, but facts are facts, and you kicked my ass, same as always."

She pumped her fist and whooped. Hauling out, it was easy to scramble up the old route, even in the dark. Her hands and feet remembered the way. She could close her eyes and be perfectly fine. In a few minutes, she was on top. Breathing a little hard, Sawyer came next to her.

She swallowed, toes flexing on the edge. "Now that I'm here, I think—"

He took her hand. "One."

"Seriously, maybe we need to—"

"Two."

"Oh God. Oh God." She was laughing. It was that or cry.

"Three."

And they leapt in unison, plunging down through the shadows, until *splash*! The river engulfed them, but even there, in the murky underworld, Sawyer's hand never left hers. And when they popped up, she only had time to catch a breath before he kissed the next one away. He tipped onto his back, bracing her hips, keeping her above him as he kicked to the shore.

"That was fun," she whispered.

"It was. And fuck, that was a lot higher than I remembered," he said.

She giggled. "I know, right? We were crazy. Correction—we still are crazy."

"I'm crazy for you," he said, stroking her hair. "And crazy proud of you for going along with that idea."

A shameless impulse seized her and she slid her hand from his loose grasp, sank it beneath the water and wrapped around his shaft. His teeth locked on his lower lip. "I did it for you. But I did it for me too."

His hips jerked and he slid heavy across her palm before easing back. "Annie, you're going to be the death of me."

She licked her lips and scooted closer. His eyes closed,

and the candlelight revealed how tight his jaw ground down. He'd been hard enough when she first touched him, but as she ran her hand up, dragging the tip of her thumb over the head of his shaft, he became granite.

"Is it difficult, for you to let me do this?"

"A little." He opened his eyes, and the intensity of his stare struck her like a shot. "This is a moment I've dreamt about for ten years."

No pressure. "And is this how you expected it to be?"

His gaze roamed her face as if committing her to memory. "No, it feels about a million times better."

She rose on her knees and he joined her. The tip of his shaft pierced the water, long, thick and every inch a man, but she couldn't shake the oddly protective sensation taking hold. As if behind that strength was a vulnerability. A man who needed love.

She slid over to him and he placed his two big hands on her back, between the dimples at the base of her spine.

He smelled too good to resist. She pressed her face into his chest and burrowed in, running her tongue over the flat of one nipple. He hissed through his teeth, so she went and did the other.

"Annie, I need you. I need you now."

"I know."

Chapter Twenty-Two

I NEED YOU NOW.

He wasn't telling her the whole truth. He didn't need her now. He needed her for always. His pulse beat in his ears, a primal rhythm like fists on a drum. Never had he been so aware of himself or another person. He sensed the lines that separated them, knew exactly where he finished and she began, and yet . . . and yet it was as if another part of him, invisible but undeniable, fused to hers.

He'd touched women before and felt lust, but this was outside of time. He'd cracked the code and realized the secret to the universe was here, in this woman he held.

"I . . . " He couldn't finish. If he tried to tell her all of this she'd think he was nuts. At worst case.

She trembled now, and he did too, his entire stomach shuddering with pent-up desire.

At best, she'd still retreat, because one doesn't simply

say, "Our souls fit together. You're the half I've been missing."

That was a lot to take in.

"Please." It was all Annie could manage with her dry throat. "Please. I . . . I . . ."

"Shhhhh, now," Sawyer murmured, his scruff rough on her neck even as his arms were gentle at her back. "I know."

"Do you . . ." She rested a hand on his cheek and felt him still. "Do you really want me?"

"Annie," he said hoarsely. "I require you."

She leaned against him, her heart pounding against his. "That's how I feel."

"It's . . . it's always been you," he said gruffly. "All the times I wondered what was missing. It was you."

"I felt the same way."

"Sometimes, I'd be out looking at the stars and I'd think 'Is Annie Carson looking at these same lights?' "

"Maybe I was."

"And now you're here."

"Right here." She slowly undid the necktie of her bathing suit and peeled it down over herself, baring herself inch by inch. When she finished, she slowly lifted her face to meet his shadowed gaze.

"Annie . . ."

She tried to speak, but no words came.

"You're goddamn gorgeous." He looped an arm under her knees and kept one on her back, carrying her to shore. Most nights were cool in the mountains, but to-night's sultry heat clung to the air. He eased her onto the blankets and she rolled on one hip as he spooned her from behind, planting a soft kiss on the back of her neck, running his hand down her hip bone, tracing where the inked birds flew across her skin. Her muscles tightened, but not in a good way. Her jaw locked.

"Hey," he rumbled. "You okay?"

"I . . . I don't know what's happening," Annie said help-lessly. She was suddenly tense, so tense, because this had to be a perfect moment. Sawyer against her, and above them a canopy of stars. This was so long in coming, it had to go exactly right, and the pressure took away some of the fun. *Oh shit, oh shit, calm down, breathe, oh shit, oh shit, oh—*

Up the hillside came a loud moo.

"What the fuck." Sawyer clutched her against him and they looked up. A cow stared at them from a rocky out-crop.

She burst out laughing and he joined her.

"That startled the shit out of me," he said.

"Runaway cow."

"From a nearby ranch. Maybe ours. I'll grab her to-morrow."

She placed a hand over her heart. "The moo."

"You jumped from your skin." He fell to the ground laughing and she joined in, and then it happened. She re-laxed, happy and free.

He slid between her legs, his fingers warm, and she offered a muffled groan when he skimmed her, turning to hook a leg over his powerful thigh.

"Hi," she said.

His eyes shone with their own light. "Hey."

"So we're going to do this."

"Yes. We are." He sat up, grabbed his bag and a box ripped open, followed by the crinkling of foil.

"Let me do it."

"Put on the condom?"

"Yes." She took it from his hand and sat, kneeling between his legs, setting the rubber against his wide tip. She slid it down and it fit, just. "Does that feel okay?" she asked, circling his base.

He managed a nod.

She crawled over him. With his size, she wanted to be on top this first time, figure out what she could realistically take. She positioned herself and . . .

"Oh." It was like her whole body formed the word and he slid through the middle of it.

"You okay?" he ground out.

She rocked in reply. Holy God, so much better than okay. He hit everything she needed to make this work, and as she rode him, he reached for her and took both her hands, pulling her close, so that her belly skimmed his taut abdomen and her breasts crushed his chest. They didn't kiss, exactly, but breathed against each other, and she knew he was doing the same as she was, feeling, concentrating on the slow slide of their bodies, absorbing the realization that this moment was happening at last.

She leaned back, savoring every stroke, letting him hit her where it was best. On and on she rode, and in the last crashing moment, right before she hit the peak, he groaned.

"Annie." The need in his voice was her undoing.

"Sawyer." She slipped over the edge, and as soon as she said his name, he joined her. She fell against his chest and he held her close, hooking his chin over the top of her head. His skin smelled of sweat and him and even her. She liked knowing that she was there, imprinted on his body.

"Your smile." His voice was thick with emotion as he traced her lips. "I love that Annie smile."

"Aren't all my smiles mine?"

He shook his head, laughter rumbling in his ribs. "This is the best one I've seen in a long time." He tucked the quilt over her shoulder. "It's what I think I've been put here for."

"What's that?" she asked, drifting. Funny how three minutes ago she was fully aware and now she was exhausted, but in a good, bone-deep way, as if she'd been used well and used in kind.

He kissed her cheek, then the other. "To make you smile that way."

There was a lot of possibility behind that simple sentence, but her eyes drifted closed, and the crickets hummed, sending her closer to stupor. "Sounds good to me."

"Does it?" He ran his thumb down her cheek. She didn't know what she was doing with her life, but if it came with Sawyer offering to give her smiles, maybe things weren't so bad.

"Are you always this good?" She poked his rib and he yelped. "Oh my God . . . " She poked again and held on tight as he wiggled back. "You really are still ticklish."

"No," he gasped. "Annie! Stop, don't."

"The big, strong sheriff is ticklish." She got him again and he roared.

"That's it, you're paying for this." He moved to grab her.

"Am I?" She tickled him again and his arms windmilled before he lunged, catching her by the waist and yanking her down, breaking her fall with his own body. Then he rolled, pinning her down with both hands, his erection hard against her hip. She rocked against it with a playful thrust. "Is this a citizen's arrest?" She gasped, wrapping her legs around him. God, his body.

And just like that, he became her willing prisoner.

"Lord, woman," he groaned when they were able to speak again.

"Mmmmm." She rolled onto one hip as he covered them with a quilt. "You should rest up. It's a big responsibility keeping all of us townsfolk safe."

"Sleep?" He traced her top lip before dipping back for yet another kiss. "I don't plan on either of us getting much sleep tonight."

As she tangled her fingers in his thick hair, reaching for a shared future, with him, seemed within her grasp. But could the power of such a moment stretch into forever?

Chapter Twenty-Three

As THEY LEFT their swimming hole the next morning, Sawyer announced his intention to take her out on the town that night, dinner and drinks at the new wine bar, Bottom of the Barrel. That was how Annie found herself stepping down from his truck at dusk and taking his hand as they ambled Brightwater's Main Street. The sidewalks were quiet, but how many eyes stared at them behind the storefront windows?

He turned as she started to pull away. "I want to hold your hand so everyone sees it."

"That's what I'm afraid of," she muttered under her breath. Why hadn't she dressed more incognito? A scoop-necked turquoise dress and lavender flats? Big dangly brass earrings? Dumb. Dumb. Dumb. Black would have been better. Something that whispered, "Don't look at me. Don't notice." Still, when she'd come downstairs after a long post-camping shower, Sawyer whistled in appreciation, and when he kissed her behind the ear, his words, "You taste as good as you smell," made everything seem all right with the world.

That well-being faded with the daylight.

She slung her purse higher over her shoulder and pasted on a grin that could win its own Best Actress Award. She'd do this. Tonight was for Sawyer. Tomorrow Atticus returned. Gregor had called this afternoon and asked if Margot could accompany him. Apparently she missed Annie as much as Annie missed her. She loved her stepdaughter, or former stepdaughter, and hated labels.

Like what was Sawyer? Not a boyfriend—exactly, and definitely a lover. But that dismissed the place he held in her heart.

What to say then?

Hello, this is Sawyer Kane. He is my everything.

Okay, a little intense. How about the piña to my colada?

Doubtful she'd be hired by Hallmark as a Valentine's Day card maker anytime soon.

She increased her grip on his hand. Earlier, as they had bumped along the gravel road, her phone had caught a signal. When she'd checked the messages there'd been one, from Hank King. A competitive offer had been made on Five Diamonds and he wanted to know if she'd come into the office tomorrow and go over the specifics. Apparently the buyer wished to remain anonymous, but the sum was staggering. Seven-figure staggering. And they were motivated.

Claire and her dad would be thrilled, so why did her own heart feel flat?

And she hadn't found a way to break the news to Sawyer either.

Not that this was bad news. Far from it. With that kind of money on the table, Atticus would have a more than ample college fund and San Francisco's exorbitant home prices wouldn't be as intimidating. She'd be able to raise her son in a place where he could fly his freak flag without judgment, she could grow her blog, and with any luck, a stable career for herself. Indeed, this was great news. She should be doing random heel-clicks and running through meadows like Maria from *The Sound of Music*.

But all she kept thinking was what if she stayed here in Brightwater?

Sawyer's own phone rang. "Sorry about that," he said, glancing at the screen. "Shit, it's the office. I need to take this." He released her hand and stepped away, walking off a short distance, speaking in low, terse tones. He kneaded the back of his neck, a gesture that indicated he was upset.

A whistle came behind her. She ignored it with an eye roll.

"Hey, it's that Carson freak. Wonder if she likes to get freaky too?"

"Damn, I'd ride that ass into the night."

Oh no they didn't. "Excuse me?" She hugged herself and turned. The three male faces went blank. One had a black mesh cap that read "Farmers Play Well with Udders," bushy red hair stuck out the sides.

They looked vaguely familiar. A couple of Sawyer's second or third cousins that she'd gone to school with.

She resisted the urge to tug down her skirt. "If you have big words to say, let's hear you say them to my face."

Then Sawyer was there, fisting Udder's shirt and slamming him against the light pole. "Did you disrespect her?"

"What the fuck, cuz? Put me down."

"Annie." Sawyer's voice was quiet, calm, and utterly terrifying. "Did this bonehead cousin of mine say something to offend you?"

"Let him down, Sawyer, it's fine." She was insulted, but Sawyer didn't deserve to get locked in his own cell because of it.

"You heard her," the big guy whined. "I didn't say nothing."

"You're not only an asshole, but a liar too." Sawyer knocked his head against the pole, and the sound of skull thwacking metal made Annie grind her molars.

"Ten years ago you got the upper hand on me. I tried to let bygones be bygones, but now here you are giving me a reason. You ready to put this right?"

The other man nodded, his face purple.

"Apologize."

"You shitting me?" His eyes bugged at Sawyer. "When are you going to learn? Who cares about her? She's a kooky Carson, man. A freak."

"Her name is Annabelle." Sawyer lifted him another

inch. "Her friends call her Annie, but I don't think you're counted as one of those."

"Sawyer, stop it," Annie said, touching his shoulder. His muscles bunched under his shirt.

"Sorry, Annabelle," Sawyer gritted out to his cousin. "This is your last chance."

"Sorry. Annabelle," the other man gasped, feet kicking the empty air.

"Boy! Boy!"

Grandma Kane plowed between the parked cars, taking the whole situation from bad to worse.

She stormed past Annie without a second look. "Boy," she shouted, and Sawyer blinked.

"Benny here—"

"I don't give a one-eyed goat for Benny. I care about my grandson making a spectacle of himself over—" She doubled over with a coughing fit.

Sawyer pat her on the back. "Grandma, are you okay?"

"Terrific," she snapped. "Never better. Got a dang frog in my throat."

Annie peered closer. Grandma Kane's skin held an unsettling pallor. She didn't look well, didn't look well at all.

Sawyer reset his hat. "I have to be rude and step aside for a little while. My deputies have a battery case and need a hand. I'm sorry this had to happen on our date."

"Date?" Grandma Kane's face did interesting things. Her paleness gave way to mottled shades of purple and red.

"Hopefully this won't take long. We've got a drunk

and disorderly in custody." He gave Annie an apologetic glance, ignoring the duck noises emanating from Grandma. "Want to go ahead to Bottom of the Barrel and order a bottle of something good? I'll be along quick as I can."

"Sounds like a plan," Annie said with forced brightness. Grandma glared at her behind his shoulders and seemed about to drag a bony finger across her throat in an age-old threat.

"Great. See you soon." He gave her a distracted kiss on the temple. "You should go home and take a nap," he said to Grandma, and strode in the direction of the sheriff's office.

Oh, Sawyer. Annie took a deep inward breath. He was perfect, but still a man. He had no idea he'd left her in one hell of a pickle.

Annie slowly turned to Grandma, who eyed her like a lion over a fallen gladiator and resisted the urge to shout, "We who are about to die, salute you."

The older woman raked the point of her tongue along the seam of her lower lip. She coughed again, but the last thing she looked like she needed was a nap. "Well, well, well, Annabelle Carson, looks like you've gone and sunk your hooks into my favorite grandson. Remember, if you break his heart, you'll be dealing with me."

Break Sawyer's heart? Funny, she'd been so focused on not breaking her own heart, she hadn't given a thought to his, except to be grateful for how strong and caring it was. But if he had the power to hurt her, it stood to reason she could hurt him too. And that was the last thing she ever wanted to do.

"Um, I should be going. Are you sure you're all right?" Annie took a step backward. The wine bar was across the street and a cab sav sounded better than good. She needed to drink and mull.

Grandma look a step closer. "Going is what your people do best, isn't it? Remember, I have my eye on you, missy, and don't forget that."

Annie hustled across the street, Grandma's gaze tracking her the whole way. It was like being in the crosshairs of a hunting mountain lion. She reached Bottom of the Barrel as the door swung open and out stepped Quincy Bankcroft redoing a cufflink.

"Daisy!" He leaned forward, giving an air kiss on both her cheeks. "I've been thinking about you."

"You have?" Annie cleared her throat. Probably didn't reflect too well for her to sound quite so surprised.

"I went on your blog the other day and it had gone quiet for the past few weeks. Are you well?"

"Yes, everything is great." She attempted a smile. It's just . . . life gets busy sometimes." The truth was that lately she didn't know what to say about anything. Feelings kept flying at her, bouncing off like bugs on a windshield. She needed to mentally pull over and figure out what she wanted once and for all.

"Do you mind passing me your details? I'd like to have a conversation soon."

"You want my number?"

"Yes, but not with anything nefarious in mind." Quincy's laugh boomed. "I have an idea that might be to our mutual benefit."

"Well, you've got my full curiosity." Annie had no idea why a media mogul would ever want to talk to her, but she reached into her purse and grabbed a *Mighty Mama* business card. "I'm easy to find."

"Wonderful. I'll be in touch."

Annie waved him off as he strolled toward a parked red Tesla standing out like a sore thumb among the pickups and battered SUVs. Then she dared a glance back across the street and, yep, Grandma Kane still stared. Slowly, the old woman forked two of her fingers into a v-shape, raising them beneath her eyes. The message was clear.

I'm watching you.

Chapter Twenty-Four

"MOMMY!" ATTICUS FLEW down the steps of the plane. Annie wrapped him in a bear hug and looked up.

"Margot!"

Her stepdaughter tossed her thick curls over one shoulder and beamed. "Surprise?"

"Welcome to the Eastern Sierras, honey." Annie gathered her in the hug too. "I'm so, so, so glad to see you."

"Thanks for letting me come. I wasn't ready to say goodbye to the little guy." Margot kept her tone bright, but her brown eyes were expressive. Everything showed on her face, always had, and something wasn't right. "I'm sorry to barge in," she whispered. "But I needed a break from both of them."

Margot didn't get along well with her parents. Annie never wanted to intervene as a stepparent, but she was a friend, and in her heart, Margot was family. "They are okay with you coming here?"

"Yeah. Dad bought the ticket and my mom could care less. More time for her and the boys." Margot's mother, Gregor's first wife, remarried a few years ago and had two more sons, pushing Margot off to one side.

"Well, you're welcome for as long as you like!" Annie said, giving her yet another hug. "I've missed you."

Margot giggled. "It hasn't been more than two months."

"I know, but when you're away from a favorite person, any time feels too long."

"Piggyback! Piggyback!" Atticus shouted, grabbing Margot's leg and hanging on tight.

"Okay, okay, Monster," Margot said, using her affectionate term for him.

Atticus insisted on Margot sitting in the backseat, and he held her hand tight the whole way home while giving Annie a running litany of all the Disneyland adventures.

"Miss Penelope let me eat two scoops of ice."

"Miss Penelope?" Annie tried to remember what movie she'd featured in.

"Dad's friend," Margot muttered with a grimace.

"Oh." *That* Miss Penelope. Atticus's former pre-K teacher? *Really, Gregor?* How many times had he played her for a fool? Even still, the idea of her ex picking up at their son's preschool, probably during their marriage, didn't hurt. Sure it felt vaguely uncomfortable. Penelope was legal—just. Sadly, there was another girl who'd soon learn a hard life lesson about broken hearts. A good thing about getting older really was getting wiser.

They pulled up the driveway.

"Whoa." Margot's voice raised three octaves. "Who's the mega hottie?"

Sawyer squatted, shirtless, on the porch roof replacing a gutter. Sweat slicked his carved torso, the air holding the muggy heat common before a storm.

"Annie. Seriously. Who. Is. That?" Margot repeated slowly.

"Oh, he's, he's . . . uh . . . he's Sawyer Kane."

"Come again?"

"Sawyer Kane, my neighbor."

"Sawyer Kane is his actual name, and he looks like . . . whoa . . . " Margot fanned her face.

Sawyer swiped his brow and threw up a hand in greeting, smiling broadly. *Whoa indeed.*

"He's the sheriff," Atticus stage-whispered. "Although he doesn't shoot bad guys."

"Um, and here I worried you'd have nothing to do," Margot muttered.

"Margot!" Annie said, pressing a hand to her cheek.

"Seriously, can I high-five you? I feel compelled to high-five you."

"That's enough, you." Annie turned around and waggled a warning finger even as her blush prickled to her forehead.

"Do you love him, Mommy?" Atticus asked.

Et tu, son?

She got out and gave Sawyer a little wave before getting Atticus from his booster seat.

"Wanted to fix the eaves before the rain came," he hollered.

"Thank you. Thank you very much."

"I'm going to repair a few shingles too. Found a spot where the roof will leak."

This man had found the spot where everything leaked. She wiped away sudden tears and blew her nose with a tissue that she had balled in her pocket. "Silly allergies," she said with forced brightness. "Let me introduce you to my stepdaughter, Margot."

"Um, hey." Margot shifted her weight on the balls of her pink Converse sneakers, uncharacteristically tongue-tied. "You, um, you're good at fixing things." She turned to Atticus. "How about you take me inside and give me a tour."

After they went inside, Sawyer jumped off the low roof, landing in a crouch.

"Sorry in advance," he said, straightening slowly.

"For what?" Annie asked.

"The fact I have to kiss you right now." He swooped her into a dip, his mouth a hot promise.

"But the children will see!" she gasped, bracing her hands on his wide back.

"Oh no they won't." He hiked her up, holding her thighs against him, and walked behind the big lilac bush her mother had long ago planted, the one that grew alongside the weatherboards in a dense hedge.

"We can't—"

"One kiss," he murmured, grazing her neck.

Her eyes closed of their own volition. "With you, it's never just a kiss."

"Your lips." He stroked her jaw with a gentle forefinger. "I might be forming an addiction to them. The way they curve here, and dip in the middle. I love it."

His eyes widened slightly as the word left his lips, and she knew hers did the same. They were venturing into dangerous L-word territory.

"Sawyer Kane." She affected a light, teasing tone, hoping to draw them onto safer ground. "You are a romantic."

"Where you are concerned?" He laughed huskily before returning to her mouth. "Guilty as charged, ma'am."

DURING LUNCH, SAWYER couldn't help but notice the way Atticus stared at him. While Margot and Annie were engrossed in a heated conversation about a Netflix show they were addicted to, the little guy waggled his eyebrows. He liked Atticus a lot. Having never been around children much, this kid put him at ease, made him feel as if he didn't have two left feet when it came to ankle-biters. But what secret signal was he trying to share?

Finally, he couldn't stand the suspense. Setting down his fork, he cleared his throat and said, "Hey, champ, how about you come outside with me? We'll go check the truck's oil."

Atticus nodded eagerly. "Sounds good!"

Annie glanced over with a distracted smile. "What are you two getting up to?"

Sawyer stood, bending to kiss her cheek. "Secret men's business. When I get back I want those dishes right where I left them. I'm washing up."

Margot stared. "You clean too?"

Sawyer shrugged. "She cooked this fine meal. It's only fair."

Atticus reached up, and Sawyer blinked at his hand a moment before realizing the boy wanted him to hold it. Aw, hell. His heart filled his whole rib cage as Atticus led him outside. Once they got away from the house, he paused. "Now are you going to tell me what's going on?"

"Can I show you something?" Atticus asked, pink-cheeked with excitement. "Course you can," Sawyer said, jerking as the kid pulled him toward the barn. For a skinny little fellow, he had one hell of a grip. They rounded the barn, and in the back was an old lean-to, probably used to store firewood way back when.

Atticus extended his pointer finger. "In there."

"What is it?"

"You'll see." Either Atticus had to pee real bad or was dancing with excitement.

Sawyer stuck his head in and let his eyes adjust to the light. On the floor, curled on her side, a pretty golden dog nursed four tiny puppies that all suspiciously looked like miniature German Shepherds.

Did Maverick have a hand in this? That sly rascal.

"Puppies." Atticus grinned.

"Yeah." Sawyer returned the smile and dropped to a crouch. "Here, sit on my knee and we can watch."

Atticus scrambled onto him, looping one arm around his neck. "This is the best thing I found in my whole life."

"Thank you for sharing it with me," Sawyer said gravely.

"Think I can keep one?"

That right there was dangerous territory. He didn't want to go committing Annie to the responsibility of a pet even though he understood the way dog love sat in a little boy's soul. "You're going to have to ask your mom."

"I hope I can." Atticus rested against his chest with a contented sigh. "And then come live with you."

Sawyer couldn't move. He could barely breathe.

"That's what I'm going to wish for on the first star I see tonight," Atticus continued, gaze fixed on the puppies, no idea how hard he squeezed Sawyer's heart. "To have one of those wiggly little puppies and live with you forever."

That's what I'm going to wish for too, champ. That's what I'm going to wish for too.

Chapter Twenty-Five

LATER THAT AFTERNOON, after Sawyer went on duty, Annie nestled in the cozy window booth of Haute Coffee watching the rain pound Main Street. Atticus stirred a fat marshmallow into his hot chocolate as Margot sipped her cappuccino.

"Oh yum. That's really good coffee." She wiped the thick dollop of foam from her top lip.

"Isn't it? The owner, Edie, knows her stuff. This could rival anything in Portland."

"Wonder what she's doing here?" Margot looked out the window at the quiet street.

"Brightwater isn't that bad." The unexpected sentence sprung from Annie's mouth, and she sat blinking at the implications.

Margot shot her a strange look. "You always said you hated where you grew up."

"We don't say 'hate' in our family," Atticus piped in. Margot rolled her eyes as Annie forced a grin.

"That's right, honey."

Strange that she raised her son not to use the word she so constantly whispered to herself. *I hate my bank account. I hate my stomach. I hate my crazy hair.*

"Well, I hate my frizz." Margot took a defiant sip.

"Mom!" Atticus looked between them, wondering who'd win.

Annie gave Margot the look. The young woman wasn't her daughter, but she'd known her for years and had sympathy for her difficult parental situation. Her mother remarried and invested in her new family, seeming to regard her first-born as unwelcome cargo from a life she no longer lived. And Gregor. Gregor only found value in the people around him reflecting his own self-image . . . and self-importance.

"You seem upset, honey."

"Meh. College stuff." Margot stared out the window. "Dad. The usual debate."

Gregor wanted Margot to attend his alma mater, an elite liberal arts college, next year, and major in philosophy, like him. Margot wanted to become a yoga teacher or study acupuncture. Margot said during the trip to Disneyland he'd made it clear in no uncertain terms that she wouldn't see a dime if she chose that direction. It wasn't Annie's role to intervene in their business, but her heart ached for her stepdaughter, who had spent the last few days moping around the property.

Suddenly Margot straightened, eyes shining despite the dull light outside. Annie glanced over her shoulder. Sawyer's youngest brother, Archer, sauntered through the front door with the slow, rolling swagger that served as his own personal calling card.

She glanced back at Margot. "Don't even think about it."

"He's really cute."

"He's way, way, way too old for you."

"I'm eighteen." Margot's face was disbelieving. "And what, he's in his twenties? I like older guys."

"We are so not having this conversation."

Margot flipped her curls over one shoulder and braced her chin on her fist, glaring at the opposite wall. "Hey, there's a concert here tonight," she said, pointing at the band poster. "Going to hear live music might be fun."

Annie hesitated. Margot was here under her care, and while she trusted her stepdaughter, she didn't trust men around a pretty young girl. From her private vantage point, she gave Archer a once-over. He leaned on the bar while Edie ground coffee beans, not taking his eyes off the back of the red-haired barista's head. He was darker than Sawyer and not quite as tall. Still, his lean muscular quality was attractive, and the dimple didn't hurt.

The Kane brothers were blessed with particularly fine DNA.

The door swung open again and Kit Kane, one of Sawyer's cousins, entered in his green and tan deputy uniform. Archer turned and gave him a fist bump. That was when they caught her staring. Annie ducked her head and sipped her mocha—extra shot, extra chocolate, extra whip, exactly how she liked it.

She couldn't hear the specifics of their fast-paced banter, but their lips moved fast and laughter came loud. No wonder Sawyer stayed quiet. Hard to get a word in edgewise around such motor mouths.

Edie turned and gave the two men a tight smile, setting their coffees on the counter before giving Annie a shy wave. She came out from around the corner, pausing at the glass cabinet and removing an extra-large slice of flourless cake.

"This piece called your name," she said, walking over to set the plate on the table and handing out three forks.

Annie almost said, "Oh you shouldn't," but Margot's presence silenced her. The girl was eighteen. She didn't deserve to hear anyone talking negative about dessert.

"Thank you," she said instead. "Please, join us for a second."

Edie scanned the shop. Haute Coffee was quiet for once. Archer and Kit stood at the counter, cracking each other up.

"You're really having The Foggy Stringdusters here?" Margot asked. "They are getting a lot of radio play back home. Indie bluegrass, right?"

"Yes." Edie's face lit up. "Amazing, isn't it?"

"How did you score that? I mean, no offense, but this is kind of the middle of nowhere."

"Quincy Bankcroft pulled a few strings," Edie said.

"He's like a fairy godmother, isn't he?" Annie grinned.

"In more ways than one." Edie gave an involuntary

glance over Annie's shoulder and flushed. Looked as if the barista wasn't immune to the charms of the Kane men either, but which one—Kit or Archer?

She hoped for Edie's sake it was Kit. Archer had the dimples, the walk, and the charm, but from what she'd heard, and she wasn't even privy to most of the town's gossip, he was a guy who didn't settle down. Truly untamed. Edie seemed gentle, reserved, and a little quiet.

"Hey! Boys! Back away from those cookies if you know what's good for you," she snapped, holding a warning finger.

Whoa. *Maybe not so quiet after all.*

Archer threw up his hands and stepped away. "Just checking to see if they were cool enough for customers."

Edie narrowed her eyes even as her lips quirked. "I have my eye on you, cowboy."

"Like what you see?" Archer drawled.

Edie snorted. "You're trouble."

Archer tipped his hat. "Trouble is my middle name."

Annie's phone rang. Hank King, her Realtor.

"Sorry, I really need to take this call. Margot, Edie, can you make sure Atticus leaves some cake for everyone else? I'll step under the awning outside."

"Yep, no problem." Edie gave Atticus a conspiratorial wink. No doubt she'd slip him another treat, but whatever, later tonight Annie would crank the music and let him dance party off the sugar rush.

The conversation didn't take long. The news was good. The best even. So why did she lean against the red brick with a sudden headache after hanging up? The sum had been raised on Five Diamonds another hundred thousand dollars with the stipulation she vacated the farm within thirty days.

That should be enough money to pave over any misgivings, so why were they still there?

"Look what the cat dragged in." Annie opened her eyes and Grandma Kane stared her down from under a black umbrella, mouth set in a permanent disapproval. "What's this about Five Diamonds having an offer?"

Was Grandma Kane Batman? Annie turned her phone over in her hands, inspecting it for bugs. "How on earth did you hear about that already?"

"I have my ways. Plus, when Hank King makes calls outside the Save-U-More he talks loud," Grandma said, nodding at the supermarket kitty-corner to them.

Inside, Archer and Kit's noisy guffaws threatened to shake the window panes. *Yeah, because your family are a bunch of shrinking violets, huh?*

"It's time you steer clear of my grandson."

"Excuse me?"

"Did I stutter?" Grandma leaned in, practically poking Annie's eye with the umbrella. "Sawyer's a good boy. He doesn't deserve to be toyed about by a kooky Carson."

"Whoa, whoa, whoa, this conversation is totally out of line."

"Look at you, with that fancy cappa-whachamacalit. This town needs to remember its roots before it's too late."

"First of all, those are your kin inside that shop drinking espresso. Second, the Carsons were on the same wagon train as the Kanes. Don't even think of trying to

Out-Brightwater me. I'm fifth-generation. You're the one who married in."

Boom, how you like those apples, Granny?

Grandma's color rose as her eyes turned to slits. "And you are willing to throw it all away, slink out of town with your money bags."

"You're upset because you want the land for yourself. You've always wanted it. When I was a kid, how many lawsuits did you file trying to encroach on access?"

Annie jumped when a large hand clasped her shoulder. She turned, and it was Archer, his mouth firm. "Are you yelling at my grandma?"

Great, out of the frying pan and into the fire.

"She's commenting on things that aren't her business," Annie responded.

"This is Brightwater!" Grandma hollered. "Everything here is my business."

"Pretty sure Sawyer won't want to hear his grandmother is disturbing the peace on his woman."

"His woman?" Annie gasped as Grandma Kane said, "Disturbing the peace?"

"Come on, Grandma," Archer said, offering her an arm. "I'm sure there's someone you can scowl at over at The Baker's Dozen. As for you"—he rose his chin at Annie—"how about you figure out what you are to my brother, and quick."

As grandson and grandmother stalked away, Annie resisted the urge to stomp in the largest puddle in sight. Instead, she turned back toward Haute Coffee. Hopefully there was an entire chocolate cake calling her name.

Her phone rang again. What now? This time an unfamiliar local number appeared on the screen. "Hello?" she said tentatively.

"Daisy, darling!" Quincy's faint accent crisped his speech.

"Oh, hello." She straightened her posture. "So good to hear from you."

"I'll cut straight to the chase. Do you want good news or better news?"

"Um, let's start with good and go up from there."

"The deal closed on *The Brightwater Bugle*. This little town paper is the newest jewel in the Bankcroft Media crown."

"Wow." A flutter of excitement ran through her. "Congratulations."

"I'm not looking to keep *The Brightwater Bugle* a rinky-dink backwoods paper. We'll still cover the local 4-H meeting and the obituaries, as those are the most popular sections, but features—that's my vision. Why let other magazines fly by night through here? We should generate our own content. Highlight Brightwater and the rest of the New West."

"New West?" Annie repeated, before face-palming. Acting like a parrot wasn't going to impress this man.

Quincy continued as if he hadn't noticed. "The old West is changing and residents need content that reflects the new landscape. These days, people appreciate a little glamor in their country. Now on to the better news. Would you like to be the *Bugle's* new Editor in Chief?"

"The . . . " Her mouth worked soundlessly, the words

unable to permeate her brain. Instead, they bounced around her skull like rogue Ping-Pong balls.

"That's right. I want you, Annabelle Carson."

"But my qualifications are—"

"Absobloodylutely what we need. Besides, I like you and your voice. I go with my gut on these decisions, and this time my gut cries out, 'Annie! Annie Carson!' "

Quincy Bankcroft's gut cried out for her? The phone trembled in her hand. "I don't know what to say."

"Say the only word I want to hear—yes."

She pressed a hand to her forehead. "How about you let me think about it?"

"I like those words far, far less."

"I'm in the middle of a few major life decisions and need to think everything through."

"Fine. You can have until the end of the week. But don't be daft, darling. You are the exact right person for the job, and something tells me you know it too."

He hung up, and she was left holding the phone, staring, as a literal tumbleweed blew down the street center. All this time she'd been telling herself how staying in Brightwater was pointless, that she couldn't advance her career or her life—that San Francisco was the only sensible option.

Now these words were thrown back in her face, but the effect was like getting dumped over the head with an ice bucket. She stepped back inside the coffee shop, determined to eat Edie's flourless chocolate cake before her words.

Chapter Twenty-Six

SAWYER SWERVED TO miss the little old lady. Scratch that. There was nothing sweet or stooped-back about the woman glaring at him from the middle of the road underneath a black umbrella.

"Grandma, are you trying to get yourself killed?" He stuck his head out the window.

She shook her finger at him. "If that's what it takes to get you to see sense, then I'll consider it a death worth dying."

A few people paused on the sidewalk, watching them curiously. Sawyer swore under his breath and drove his squad car to the curb, then parked it, got out and slammed the door. He set his hand on Grandma's bony elbow and led her out of the middle of the street.

"Jay-walking is a crime."

"Good, that was the idea. Book me. Take me in."

"You want me to arrest you?"

"This is a one-woman protest."

"It looks like you might need a nap and cup of tea."

She shrieked in outrage. "Don't you dare talk to me that way. I remember changing your diaper."

Sawyer grimaced. "For that, I'm sorry."

"Bring me in and maybe I'll be able to talk some sense into that numbskull head of yours."

"Grandma, I'm the sheriff."

"And I'm your elder." She looked up at the sky. "It's going to start raining like a cow pissing on a flat rock again any second, so let's cut to the chase. Annabelle Carson sold Five Diamonds."

Her words hit him like a slug to the gut. "What?" He'd failed.

"Did I stutter? She's sold the place, and to the worst person you can imagine. I heard that old fat cat King make the call. Ruby preened next to him smug as a cat who got into the cream."

Sawyer took off his hat, rubbing his forehead. That didn't make any sense. "Annie would never sell the farm to Ruby."

"The price was more than right. Your little girlfriend doesn't care about the farm, or the fact that Ruby will lock it up, tear it down and build a sunken pool, and tennis courts to entertain her Hollywood friends. All that prime land will get mowed under to put in a nine-hole golf course."

Sawyer's insides were scoured empty. Ruby said she wouldn't let him go without a fight, but he never expected this.

"I'll talk to Annie." That was it. That was what he'd do. Once he laid out his feelings, she'd see sense and stay.

Wouldn't she?

AFTER ANNIE STUMBLED back inside the coffee shop, she discovered Margot had wheeled Edie into letting her help behind the counter during tonight's concert and then sleep over in her above-shop apartment afterward. Atticus was tucked in bed, and now the house was too quiet by half.

Truck tires ground up the gravel. She set down the book she wasn't reading anyway and went outside as Sawyer parked his truck. The nearby pine grove looked dark but not forbidding, and for once the peaks didn't make her feel lonely. The landscape had a hushed quality, a night for futures to be decided.

Grandma Kane might have spewed mean, hurtful words in town today, but they weren't anything she hadn't thought herself. For so long she'd let things happen. Terrible things. Mundane things. Until she'd gone numb. Never asking for what she needed. Ignoring what she wanted.

The truck door slammed.

She grabbed her want and found the feeling fit perfectly. She didn't have to suck it in or shimmy.

"Annie?" Sawyer called out, a trifle wary as she stood and approached. "I heard you and Grandma had words."

"I don't care about what your grandma thinks of me, Sawyer." Annie wrapped her arms around him. "Follow me." She led him inside, pointing at the giant blanket fort strung up in the living room. "Atticus and I built it earlier, just like Claire and I used to do."

"We can't fit in there, can we?"

"We might have to get cozy, but it's better here. He's sleeping upstairs."

"You convinced me." They crawled inside and he eased her on top of him, swearing. "Shit, what's that?" He reached beneath and pulled out a flashlight. He flicked it on and her eyes constricted from the light.

"Sorry." He lowered the beam so it hit directly on her breasts. "Wow."

Her shirt had popped a button and a lot of cleavage showed. "I kind of have that whole heaving bosoms thing going on, huh?"

"Whatever you want to call it, they look all right."

"All right?" She giggled. "That's the best you've got?"

"Your bosoms—your heaving bosoms—look incredible."

"Incredible, really?"

"Would you prefer fucking hot?"

"I'm like a heroine in my own romance novel, the coy down-on-her luck single mom who is plucky." She palmed a breast and arched a brow. "And perky."

"Works for me."

"And you're the hero, obviously. Strapping. Sexy. A sheriff, even. Oh my God, we are a cliché." She reached for his belt. "Do you have a throbbing member?"

"Jesus, Annie." He looked torn between choking and laughing.

"A rampaging cockstand?" She opened the buckle.

"That sounds dangerous."

"What about . . . " She lowered her voice with dramatic flair. "A quivering member?"

"Annie, you know I love talking to you, right? But I'm going to have to shut you up." He kissed her hard then, and whatever it was that rampaged, quivered or throbbed pressed against her. The flashlight rolled from his grasp as he fisted her hair and she did the same. They kissed each other hard, grabbing as if they tried hard enough they'd merge into one self.

Annie undid his zipper and didn't think. Tonight she knew exactly what she wanted, and it was high time she had it. Lowering her head, she took him down as far as she could go, her mouth hitting a point where it was full of Sawyer, everything he had to give. Then she drew back, kissing him along his shaft as his mangled words distilled to one refrain.

"Annie. Annie. Annie." He tried to pull away. "Stop. Please, you don't have to . . . Aw, shit—"

She shook her head, and the side-to-side motion pushed him in deeper, making him swear again.

"Annie." He hauled her up against him.

"Why'd you stop me?" She touched her lips, swollen, a little puffy, but in a good way. "Wasn't it okay?"

"You're goddamn amazing, but there's a rule I have."

"A rule?"

"With you."

"Okay." She had no idea what he'd say.

"You come first."

"What?"

"That's my rule. I get you off first."

"Oh . . . " Her brain exploded in a silent burst. She was vaguely aware that he pulled a condom out of his wallet, that her underwear came off, and that the diffuse flashlight glow caught flecks of gold in his green eyes.

"So good watching you respond to me." He parted her legs, teasing her with the tip, grinning as she squirmed, helpless, shamelessly begging with her body for more. "So good hearing you make those little sounds when I do this." Inch by inch he buried deeper as she let out an incoherent moan.

He withdrew, but the absence couldn't even be missed because then he was there, plunging again. Her mind was right there, in this moment. His gaze didn't leave hers as his hands gathered her hips, tilting them so he could plunge impossibly deeper. This man was inside her, and yet he'd always been there in his own way. She'd carried a piece of him all these years, so now having him here in truth only intensified the experience.

He made a low rasp in his throat and she shivered. She was normally the one gasping and crying out, he was always so focused. What would it be like to get him going? She sucked in a sharp inhalation, clenched around him and whispered the only two words that mattered in this moment. "Sawyer. Yes. Sawyer."

A definite groan this time. He rode her harder as she leaned up and sucked at the hollow of his neck. His skin flavored with sweat and need.

"You feel so good," she murmured, and his throat worked hard.

"Fuck," he muttered through his teeth as she reached to hold his sac in a featherlight caress.

"I have rules too," she said. His eyes rolled back in his head. She had forgotten the part of her that was playful, liked to try things out, have fun. She'd never been able to be this close to someone while having sex. "My rule is tonight, we come together," she panted. "Same time."

"Annie." He adjusted her so her legs were on the outside, his on the inside and every movement went from amazing to mind-blowing. His pelvis skimmed her clit as his rough callused fingers circled the softest, slickest, most sensitive part of her. When he flicked his tongue against the side of her mouth she opened, let him slide the curve of his lower lip against hers while she gripped his biceps.

It wasn't a flame within her, it was a conflagration, as if she'd thrown her mask on a bonfire and given him her truest face, and he showed her his. Memories flashed. The long ago day the tall, beautiful boy, all big hands and feet, stared but didn't speak in the freezer section of the grocery store. She'd glanced at him through the open door and frozen herself, until the glass between them fogged and she dropped her head in embarrassment. The next time he approached she'd been in the river, and she hadn't understood the look on his face, but liked the way that he'd watched her.

She wrapped her legs around him and pressed her forehead against his chest as he increased the rhythm.

"Eyes on me, Annie Girl." He gritted his teeth, his one bracing arm shuddering as his strokes took her to the edge. She hovered a moment, toes curling. One last rolling thrust and she jumped, knowing he fell alongside her, holding her hand the whole way down.

Afterward, she lay with her head on his shoulder, fingers entwined. They hadn't said much. Words seemed strange, useless things to describe the journey they'd taken.

This man lit up her life like the North Star, yet on the kitchen table sat an offer of sale for the house. What to do? Stride forward toward the light, even as it seemed so high, painfully beautiful and unattainable, or spin and spin and find herself in a new place, with a new start, a new life?

"I . . . " Sawyer smoothed back her hair and wrapped his arms around her. The house was quiet. They hid in their blanket fort inside this stolen moment of time. "I don't always have an easy way with words."

She squeezed his hand. Something told her he'd opened up to her more in the last few weeks than he ever had with anyone. "It's okay."

"But sometimes there are things that need saying." He rolled her gently onto her side, wincing as they separated. His hard pectoral muscles tightened. "I need to tell you that I'm falling—" His phone rang and he muffled a curse. "That's work. I have to take this." He tugged his phone out of his pocket and answered, "Kane here. What? Shit. On my way." He hung up and looked over.

"Duty calls?"

"Yeah, a car accident got called in outside town. I'll be back as soon as I can, okay?" He gave her a kiss on the forehead.

"Of course."

He sighed and kissed her again, a light brush on the lips. "You know how hard it is to leave when you look like this?"

She patted her head. "A half-drunk porcupine?"

"Nah. Like a woman who's been well-loved." And with that he was gone, and the blanket fort was hers alone.

Falling. He was falling. She was too, but the thing about falling was eventually you hit, splattered, and then the fun was over.

She pressed her hands over her face, couldn't bear to wake from this dream. Falling in love was one thing, but what happened after the fall was the scary part.

Chapter Twenty-Seven

ANNIE WAITED BUT Sawyer didn't return. At four in the morning, she wandered into the kitchen and flicked through the deed of sale. Who was this mystery buyer? This was a big decision, and to pass the farm off to a nameless stranger made it seem as if she cared far less than she did. There was a lot of money at stake, and even more family pressure, but how could she leave Sawyer?

The laptop sat on the table, and she flicked through old blog comments that did nothing to make her feel better. Everyone expressed positivity, validated her choices, but they didn't know anything about her, the real her. She might as well be a fictional character. It was amazing and kind that they took time to reach out, but maybe it was time to be honest. Show her life, warts and all.

Joy of joys—Ms. Hootenanny had left another comment. *I don't believe in you.*

"I don't believe in me either," Annie said out loud.

Dad had sent a new email.

Any update on the sale of Five Diamonds? Found a place here in Mexico I want to buy. Send an update asap because I can't make an offer until I know what we can expect to earn.

Her heart sank. Even if she didn't want to sell the farm there were still two others in her family who'd profit and who didn't have their hearts beating in a fast rhythm because Sawyer had touched them in the mysterious space between the soul and heart.

Why couldn't life be a simple straight line for once?

She bent, crying soundless tears into her hands when the back door shut.

"Hey," Sawyer said, stepping inside the kitchen.

She wiped her eyes. Why did he hover, his face so tense and pale? "What's the matter?"

He braced his hand against the fridge. "The car accident tonight—it involved Margot."

"No." She tried to stand and fell back against the chair. "No!"

"I'll be okay," Margot chimed in, ducking under Sawyer's arm. Her eye was bruised black, her right arm in a sling.

A low sob escaped her. "You're okay?" She rose, this

time keeping a firm grip on the table. "Why didn't anyone call me?"

"I tried to. You never picked up. She'll be fine. The wrist sprain is the worst of her injuries. I had her checked from head to toe."

How had she not heard the ring? Annie grabbed her phone. "Crud. The battery's dead. What happened?"

"We were hit," Margot said, giving Sawyer an uncertain look.

Annie dug her fingers into her temple. "We? You were supposed to be spending the night with Edie."

Margot shifted her weight and stared out the window.

"She was with my brother," Sawyer said with a tired frown.

"Archer? Margot, you were out driving with Archer? Alone?"

"Yes, but . . . " Margot shook her head, curls bouncing around her shoulders. "But it's not like it sounds."

"No buts. I'm responsible for you while you're in Brightwater."

"First—I'm eighteen," Margot said, like a stubborn child. "Second—he wasn't . . . we weren't . . . "

Sawyer clasped a hand on Margot's shoulder. "Why don't you go upstairs, take the pain pill prescribed by the doc and go to bed?" The younger girl flounced out without a backward look.

"I was handling that," Annie snapped. "You shouldn't have interfered."

"You were misunderstanding the situation. Archer

was taking her home. Edie got one of her migraines during the concert."

Annie gave a huffy laugh. "That's what he says. You know what he's like."

"My brother might be a lot of things, but he's no liar," Sawyer said tightly. He sat heavily and focused on the real estate papers spread across the kitchen table. "So it's true then. You've been made an offer."

"How did you—"

He looked straight at her, his gaze almost furious. "A private buyer, very discreet?"

Annie nodded uncertainly. What was going on?

"I was going to talk to you about this earlier, before we got distracted. Your buyer is Ruby." His smile was humorless. "You are selling Five Diamonds to Ruby, Annie."

"What?" Annie jerked with surprise. "I didn't know, I swear."

Sawyer set his hat on the table with a heavy sigh. "Maybe not, but that's what's happening. She was also driving the car that hit Archer and Margot, and blew twice the legal limit. She's damn lucky no one was killed."

Ruby had driven drunk and hit Margot? Red rage rose behind Annie's eyes. "I am going to murder her with my own bare hands."

"She's at the station with Leroy, I recused myself before I did just that. Annie, I've tried not to push you on this, but why? Why do you have to sell?"

"It—It's so much money, Sawyer. Insane money, the kind that can set you up for a whole new life."

"But money isn't what matters to you, Annie. I know you."

"Be fair. The property isn't only mine, Sawyer. Claire owns a stake, and so does my dad. There's no way I'll sell to Ruby." She reached out her hand. "But I have to sell. I *have* to."

"Tell me. What am I?" He stepped away until all she had in her grasp was empty air. "Someone good enough to fuck but not good enough to settle down with?"

"Sawyer." She flinched. "No, stop."

"I've tried to be patient and take it slow. And where has it gotten me? I've been here before. But with you, it hurts a lot more." He turned around and kissed her hard, past the point of sense. His tongue, angry and demanding, tangled with hers and drew out a response despite any wish to the contrary. She was fisting her fingers into his hair before she could form a coherent thought, and then he tugged her free and stepped away.

"Anyone can do that, fit their body parts together," he growled, breathing hard. "It doesn't mean anything. That's what people say about flings, right? We do what feels good in the moment and walk away."

"Sawyer," Annie gasped. "Listen to me. You aren't a fling."

"I think that's exactly what I am. But I'm not sticking around to watch another woman walk out of my life because Brightwater isn't good enough—because I'm not good enough. Especially not if that woman is you. I can't do that—I won't."

"Sawyer, I don't know what to do. I don't know what's right." Her voice was quivering.

"Do what you need to do." He bunched his hands into fists. "Sell and leave Brightwater, Annie. Go to San Francisco and chase your perfect dream. But tonight? I'm the one who is walking away."

Chapter Twenty-Eight

ANNIE SAT UNTIL dawn, hollowed by a lack of sleep and faith. Five Diamonds would never go to Ruby. Time to hire another real estate agent because Mr. King had a serious conflict of interest representing his daughter in the deal without making a full disclosure.

Sawyer didn't return, not that she expected him to. The look on his face before he'd slammed the back door dashed all her hopes about their future. She'd strung him on for too long and he finally cut ties. Maybe she needed to do the same. She opened her laptop, went to her blog and hovered her finger over the delete button.

Wait.

What if . . . what if she tried one last thing?

Her fingers inched toward the keyboard and the words started flying.

Dear Readers,

Hey there! So from here on out I'm going to make some changes on the blog. What I've shown to date has been my life, but only the very best parts. And you know what? I think that's okay. I think people can share whatever they choose about themselves, whenever they want. But here's the thing. For a long time, I've wondered if maybe I need to share a little more balance. Not my dirty dishes in the sink. You probably have enough in yours, but at least acknowledge that I have them. Or that sometimes I get so tired that I've fallen asleep eating my dinner while my son talks to me. Or that I am not perfect.

My life is far from perfect.

I made this space to celebrate the little things in my day because it's hard work to parent, to be a woman. But we all need to be kinder to each other. To take a break. To stop judging and comparing. If your grass is green, that doesn't make mine brown. If I'm having a win, that doesn't mean you need to lose. I'm sorry if I've ever projected something that made people here feel inadequate, but at the same time, if I have, was it really me? Because no one can make you feel anything except for yourself. Only you are the boss of you, and I am the boss of me. I am 100% stealing this language from Atticus, by the way. He very much wishes he could be the boss of me. And to eat cupcakes for breakfast every morning.

It's time to stop portraying things how I wish they would be. I want to find joy in how they actually are, and sometimes that truth is messier, less lovely, more raw. Some days I might not be able to post here, because I want to take my son for a hike and not bring my camera, just a packed lunch and a butterfly net.

Since I've been in Brightwater, something's happened to me. I've fallen in love. No, even that's not the right word. I've remembered love. I've remembered myself and found the courage, banged up and rusty, from my youth, of when I'd jump. I used to cliff jump. Can you believe it? I would climb high over the swimming hole and laugh the whole way down.

Falling is scarier now. There seems to be more at stake. More to lose. More opportunity for things to go wrong and break, like Humpty Dumpty.

But no one said falling is easy, or even that it always has to be fun.

And when you find yourself, sometimes there might be things there that you don't want to see, maybe truths about yourself that you wish weren't there. Life has a funny way of denting us all in ways that will never fully be fixed. But if you are lucky, one day you might find someone who loves those banged-up parts.

They might even see you make terrible mistakes and forgive.

I've been hurt by the person that I love here. But I do forgive. And now I have nothing to offer but my own imperfect self who is ready to love him with my whole heart.

She hit send and held her breath.

So, there was that.

Done.

Atticus screamed from the yard, a good scream, a happy sound. She ran to the back door and saw him rolling around on the ground with Maverick and a host of little puppies that uncannily resembled the German Shepherd. First, where on earth had they come from? And second, how amazing. Her little boy, once terrified of dogs, took a chance, and he'd turned out better for it.

She looked around but saw no sign of Sawyer.

Her heart pounded in her ears. Where was he? He must be close because he'd never let his dog run free.

Maverick danced around the yard, scampering, wagging his tail and looking decidedly pleased with himself. The golden dog she'd seen before in the barn trotted around the corner and nuzzled the big German Shepherd before turning to round up the puppies and march them around the side of the house.

Well, well, well. It looked like Maverick had his own canine romance happening.

"Roo roo roo," answered Maverick, adding mind-reading to his list of tricks.

"Oh, you are a naughty one," Annie said, and Maverick wagged his tail harder.

"Morning." Annie turned, and Margot hovered in the doorway.

"Hey."

"So about Archer—"

"Look, I need to say something," Annie said. "I trust you." Last night, she'd let panic override common sense. Margot never lied to her in the past, so there was no good reason for her to start now. "I'm sorry for the things I said. I was afraid of you being hurt, and I feel responsible. You aren't my daughter, but I love you like one."

Margot ducked her head. "I wasn't trying to do anything wrong. Besides, you don't have to worry about Archer."

Annie walked up the stairs and wrapped her in a big hug. "I'm protective of you, and he has a reputation."

"He's cute and fun and funny, but trust me, whenever *she's* around, she's all he sees."

"She?"

"Edie. The owner of Haute Coffee. Archer is totally in love with her."

"That's crazy." The quiet refined barista and Sawyer's bad-boy cowboy brother? The idea didn't compute.

"It's true. He loves her. But you know what? She won't look at him. I watch him, watch her. No one is happy."

"Who . . . who does Edie watch?"

"Nobody. She just looks away. I don't get it. I thought that when you're older, you figure life out."

"Oh, honey." Should she tell her it got easier? No—no lies. "Love is so much more than the rush of attraction. That's a fun part, no doubt, but it's not the sum total."

"So what is it? Tell me what love is, and don't say I'm too young to understand."

"Tell you what love is?" *Jesus, no pressure.* "It's . . . it's what's left, what remains even on the days you don't feel pretty or want to laugh or even try. One day you'll find a guy who will see you at your worst, but all he'll remember is you at your best. That's love, true love."

"Is that how it is with you and Sawyer?"

"I think . . . yeah. It is."

"So what are you going to do? I heard you guys fighting last night."

Annie looked out at Maverick in the yard. He lifted his head and tilted back his ears.

Shit, I really screwed things up, didn't I?

Maverick gave a low woof, as a further reproach or encouragement? Hard to say.

"I'm going to go next door and see him. Because he needs me as much as I need him. He's been there for me and I need to be there for him too."

Margot smiled. "Go. I'll watch Atticus."

"You sure?"

"Yep. I'm going to eat a pint of ice cream out in the sunshine while he plays with the puppies."

"That sounds nice."

Margot gave a slow smile. "It does. And, Annie, good luck. I hope everything works out for you."

"No boy, not that way!" Annie patted her leg, eyeing the open door into Grandma Kane's farmhouse. "Don't go in there. Don't . . . "

Apparently Maverick was the boss of himself too. He trotted straight into the old ranch house, tail high.

Crap and crud. Maybe she could leave him there and run for it. But she needed to see Sawyer and couldn't turn up without his dog.

She trudged toward the door, the musical score from

The Exorcist playing in her mind. The closer she got to the house, the more her heart rate increased. It was a beautiful summer day. The sky a vault of blue. Butterflies flitted from bush to bush. The sun spread warm along her neck like warm molasses. The door only two feet away. Inside came an ominous creak.

Grandma Kane stuck her head out and Annie shrieked, pressing a hand to her heart. Holy buckets, if the woman said, "Heeeeeere's Johnny," all bets were off. She'd run screaming over the mountains.

Screw up your courage. Hold your ground, soldier. Need to recover Maverick. No pooch left behind.

"Sawyer's dog ran off."

"So I see."

"I'll go get him."

The German Shepherd appeared next to Grandma, nose high in good cheer. "Roo roo roo," he said.

Was he messing with her?

"Come on, boy." She stepped forward and realized Grandma's posture was odd. She was a skinny woman but she obviously tried to fill the doorway. What did she have to hide? Oh, lord. Maybe there really were a pile of chicken bones in there. She shouldn't look. She should go, get out while the getting was good. Otherwise she might find herself auditioning for the role of Bluebeard's unlucky lady love.

Instead, she was Lot's wife. Her gaze swung back, almost of its own volition, and connected to a desktop in the living room.

The fact Grandma had a computer wasn't what made

her gasp. Older people often surfed the web, read the news, did all the things. Technology could help increase accessibility, had all sorts of benefits for senior citizens.

Except what was on the screen wasn't recipes, or an Amazon book order, or even a page titled "Chicken Killing Made Easy."

It was *Musings of a Mighty Mama*.

A chill swept through Annie's bones and rattled her teeth.

"You read my blog?"

"No."

Annie pointed at the computer. "It's open on your screen."

"It's not." Grandma Kane's eyes narrowed as she channeled a strange intensity.

"Are you trying to Jedi mind trick me?" This was weird, too weird to handle. Better she get away before saying something she'd regret. "Never mind. I need to go home," Annie said, moving to leave.

"What do you know about home?" the older woman retorted.

"Please." Annie turned back, setting her jaw. "I don't want trouble." But she wouldn't back down to this old woman either.

"I don't think you know the first thing about what you want."

Tonight as she was trying to fall asleep, no doubt the perfect snappy retort would come. For now, she had nothing, so might as well offer up the truth. "You're right."

Grandma Kane ducked her chin, visibly taken aback. She peered through her bifocals. "Who are you, Annabelle Carson?"

"Good question."

"Because I see someone who is trying herself on, but you're not a pair of shoes. I knew your grandparents, I didn't like them, but they worked hard."

"They did."

"So did the people before them."

"Yes. I know," Annie replied testily.

"And you're going to sell it off." Grandma's voice was thick with disgust.

"I don't have a choice."

"There's always a choice." She paused, overwhelmed by a coughing fit. "What are you doing with my grandson?"

"I don't think that's your business," Annie snapped.

"He's blood—that makes it my business. I haven't gotten to where I have by letting people mess with me and mine."

"Does everything around here have to be so dramatic? God, you'd think we were in a Francis Ford Coppola movie. We're neighbors, not Mafioso."

Grandma cleared her throat. "You're a fine one to talk about drama."

"What's that supposed to mean?"

"What you post on the computer. Those stories about yourself, your day, who you are, what you do. That's not who you are, Annabelle. Not all of you anyway."

Realization threatened to strike her dumb. "You. You are *her*."

Grandma folded her arms and glared.

Everything clicked into place. The mean messages she'd been receiving on the blog, those were all Grandma Kane. "You are Ms. Hootenanny, aren't you?"

"Maybe I am, maybe I'm not."

"Does Sawyer know?"

"That boy doesn't even have a Tweeter account."

"Twitter."

"You get my point."

Annie shook her head. "Why would you send all those mean comments to me? Seriously, what have I ever done to you?"

"Are you deaf?" She coughed again. "None of this is about me."

"I don't understand."

"I'm not going to be around forever." Grandma coughed again, pounding her chest with a fist. "I love two things in this world—this ranch and those three boys. Sawyer deserves someone real. Someone worthy of him. Look at you, the way you take those pretty pictures, showing all the good things and none of the bad."

"Isn't that what everyone does? In a conversation, if someone asks how you are doing, you don't answer, 'I have a headache, my son wet the bed at three a.m., and my husband divorced me to finger strangers.'"

Grandma Kane's mouth had been working double time to get a word in edgewise but the last part of the sentence shut her up.

"Sorry." Annie said on autopilot. "No, you know what? I'm not sorry. No one heard the stay-at-home mother's

voice a generation ago. And I do have journalist creden-
tials, not that it even matters. What you are doing is tan-
tamount to bullying, and you know what happens when
you sling dirt. You get dirty."

"You are leaving town and selling your history to a
woman who couldn't care about it less, a woman who dis-
respected my Sawyer, *your* Sawyer, and who will respect
the land even worse than your father."

"I'd think you'd be happy to see the door slam on the
kooky Carsons once and for all."

"Is that it?" Grandma narrowed her eyes, coughing
into her handkerchief. "Or is it that you don't want us?"

"Of course I want into the Brightwater club. It's what
I've always wanted. A place to belong. A place where
people know my name. Care about me. Care about my
family. My life. I had that on Five Diamonds but never in
town. And how I feel toward your grandson is . . . is . . . is
the best part of me. I love him."

"Annie."

She closed her eyes, hearing Sawyer's deep voice
behind her. Grandma knew he was there? Maverick knew
and hadn't so much as wagged a tail.

She was tricked into confessing her love for Sawyer,
and worse, she'd told his grandma, not him.

"I do. Okay." She threw up her hands. "I love you,
Sawyer. There. I said it. Happy?"

"No. I'm not happy," he said quietly. "Because you are
leaving."

She cried now, in public, on the steps in front of his
crazy grandma. "You are the best man I've ever known.

Will ever know. You fix all my broken pieces, and what you put back together feels better than the way things were before. Stronger. Sturdier. A little worn, but hey, that's the fashion. You . . . you repurpose me."

"But you want to move to the city, start again."

"Because I'm afraid—afraid of staying here, and having the town hate me. Never being welcome because of my last name. Imagine family reunions, picnics, everyone ostracizing me, and worse, Atticus. I can't do that to a sensitive little boy."

"But this is your home," he said softly.

"No, you are my home," she answered, wiping her eyes. "But I love you too much to ask you to sign on to something that's going to be too hard."

"See, what did I say?" Grandma Kane sounded smug. I've always known Carsons are damn fools. This land is for working people, and that's what love is—it's hard work."

Annie whirled around. "I want to make him happy, more than anything, but the family, the feud . . ."

Grandma regarded her steadily. "This town listens to me. If I say we are accepting the kooky Carsons, it's as good as done."

"You . . . you'd do that?"

"If you don't sell the land."

"That's the deal. You want my farm? And in return you'll give me Sawyer and peace."

"Grandma—" Sawyer stepped forward. "That's not okay."

"What?" the old woman snapped. "Why does everyone suspect me of dealing so dirty?"

"Because you are The Don of Brightwater," Annie answered testily. "Besides, you were my blogging stalker."

"What?" Sawyer looked between them.

"I wanted to test your mettle," Grandma said unapologetically. "See what you were made of."

"You wanted to get to know me? You could have invited me over for a cup of coffee."

"So what say you? Don't sell the farm and you get Sawyer and my blessing."

"What about me? I'm standing right here," Sawyer said tightly.

"I'm handling this, boy," Grandma snapped.

"He's not a boy." Annie stepped forward. "He's a man. He's my man. And I don't need your permission to be with him." Here she was, staring down the heart of the matter, and all she could see was Sawyer. The rest was details. "If you want to set the whole Kane family on me, I'll take it. I was wrong to care about all that. And as for Atticus, what he really needs more than anything in his life is love. And he'll see that, between me and Sawyer. Real love. I've been scared of all the wrong things."

A hand gripped her arm and she turned, staring into Sawyer's face, his expression tight with restrained emotion. "Are you saying—"

"Ruby doesn't get to win," she whispered, placing a hand on his cheek. "Not on Five Diamonds or continuing to harass you. Quincy Bankcroft offered me a position as editor in chief of the *Brightwater Bugle*, and I'll accept it. We're going to complement it with online lifestyle stories.

A good idea, seeing as most everyone and their grandma out here uses a computer."

Grandma Kane at least had the good sense to look abashed.

Sawyer cupped her chin in his hands. "You mean it." His eyes shown. "You will stay in Brightwater? Give us a shot?"

"There's no shot." Annie covered his hands with hers. "I'm an all-in kind of girl, remember? I don't wade. I jump."

He kissed her hard then and it felt like falling, and strangely enough, falling felt exactly like flying.

Grandma laughed. "Go on then, get."

"What's so funny?" Sawyer asked.

Grandma chortled. "You two."

"You act like everything is going to your wishes," Annie said.

"Because it is," she responded haughtily.

Annie shook her head. "I'm not giving you Five Diamonds."

"Maybe not me, but you forget, I care about family, not soldiers. You marry Sawyer and you become a Kane. Then the Kanes get Five Diamonds no matter what," she said with a cackle.

"Grandma," Sawyer said, warning in his voice.

"I've got this handled." Annie released Sawyer and walked toward the old woman, still snickering at her cleverness.

Annie froze at the bottom step. "You're right. What I have will be Sawyer's, but you forget, what is Sawyer's will also be mine." She looked around at Hidden Rock Ranch. "Home sweet home. I've always liked this place."

The laughter dried in Grandma's throat. "Now you see here, missy."

Sawyer started laughing. "She's got you there, Grandma. And little grandbabies will be running around someday with both our blood. Who knows, maybe they'll inherit everything."

Annie walked back toward him. "I always have wanted more children. And I have the perfect name for our first one. Carson. Little Carson Kane."

"At least I've got other grandsons. I'll get them fixed up right." Grandma walked back toward the house shaking her head.

Sawyer smiled at her, and the joke swelled her heart, because as she said it she knew this was real. She'd have more children with him, build a life. And this time when they both started laughing, it was real, and it was good. So very good.

"I need to call my dad and tell him I'm refusing the offer. He's going to freak out, but I don't know what to do," she said, taking his hand.

He gave her a reassuring squeeze. "I can come live at Five Diamonds."

"But you have your cabin. You love it. I love it too." She looked out at the mountains. "I have to believe again."

"In what?"

"Magic. Let's go back to the farm. I'm going to call my sister. She'll help me break the news."

As ANNIE PUT down the phone, Sawyer frowned, unable to read her face. "What's happened?"

"A miracle," Annie whispered. "My sister, Claire, is going to buy Five Diamonds from Dad—offer enough so he can get his place in Mexico."

His stomach twisted even as his chest swelled. "Come again?"

"She said after she was here that she reconsidered her priorities. Once she heard I wanted to stay in Brightwater, she said we could still make our plan work, the one where we are neighbors."

"But her job in San Francisco . . . "

"She'll keep doing it for now. But she'll come out every chance she gets. She wants to remodel the main house and get to work hiring a contractor. I can live here for now with Atticus, and then soon . . . "

He liked how she flushed. "Yeah. I want my home to be yours too."

"I like the sound of that."

He enfolded her in his arms and breathed deep. "Annie Girl."

"So we are doing this, me and you, for real?"

He kissed her slow. "Forever."

Epilogue

ATTICUS THREW A stick for Maverick and the dog ran long, leaping to catch it in his mouth.

"Score!" Atticus threw his hands up in victory before chasing after him. He had been allowed to select a puppy from the litter before the rest were adopted into neighborhood homes, and he'd chose the runt, naming it Orion after the first constellation Sawyer taught him.

Maverick turned and tackled Atticus, licking him from chin to forehead. Annie froze, heart in her mouth, but her son only shrieked with laughter, hooking his arms around the big dog with glee. Orion yipped and jumped on Atticus's stomach.

The sun dropped behind Mount Oh-Be-Joyful and the peak reflected the fire that grew in Annie's heart, the warm crackle of a hearth. She realized she hummed under her breath.

Sawyer left the telescope he'd set up, walked over,

helping her to her feet. He led her in a few dance steps while she kept up the tune.

"You bet I could never get you to dance." She curved her mouth into a coy smile. "Looks like you owe me."

"This is true." He grinned in that easy way that made her melt. "Name your price."

She tapped her chin. "I demand a kiss, Sheriff."

"Guess I better pay up." Sawyer stepped back and pulled her to the quilt.

"Mmmm, good idea." She snuggled against his broad chest, craving the body heat radiating through his flannel button-down. "Don't want you getting in trouble with the law."

"Yeah, better not mess with those guys."

"Well," she whispered against his ear. "I'd kind of sort of planned to mess with one of them."

"Got to say"—he leaned close and traced his index finger under her chin, brushing the sensitive skin beneath her jaw—"it's not a chore being in your debt." His kiss tasted of warm apples and cinnamon sugar with enough spice to send her bare toes curling into the dewy grass.

"Don't you think it's kind of funny?" She held him as tight as he held her. "To think all this time my happy ending was waiting here, at home, with you?"

He shook his head. "Our story isn't going to end, Annie Girl. When those mountains out there become nothing but empty spaces, and this world stops spinning, it won't matter, because we'll be somewhere else, somewhere better, forever burning bright."

Right on the horizon, where night and day met, a shooting star blazed, the glittering trail of dust illuminating the dark. "You make me believe in magic again," she said.

"I believe in us." Sawyer's steadfast gaze held infinite promise.

Keep reading for a sneak peek of Lia Riley's next fantastic
Brightwater novel

RIGHT WRONG GUY

Sometimes two wrongs can make a right. . .

Bad-boy wrangler Archer Kane lives fast and loose.
Words like "responsibility" and "commitment" send
him running in the opposite direction—until a wild
Vegas weekend puts him on a collision course with
Eden Bankcroft-Kew, a New York heiress running away
from her blackmailing fiancé . . . on the morning of their
wedding.

Eden has never understood the big attraction of cowboys.
Give her a guy in a tailored suit any day of the week. That
is, until all she can think about is Mr. Rugged Handsome, six feet of sinfully sexy country charm with a pair
of green eyes that keep her tossing and turning.

Archer might be the wrong guy for a woman like her, but
she's also wrong to think he'll walk away without fighting
for her heart. And maybe, just maybe, two wrongs can
make a right.

Available August 2015

An Excerpt from
RIGHT WRONG GUY

ARCHER KANE PLUCKED a dangly gold nipple tassel off his cheek and sat in the king-sized bed, scrubbing his face. The trick lay in not disturbing the two women snoring on either side of him. Overturned furniture, empty shot glasses and champagne flutes littered the hotel room while a red thong dangled from the flat screen. He inched his fingers to grab the Stetson resting atop the tangled comforter. Vegas trips were about fillies and fun--mission accomplished.

Right?

"What the—" A dove dive-bombed him, swooped to his left, and perched on the room service cart to peck at a peanut from what appeared to be the remnants of a large hot fudge sundae. Who knew how a bird got in here, but at least the ice cream explained why his chest hair was sticky, and farther below, chocolate-covered fingerprints

framed his six-pack. Just to be on the safe side, he tugged
the sheet lower for a status check. Looked like he'd had
one helluva night. Too bad he couldn't remember a damn
thing. He should be high-fiving himself, but instead, he
just felt dog-tired. This Vegas trip hadn't been like the
others and waking in strange women's hotel rooms didn't
hold the same old thrill.

He emerged from beneath the covers and crawled to
the bottom of the bed, head pounding like a bass drum.
As he stood, the prior evening returned in splintered
fragments. Blondie, on the right, cuddling his empty
pillow, was Crystal Balls aka The Stripping Magician.
The marquee from her show advertised, "She has nothing
up her sleeve." Dark-hair on the left had been the assis-
tant . . . *Destiny? Dallas? Daisy?*

Something with a D.

How in Houdini they'd all ended up in bed together
was where the facts got fuzzy.

A feather-trimmed sequined gown crumpled by the
mini bar and an old man ventriloquist's dummy appeared to track his furtive movements from the corner.
Archer stepped over a shattered champagne bottle and
crept toward the bathroom. Next mission? A thorough
shower followed by the strongest coffee on the strip.

Coffee. Yes. Soon. Plus a short stack of buttermilk
pancakes, a Denver omelet and enough bacon to require
the sacrifice of a dozen hogs. Starving didn't come close
to describing the hollow feeling in his gut, as if he'd
run a sub-four-hour marathon, scaled Everest and then
wrestled a two-ton longhorn. His reflection stared back

from the bathroom mirror, circles under his green eyes and thick morning scruff. For the last year a discontented funk had risen within him. How many times had he insisted he was too young to be tied down to a serious committed relationship, job . . . or anything? Well, at twenty-seven he might not be geriatric, but he was getting too old for this bed-hopping shit.

"What the hell are you doing?" he muttered to himself.

Mr. Brightwater wasn't looking his best. His cousin, Kit, had given him that nickname after he'd graced the cover of a "Boys of Brightwater" town calendar last year to support the local Lions Club. He'd been February and posed holding a red cardboard heart over his johnson to avoid an X-rating, although, as his big brother Sawyer had dryly noted, "Not like most women around here haven't already seen it."

In fairness, Brightwater, California, didn't host a large population. For a healthy man who liked the ladies, it didn't take long to make the rounds at *The Dirty Shame*, the local watering hole. Trips to Vegas meant variety, a chance to spice things up. Although a threesome with Crystal and Diamond—*Deborah? Deena? Dazzle?*—was akin to swallowing a whole habanero.

He reached into the shower and flicked on the tap as a warm furry body hopped across his foot. "Shit!" He vaulted back, nearly going ass over teakettle, before bracing himself on the counter. A bewildered white rabbit peered up, nose twitching.

"You've got to be kidding me." He peered into the

steam with increased suspicion. Hopefully, Crystal's act didn't also involve a baby crocodile or, worse, a boa constrictor. He hated snakes.

The coast was clear so he stepped inside, the hot water sending him halfway to human. There was a tiny bottle of hotel shampoo perched in the soap dish and he gave it a dubious sniff. It smelled like flowers but would do the job of rinsing away stale perfume and sex. He worked a dollop through his thick hair, shoulder muscles relaxing.

He'd always prided himself in being the kind of good-time guy who held no regrets, but lately it seemed like there was a difference between dwelling on past mistakes, and reflecting in order to avoid future ones. Did he really want to live out these shallow morning-after scenarios forever like some warped version of Groundhog Day?

The hair on the back of his neck tingled with the unmistakable sensation of being watched. He swiped suds from his eyes and turned, nearly nose to nose with the blank stare of the old man ventriloquist's dummy.

"Fuck," he barked, any better word lost in the shock.

"Great Uncle Sam don't like it when menfolk cuss," the dummy responded in a deep, Southern drawl. Other than the puppet on her hand, Dixie-Dorothy-Darby wore nothing but a suggestive smile.

"Uh . . . morning." He plastered on his trademark grin. Time to charm his way out of here.

"No one's ever made me come so hard." The puppet's mustache bobbed as he spoke, and more of last night's drunken jigsaw snapped into place. Desdemona-Diana-Doris had gone on (and on) about her dream to become a professional ventriloquist. She'd brought out the puppet and made Old Uncle Sam dirty talk, which had been hilarious after Tequila Slammers, Snake Bites, Buttery Nipples, and 5 Deadly Venoms, plus a few bottles of champagne.

It was a whole lot less funny now.

"Hey, D, you mind giving me a sec? I'm going to finish off here." When in doubt, refer to a woman by their first initial. Made you look affectionate instead of like an ass-hole.

"D?" rumbled Great Uncle Sam.

Damn. Apparently an initial wasn't going to cut it.

Okay think . . . Dinah? No. Two rocks glinted from her lobes—a possible namesake. "Diamond?"

Great Uncle Sam slowly shook his head. Maybe it was Archer's imagination, but the painted eyes narrowed fractionally. "Stormy."

And so was her expression.

Shit, not even close.

"Stormy?" he repeated blankly. "Yeah, Stormy, of course. Beautiful name, makes me think of rain and . . . and . . . rainbows . . . and . . . "

"You called it out enough last night, the least you could do is be a gentleman and remember it in the morning!" Great Uncle Sam head-butted him. Terrific, add splitting headache to his current list of troubles.

Archer scrambled from the shower before he got his bare ass taken down by a puppet. You didn't fight back against a woman, even if they were trying to bash your brain in with Pinocchio's deranged elderly uncle.

"Get the hell out," Stormy said in her own voice, which sounded a lot more Jersey Shore than gentile Georgian peach farmer. She wasn't half bad at the whole ventriloquist gig, but now wasn't the time to offer compliments.

He threw on his Levis commando style while Stormy eyed his package, ready to go full-scale hurricane on his junk. Scooping his red Western shirt off the floor, he made a break for the bedroom. His boots were by the door but his hat was still on the bed, specifically, on Crystal's head. Her sleepy expression gave way to confusion as Stormy sprang from the bathroom, Great Uncle Sam leading the charge.

"What's going on?" Crystal said just as Stormy bellowed, "I'm going to kick your ass back into whatever cowpoke hole you crawled from."

Hat? Boots? Hat or boots? Archer only had time to grab one. He slung his arms through the shirt, not bothering to snap the pearl clasps, and grabbed the hand-tooled boots while hurtling into the hall. Yeah, definitely getting too old for this shit.

"Lovely meeting you fine ladies," he called over one shoulder as the dove swooped.

He bypassed the elevator bay in favor of the stairwell. Once he'd descended three floors, he paused to tug on his boots and his phone rang. Pulling it out from his back pocket, he groaned at the screen. Grandma Kane.

He could let it go to voice mail. In fact, he was tempted to do just that, but the thing about Grandma was she called back until you picked up.

With a heavy sigh, and a prayer for two Tylenol tablets, he hit answer. "How's my favorite grandma in the world?" he boomed, propping the phone between his ear and shoulder and snapping together his shirt.

"Quit with your smooth talk, boy," Grandma snapped. "Where are you?"

"Just leaving church," he lied smoothly.

"Better not be the Little Chapel of Love."

"What do you—"

"Don't feed me bullhickey. You're in Vegas again."

Sawyer must have squeaked. As Brightwater sheriff, he was into upright citizenship and moral standing, nobler than George Washington and his fucking cherry tree.

"Did you forget our plans this weekend?"

"Plans?" He wracked his brain but thinking hurt. So did walking down these stairs. Come to think of it, so did breathing. He needed that coffee and bacon in a hurry.

Grandma made a rude noise. "To go over the accounts for Hidden Rock. You promised to set up the new purchase order software on the computer."

Shit. His shoulders slumped. He had offered to help. Grandma ran a large, profitable cattle ranch, but the Hidden Rock's inventory management was archaic, and the accounting practically done by abacus. In his hurry to see if an impromptu Vegas roadtrip could overcome his funk, the meeting had slipped his mind. "Let me make it up to you—"

"Your charm has no currency here, boy." Grandpa Kane had died before Archer was born and Grandma had never remarried. Perhaps he should introduce her to

Stormy's Great Uncle Sam. Those two were a match made in heaven. They could spend their spare time busting his balls.

He closed his eyes and massaged his forehead. "Guess I forgot."

"Funny—guess you're too busy using women like disposable silverware." Grandma's tone sounded anything but amused. "Even more funny will be when I forget to put you in my will."

Grandma's favorite threat was disinheriting him. Who cared? The guy voted "Biggest Partier" and "Class Flirt" his senior year at Brightwater High was also the least likely to run Hidden Rock Ranch.

The line went dead. At least she didn't ask why he couldn't be more like Sawyer anymore.

Whatever. Archer had it good, made great tips as a wrangler at a dude ranch. His middle brother took life seriously enough and he hadn't seen his oldest one in years. Wilder worked as a smoke jumper in Montana. Sometimes Archer wondered what would happen if he cruised to Big Sky Country and paid him a surprise visit--maybe he had multiple sister wives or was a secret war lord.

Growing up, after their parents died in a freak house fire, they all slipped into roles. Wilder withdrew, brooding and angry, Sawyer became Mr. Nice Guy, always the teacher's pet or offering to do chores. Archer rounded things out by going for laughs, practical jokes and causing trouble because someone had to remind everyone else not to take life so seriously. None of them were getting out alive.

Archer kept going down the flights of stairs, tucking in his shirt. Grandma's words played on a loop in his mind. "Using women like disposable silverware."

A good time was all he wanted. And Lord knew, those women used him right back.

It was fun, didn't mean anything.

Meaningless. He ground his jaw so tight his teeth hurt. Casual sex on pool tables, washing machines, countertops, and lawn chairs filled his physical needs, but these random hook ups were starting to make him feel more and more alone.

On the ground floor, he pushed open the door with extra force. There were two corridors. He turned left for no reason other than that was the hand he favored. Seemed as if he chose wisely because a side entrance was just ahead. He walked outside, wincing at the morning sun even as he took a gulp of fresh air. Well, fresh for the Vegas Strip, but a far cry from the Eastern Sierra's clean mountain breeze. His heart stirred. He'd have his breakfast and get on the road. As much as he liked leaving Brightwater, he always missed home.

Archer reached to adjust his hat and grabbed a handful of wet hair instead. Twelve stories above, a stripping magician had found herself a mighty fine Stetson. Everyone wanted him to take more responsibility, but someone had to have the fun.

He stepped onto the street, jumping back onto the

curb when a city bus turned, the side covered by a shoe ad poster and the slogan, "Can You Run Forever?"

Sure. Hell, he'd been running from accountability, stability, and boring routines his whole life.

Another thought crept in and sank its roots deep. Was he running from those things, or letting his fears of commitment and responsibility run him instead?

About the Author

After studying at the University of Montana-Missoula, LIA RILEY scoured the world armed with only a backpack, overconfidence, and a terrible sense of direction. She counts shooting vodka with a Ukrainian mechanic in Antarctica, sipping yerba mate with gauchos in Chile, and swilling fourex with station hands in Outback Australia among her accomplishments.

A British literature fanatic at heart, Lia considers Mr. Darcy and Edward Rochester as her fictional boyfriends. Her very patient husband doesn't mind. Much. When not torturing heroes (because c'mon, who doesn't love a good tortured hero?), Lia herds unruly chickens, camps, beach combs, daydreams about as-of-yet unwritten books, wades through a mile-high TBR pile, and schemes yet another trip. Right now, Icelandic hot springs and Scottish castles sound mighty fine.

She and her family live mostly in Northern California.

Discover great authors, exclusive offers, and more at hc.com.

Give in to your Impulses . . .
Continue reading for excerpts from
our newest Avon Impulse books.
Available now wherever e-books are sold.

HEART'S DESIRE
By T.J. Kline

DESIRE ME NOW
By Tiffany Clare

THE WEDDING GIFT
A SAVE THE DATE NOVELLA
By Cara Connelly

WHEN LOVE HAPPENS
RIBBON RIDGE BOOK THREE
By Darcy Burke

An Excerpt from

HEART'S DESIRE
by T.J. Kline

Jessie Hart has a soft spot for healing the
broken, especially horses and children, but her
business is failing. The one man who can save
Heart Fire Ranch is the last man she wants to see,
the man who broke her heart eight years ago . . .

Jessie heard the crunch of tires on the gravel driveway and stepped onto the porch of the enormous log home. Her parents had raised their family here, in the house her father had built just before her brother was born. The scent of pine surrounded her, warming her insides. Even after her brother and sister had built houses of their own on either end of the property, she'd remained here with her parents, helping them operate the dude ranch and training their horses. She inhaled deeply, wishing again that circumstances hadn't been so cruel as to leave her to figure out how to make the transition from dude ranch to horse rescue alone.

Leaning against the porch railing, she sipped her coffee and enjoyed the quiet of the morning. When a teen girl walked toward the barn to feed the horses, she lifted her hand in a wave. The poor girl was spending more time at the ranch than away from it these days, since her mother had violated parole again, but Jessie loved having her here. Aleta's foster mother, June, had been close friends with Jessie's own mother, and she understood the healing power horses had on kids who needed someone, or something, just to listen. Now that Aleta was living with June again, she was spending a lot of time at the ranch.

Jessie looked down the driveway as Bailey drove her truck closer to the house. She could just make out Nathan through the glare on the windshield. The resentment in her belly grew with each ticking second at the sight of him. Clenching her jaw and squaring her shoulders for the battle ahead, Jessie walked down the stairs to meet Justin's former best friend and the man who'd broken her heart.

The truck pulled to a stop in front of her, and Bailey jumped from the driver's seat wearing a shit-eating grin. Jessie narrowed her eyes, knowing exactly what that meant—she was in for a week of hell from this pain-in-the-ass, penny-pinching bean counter.

She didn't understand why he'd insisted on returning to the ranch. If Justin hadn't begged her to give Nathan a chance to help, she would have been perfectly content never to speak to his lying ass again.

She watched him turn his broad shoulders to her as he removed his luggage from the back seat. When he faced her, Jessie was barely able to contain her gasp of surprise. After he left, she'd avoided any mention of Nathan Kerrington like the plague, going as far as changing the channel when his name was mentioned on the news. She'd been praying that the past eight years had been cruel, that he'd gained a potbelly, or that he'd developed a receding hairline. She pictured him turning into a stereotypical computer geek.

This guy was perfection. Well, if she was into muscular men who looked like Hollywood actors and wore suits that cost several thousand dollars. Every strand of his dark brown hair was combed into place, even at six in the morning, after a flight from New York. There wasn't a wrinkle in his stiffly starched shirt.

His green eyes slid over her dirty jeans and T-shirt before climbing back up to focus on her face. Memories of stolen kisses and lingering caresses filled her mind before she could cast them aside. His slow perusal sent heat curling in her belly, spreading through her veins, making her feel uncomfortable. Was he just trying to be an ass? If so, it was working. She felt on edge immediately, but she wasn't about to let him know it. She crossed her arms over her chest and kicked her hip to the side.

"Nathan Kerrington. You've got some brass ones showing up here."

An Excerpt from

DESIRE ME NOW

by Tiffany Clare

Amelia Grant has just escaped her lecherous
employer with nothing but the clothes on
her back. In the pre-dawn hours of London,
a horse and carriage comes barreling
down on her, and a stranger rushes to
her aid, sweeping her off her feet . . .

"**W**hy did you kiss me?" She wasn't sure she wanted to hear the answer, but a part of her needed to know. And talking was safer right now.

"I have wanted to do that since you first stumbled into my path. Do you feel something growing between us?"

She'd been ignoring that feeling, thinking and hoping it would pass with time. She'd assumed she'd developed hero worship after Mr. Riley had rescued her and then taken care of her when she'd been at an ultimate low.

She couldn't deny the truth now. She did feel something for him; something not easily defined as mere lust but a deep desire to learn more about him and why he made her feel so out of sorts with what she thought was right.

Not that she would ever admit to that.

Who was she to garner the attention of this man? Women probably threw themselves at his feet and begged him to ruin them on a regular basis. That thought left her feeling cold. She eyed the door, longing for escape.

"Do not leave, Amelia." He stepped closer to her, near enough that she could kiss him again if she so desired. She ignored that desire. "Work for me as we planned. Just stay."

There was a kind of desolation in his voice at the thought

of her abandoning him. But that was impossible. And she was reading too much into his request. Logically, she knew she couldn't feel this sort of attachment to someone she had just met. Someone she didn't really know.

"I am afraid of what I will do," she admitted, more for herself than for him.

"Then do not think about it. Go with what your instincts tell you. If there is one thing I have always done, it is to follow my first inclination. I would not be in the position I am today, had I ignored those natural reflexes."

He caressed her cheek again. She nearly nestled into his palm before realizing what she was doing. With a heavy sigh, she pulled away from him before she made any more mistakes. This was not a good way to start her first official day as his secretary.

She couldn't help but ask. "And what do your instincts say about me?"

"I do not need my instincts to tell me where this is going. It is more base than that. I desire you. And there is nothing that can stop me from fulfilling and exploring what I want. You will be mine in the end, Amelia."

Her heart picked up speed at his admission. Her breathing grew more rapid as she assessed him. She desired him too. She, Amelia Marie Somerset, who wanted nothing more than to escape one vile man's sick craving to marry her and claim her, was willing to let the man in front of her ruin her, only because she felt different with him than she had with anyone else.

What would she lose of herself in the process of courting dangerous games with this man? Focusing on the hard angles of his face and the steady expression he wore, one thing was certain.

This man would ruin her.

And more startling was the realization that she would do nothing to stop him.

An Excerpt from

THE WEDDING GIFT
A Save the Date Novella
by Cara Connelly

In the next Save the Date novella, mousey
Jan Marone finally allows herself to live,
laugh, and love . . . with a sexy fireman
during a weekend wedding in Key West!

"I'm sorry, ma'am, there's nothing I can do."

Jan Marone wrung her hands. "But I have a reservation."

"I know, I'm looking at it right here." The pretty blonde at the desk tapped her screen sympathetically. "I'll refund your deposit immediately."

"I don't want my deposit. I want a room. My cousin's getting married tomorrow, and I'm in the wedding."

The girl spread her hands. "The problem is, when one of the upstairs tubs overflowed this morning, the ceiling collapsed on your room. It's out of service for the weekend, and we're booked solid."

"I understand," Jan said, struggling to remain polite. Hearing the same excuse three times didn't make it easier to swallow. "How about a sister hotel?"

"We're independently owned. Paradise Inn is the oldest hotel on the island—"

Jan held up a hand. She knew the spiel. The large, rambling guesthouse was unique, and very Old Key West. Which was exactly why she'd booked it.

"Can you at least help me find a room somewhere else?"

"It's spring break. I'll make some calls, but . . ." A discouraging shrug and a gesture toward the coffeepot.

The girl didn't seem very concerned, but Jan smiled at her anyway. "Thanks, I appreciate you trying."

Parking her suitcase beside the coffee table, she surveyed the lobby wistfully. The windows and doors stood open, the wicker furniture and abundant potted plants blurring the line between indoors and out. The warm, humid breeze drifted through the airy space. Her parched Boston skin soaked it up like a sponge.

To a woman who'd never left New England before, it spelled tropical vacation. And it was slipping through her fingers like sand.

Growing ever gloomier, she wandered out through a side door and into a lush tropical garden—palm trees, hibiscus, a babbling waterfall.

Paradise.

And at its heart, a glittering pool, where six gorgeous feet of lean muscle and tanned skin drifted lazily on a float.

Ignoring everything else, Jan studied the man. Thick black hair, chiseled jaw, half smile curving full lips. And arms, perfect arms, draped over the sides, fingers trailing in the water.

He seemed utterly relaxed, the image of sensual decadence. Put him in an ad for Paradise Inn, and women would flock. Gay men would swarm.

As if sensing her attention, the hunk lifted his head and broke into a smile. "Hey Jan, getcha ass in the water!"

Mick McKenna. Her best and oldest friend.

He rolled off the float and jacked himself out of the pool. Water streamed from gray board shorts as he crossed the flagstones.

Stopping in front of her, he shook his hair like a Labrador.

"Geez! Don't you ever get tired of that?" She brushed droplets off her white cotton blouse.

He laughed his big, happy laugh. "Never have, never will. Get your suit on. The water's a perfect eighty-six degrees."

"I can't. They don't have a room for me."

The grin fell off his face. "What the hell?"

"Water damage." She shrugged like it wasn't tragic. Like she hadn't been anticipating this weekend for months.

"They must have another room." Mick started to go around her, no doubt to raise hell at the desk, McKenna-style.

She stopped him with a hand on his arm. "I tried everything. They're digging up a room for me somewhere else on the island."

He tunneled long fingers through his hair. "Take my room," he said.

An Excerpt from

WHEN LOVE HAPPENS
Ribbon Ridge Book Three
by Darcy Burke

In the third Ribbon Ridge novel from
USA Today bestseller Darcy Burke,
Tori Archer is about to discover that even the
best kept secrets don't stay buried for long . . .

Tori Archer sipped her Nocktoberfest, Dad's signature beer for the annual Ribbon Ridge Oktoberfest, which was currently in full swing. She clung to the corner of the huge tent, defensively watching for her "date" or one of her annoying siblings that had forced her to go on this "date."

It wasn't really a date. He was a professional colleague, and the Archers had invited him to their signature event. For nine years, the family had sponsored the town's Oktoberfest. It featured Archer beer and this year, for the first time, a German feast overseen by her brother Kyle, who was an even more amazing chef than they'd all realized. Today was day three of the festival and she still wasn't tired of the fondue. But really, could one ever tire of cheese?

"Boo!"

Tori jumped, splashing a few drops of beer from her plastic mug onto her fingers. She turned her head and glared at Kyle. "Did you sneak through the flap in the corner behind me?"

"Guilty." He wore an apron tied around his waist and a custom Archer shirt, which read CHEF below the bow and arrow A-shaped logo. "How else was I supposed to talk to you? You've been avoiding everyone for the past hour and a half. Where's Cade?" He scanned the crowd looking for her not-date, the engineer they'd hired to work on The Alex, the hotel and restaurant venue they'd been renovating since last spring. With a special events space already completed, they'd turned their focus to the restaurant and would tackle the hotel next.

Tori took a drink of the dark amber Nocktoberfest and relished the hoppy flavor. "Don't know."

Kyle gave her a sidelong glance. "Didn't you come together?"

"No. Though it wasn't for your lack of trying. I met him here. We chatted. He saw someone he knew. I excused myself to get a beer." *An hour ago.*

Kyle turned toward her and frowned. "I don't get it. Lurking in corners isn't your style. You're typically the life of the party. You work a room better than anyone I know, except maybe Liam."

Tori narrowed her eyes. "I'm better at it than he is." Their brother Liam, a successful real estate magnate in Denver, possessed many of the same qualities she did: ambition, drive, and an absolute hatred of failure. Then again, who *wanted* to fail? But it was more than that for them. Failure was never an option.

Which didn't mean that it didn't occasionally come up and take a piece out of you when you were already down for the count.

Kyle snorted. "Yeah, whatever. You two can duke it out at Christmas or whenever Liam decides to deign us with his presence."

Tori touched his arm. "Hey, don't take his absence personally. He keeps his visits pretty few and far between, even before you moved back home. Which is more than I can say for you when you were in Florida."

Kyle's eyes clouded briefly with regret and he looked away. "Yeah, I know. And hopefully someday you'll stop giving me shit about it."

She laughed. "Too soon? I'm not mad at you for leaving anymore. I get why you had to go, but I'm your sister. I will always flip you shit about stuff like that. It's my job."

He returned his attention to her, his blue-green eyes—nearly identical to her own—narrowing. "Then it's my duty to harass you about Cade. He's totally into you. Why are you dogging him?"

It seemed that since Kyle and their sister Sara had both found their soul mates this year, they expected everyone else to do the same. Granted, their adopted brother Derek had also found his true love, and they'd gotten married in August. What none of them knew, however, was that Tori was already spoken for—at least on paper.